IT'S NOT ME, IT'S YOU

JO LOVETT

Boldwood

First published in Great Britain in 2025 by Boldwood Books Ltd.

Copyright © Jo Lovett, 2025

Cover Design by Head Design Ltd

Cover Images: Shutterstock

A CIP catalogue record for this book is available from the British Library.

Paperback ISBN 978-1-83656-127-9

Large Print ISBN 978-1-83656-126-2

Hardback ISBN 978-1-83656-125-5

Trade Paperback ISBN 978-1-80656-040-0

Ebook ISBN 978-1-83656-128-6

Kindle ISBN 978-1-83656-129-3

Audio CD ISBN 978-1-83656-120-0

MP3 CD ISBN 978-1-83656-121-7

Digital audio download ISBN 978-1-83656-124-8

This book is printed on certified sustainable paper. Boldwood Books is dedicated to putting sustainability at the heart of our business. For more information please visit https://www.boldwoodbooks.com/about-us/sustainability/

Boldwood Books Ltd, 23 Bowerdean Street, London, SW6 3TN

www.boldwoodbooks.com

To my parents

1

FREYA

'Go, Freya.' Maud, my eighty-one-year-old neighbour, fist-bumps me. 'You're going to smash it.' (She learns what she calls 'young-person vocab', and her supportive fist actions, from avid Netflix watching.) 'I've already got the TV on waiting for your appearance. Don't want to miss you.'

I smile at her. We both know that *Wake Up Britain* doesn't start for another hour, and my slot isn't for another three hours.

It's Valentine's Day and I've been invited onto the nation's most-watched daytime TV show to talk about love (I'm a romance novelist) together with a divorce lawyer (I'm guessing he's there to provide a balance, talking about the opposite of love). I've been on TV a couple of times before, to talk about my books, but this is the first time it's been such a high-profile slot (in Maud's eyes, anyway; she's a *huge* fan of the show).

'Thank you.' I hug her. 'I'll come straight round when I get home and fill you in on all the details.'

'I can't wait. Remember: try to get a look at Sonja's label.' Maud likes to know where celebs buy their clothes, to feed her online shopping habit. She orders a *lot* of clothes, tries them on and does fashion parades for me, and then I return about ninety-five per cent of them for her. Luckily, the post office is only just round the corner. Sonja, the *Wake Up Britain* host, famously espouses the 'I am not about my clothes and I will therefore not tell the media where I bought them' approach, while simultaneously wearing very statementy garments at all times, even when papped nipping to her local shop for a pint of milk.

'On it,' I say, as my phone pings to tell me that my Uber's arrived. *Wake Up Britain* are very generous on taxis it seems.

'Also, don't forget my autograph,' Maud calls after me.

'On that too,' I shout as I disappear out of her front door.

* * *

Two and three-quarter hours later, I'm at the studio in full make-up and a dress from the show's wardrobe, ready to go. They've slapped on a *lot* of make-up, but obviously they know best and, frankly, after getting up at the crack of dawn I can do with any help I can to look human; I *never* usually have to get up early – one of the perks of being a writer and setting my own schedule – and the bags under my eyes this morning were *big*. The dress they've chosen for me is very cleavagy but again apparently they know best and that's what will work for TV. (I've noted the label for Maud's benefit. Apparently it's a good one: aspirational but attainable.)

'Time to come and meet Jake Stone,' says Soraya, the very nice girl who brought me some super-strong coffee earlier when I was nodding off in the make-up chair. Jake is the divorce lawyer I'm being interviewed with.

'Great, thank you.' I practise one last warm smile in the mirror in front of me (I'm beginning to feel a little nervous now and I do *not* want to freeze on live TV) before following her down a corridor and into a room holding one other person, who I presume is the lawyer.

He has his back to me, and I can't help noting that it's a particularly fine back. In my defence, I do *have* to note these things. It's literally part of my job. I need inspiration for my male protagonists. This man's back is, well, yes, gorgeous. He's tall (not a complete prerequisite for a romantic hero but definitely helpful) and broad-shouldered and slim-hipped, and as he turns to greet us I catch a glimpse through his smart navy jacket of muscle flexing (or rippling, one might say if writing romance).

As he faces me, I do my absolute best not to look as though I'm ogling him or reacting at *all* to the fact that from the front he's just as good swoon-worthy-hero material as he is from the back. Your basic classically handsome, strong-jawed, tanned-skinned, brown-eyed, great-haired hero. (His hair is thick, slightly curly and dark brown.)

Mid-thirties, two or three years older than my thirty-three, I'd guess. A very good age for a romantic hero. (For my books, not for me: I do not do real-life romance.)

I like the way he has his hair slightly long but not too long, just curling over his collar, and how when he begins to speak his mouth quirks slightly irregularly. The tiny imperfection makes him even more gorgeous.

I am, I have to admit, ogling.

Until his perfect lips form into the hint of a sneer, and he says in an incredibly frosty tone, 'Freya Cassidy, I presume?'

I don't like his weirdly unpleasant manner, but I do note that his voice is ideal for a hero: deep but not uncomfortably so.

'Yes.' I smile politely, deciding to ignore his strange coldness. 'Jake Stone?'

He nods, and then, after a slightly too-long pause, proffers his hand in pre-shaking position. The way he holds it does not look as though he's going for a polite handshake, it looks as though someone's forcing him to receive something like a bag of very grim dog poo. I put my own hand into his anyway. Our shake lasts for approximately a quarter of a second before he releases my fingers. All I can think is that I'm glad that didn't happen on national television. We'd both look like idiots.

I really cannot understand why he seems to dislike me on sight.

Ohhhh. Maybe he caught a glimpse of my ogling. Whoops. Well, whatever. It isn't like I *know* him. We just have to be pleasant to each other during our interview and then we'll never see each other again. And with no further ogling evidence he'll probably think that he was mistaken, and defrost towards me.

'Great that you already know who you both are,' says Soraya brightly. 'I'll leave you to get to know each other for a few minutes before I come and collect you to take you on set.'

'Thank you,' I say, equally brightly.

Jake smiles in very pleasant, hero-like fashion, at Soraya, before nodding totally unsmilingly in my direction and taking himself over to a sofa on the opposite side of the room and arranging himself on it in such a way that I couldn't possibly share it with him without intruding very weirdly into his personal space.

So I sit on one of the two extremely uncomfortable upright chairs next to me.

The silence that spreads between us is *peculiar*, so after a minute or two I say, 'I understand that you're a divorce lawyer.'

He raises one eyebrow, like *how dare you speak to me*, and then says, 'Correct.'

I'm beginning to feel really quite irritated. What's *wrong* with him? I mean, this is just *rudeness*.

I'm going to slay him with polite courtesy, I decide.

'I write romantic fiction,' I say, with a politely courteous smile.

'Right.' He manages to make the word sound very similar to *fuckoff*. Frankly, I'd just like to swear back at him, because this is ridiculous. I am, however, going to continue to rise above his unfriendliness.

'It's beautiful weather today,' I venture, the smile still fixed.

He raises the eyebrow again, like *wow you're very boring*, before saying, 'Yep.'

And that's it. I decide not to say anything else because I'm edging towards *serious* irritation now and I don't feel as though it would be good to have an argument with someone straight before I go on live TV with them. Also, I'm very confused. I don't argue with people, and I'm literally thinking about arguments with this person after having exchanged max thirty words with him. He's crazy, I decide. Or a massive misogynist. Or he has a migraine and hates all people today. Or something.

Whatever. We'll do the interview and then that will be that.

I take a deep, calming breath, and stare out of the window at the featureless building opposite.

This is going to be *fine*. This man will definitely, *definitely* not behave like this on actual TV. Nothing is going to go wrong. Maud, my family, my friends, my *readers*, they will all see me (gaaaah) and it *will* be fine.

2

JAKE

I have no interest in making polite conversation with Freya Cassidy. The woman's a homewrecker. Well, her books are. And clearly her books are an extension of her.

This is a lesson in thinking before saying yes, however busy I might be in that moment. When I was asked to do this interview, I should have spent ten seconds considering who my unnamed co-interviewee might be. It does of course make complete sense to include a divorce lawyer and a romance writer on the same 'let's talk about everlasting love' Valentine's panel. I could have foreseen that, or at least asked.

Ms Cassidy clears her throat and uncrosses her neatly crossed ankles and recrosses them the other way round. I hold an imaginary bingo card at the ready to see what banality she will come out with next. Weather? Travel? Whether I've been on TV before?

It's surprising. You'd think an author who'd sold millions of books would have better conversation. Although, to be fair to her, I'm giving her absolutely nothing to work with.

'Did you have far to travel this morning?' she asks. Bingo.

'Not really,' I say repressively.

She raises one perfectly shaped eyebrow, just very slightly, implying, I think, that she believes me to have been unnecessarily rude.

I feel a flash of annoyance. I am not a rude person. Ever. Except... yes, apparently I *have* just been rude. I'm talking to Freya Cassidy though; and, while I haven't met her before, I do know that I don't like her. Or, more specifically, that I don't like her *work*. I should really be mature enough to make polite conversation, however.

'A half-hour journey,' I elaborate. And then I add, 'How was your journey?'

Her – objectively (and annoyingly) beautifully shaped – lips curve into a small smile. I do not, of course, know her personally, but I would say that's a victorious smile. I'm guessing she was doing her best to goad me into actual conversation. I find my own lips twitching in response, which annoys me.

'Very good, thank you.' She gives me a long, appraising look for a moment, before continuing, 'I'm not an early riser. On the occasions that I *am* out and about at the crack of dawn, I do enjoy seeing London waking up.'

'Yeah,' I agree politely. 'That is cool.'

She nods. I nod too. (I don't know why.) And then we settle back into silence. I take my phone out and check my emails and mentally run down what I'll be doing for the rest of today, until I'm dragged back to now by a young woman knocking on the door and coming into the room.

'Hi, Soraya.' Ms Cassidy greets her with a beam, as though they're best friends. I presume they only met this morning, though.

Soraya returns her smile and says, 'I hope you've had a lovely time getting to know each other. Just letting you know that you'll be on in a couple of minutes.'

'Great,' we reply simultaneously, as Soraya disappears again.

'Have you been on TV before?' Ms Cassidy asks.

'Yes, but not on this kind of show.' I have some very high-profile clients so sometimes I have to read statements out to the media, but I see no reason to mention that now. 'You?' I'm genuinely interested, despite myself, in how much media exposure she's had.

'Yes, a few times, on local news programmes and a few other chat and magazine type shows like this. My publisher has a very good publicity department and they're fantastic at getting authors slots like this.'

To maximise the number of people who will get sucked into reading her books and thus have their perception of reality warped.

'Good for them,' I say with great insincerity.

'Yep.' She stands up and smooths the skirt of her dress, which makes me wonder whether she's a little anxious about the interview.

I'm not nervous, just keen to get the interview out of the way and then get on with the rest of my over-busy day; I'm here because no publicity is bad publicity, according to my fellow partners at work. The more people have heard of us, the more they'll send their business our way. I already have enough business but thought how hard can it be, and said yes anyway, for the greater good of the firm, when everyone else decided I'd be the best person for the job. Mistake.

The door opens; Soraya's back.

'Let's go,' she says.

Ms Cassidy does the skirt-smoothing again and also gives both sides of the chest of her dress a little inwards tug. It's quite revealing on the top half; I'm guessing from the way she seems to be trying to rearrange the dress that she isn't comfortable with that. Presumably she was given it to wear by the wardrobe people.

'You look beautiful, Freya,' Soraya tells her, obviously having noticed that she doesn't look entirely at ease. She's right. Objectively, she *does* look beautiful. She has very thick, long hair, mainly down but with some bits up, which frames her heart-shaped face very attractively. And whoever chose the dress and high heels she's wearing did a good job; I can't imagine anyone else wearing them better, frankly. The dress has deep pink and red flowers, presumably in a nod to Valentine's Day (I was told to either bring a pink tie of my own or borrow one from them; I brought one), and suits her dark blonde hair and creamy skin, and the heels are red and shiny, and combined with the swishy skirts of the dress reveal excellent legs.

Wow. I have *no* idea why I'm cataloguing what the woman is wearing. She's been thanking Soraya, and they've been chatting about nail varnish while I've been lost in my own peculiar thoughts.

Make-up people swoop towards us. I tell them I am absolutely fine, thank you; Ms Cassidy submits to having something powdery brushed on her cheeks and forehead and black eye stuff touched up, while the woman wielding the brushes gives her some advice about how to hold herself on camera. When the woman's finished, I can't see a difference if I'm honest. Ms Cassidy looked ridiculously beautiful before; she still does.

I have *no* idea why I can't think of her as Freya. We aren't in the nineteenth century. I'm just too *irritated* by her actual existence, though.

Right. We're finally going on. As we walk down the corridor, Soraya calls, 'Enjoy!' after us.

I look at Ms Cassidy's perfectly proportioned profile and feel yet another wave of *real* annoyance that she has this butter-wouldn't-melt look while she's regularly ruining people's lives.

When she smiles at me, and says with an ironic little eye-roll, 'Well, let's have *fun*. Here's to love and Valentine's Day,' all I can do is respond with an eye-roll of my own. *At* her, though, not *with* her.

3

FREYA

'Freya Cassidy. Writer of romance. Purveyor of happily-ever-afters.' Maud's heroine, Sonja, the national-treasure, longest-standing presenter of *Wake Up Britain*, smiles at me, and I dutifully return the smile, remembering to project my chin forward as I do so. The chin projection is surprisingly difficult but – according to the make-up artist who dusted powder over my face just now – worth it as it's the best way to ensure as flattering a camera angle as possible at all times. 'What are your tips for finding a forever love? Your *personal* tips.'

Accept there's no such thing and move on, I think.

'Well,' I say. 'Everyone is different, and every love story is different.' I look at Sonja. She famously likes actual answers to her actual questions; clearly I'm not going to be able to leave it there. 'And you're asking how each person can find their own individual love story.' In my experience you can sometimes divert interviewers by repeating their question back at them.

'Exactly.' Sonja leans in towards me, her head tilted to one side, an interested, enquiring expression on her face. She's *good*; I now genuinely almost do want to answer her truthfully. Except, also, I do not want to upset my readers, to whom I am very grateful, and about whom I care a lot; and no-one enjoys having illusions shattered, and they think that I very much believe in love and am waiting with bated breath for my own Prince Charming to come along. So I'm going to continue to hide the truth behind platitudes.

'I think you just have to let it happen,' I say soulfully, still chin-projecting.

A discreet but definite snort comes from my left. Jake. I freeze for a moment in slight shock – it's one thing someone being rude to me one on one, behind the scenes, and quite another them snorting at me on national television – before realising that, frustratingly, my only option is to ignore him if I want to retain my dignity.

Sonja does not ignore it. 'Jake Stone. Divorce lawyer to the stars. You look – and sound – sceptical. Are you suggesting that there's no such thing as "just letting it happen"? I take it you don't believe in love?'

Well, of course he doesn't. Surely all divorce lawyers have seen so many warring couples that it would put them off love for life. Presumably that was why they asked him on the show in the first place, to provide a balance to the pro-finding-love comments they knew I would make.

However. 'On the contrary,' says snorty, over-smooth and over-handsome Jake. 'I do believe in love. I believe that most of my clients have just been unlucky and there's no reason they shouldn't eventually find true love. Or perhaps they *were* truly in love when they married, but they've genuinely grown apart due to circumstance or differing personal development. So, yes, I do believe in love.'

I find myself nodding in reluctant appreciation. Despite how extremely annoying he is, I do have to give it to him: that was a very good marketing spiel. And almost genuine-seeming. If someone's hurting from the breakdown of their marriage and wants to go back for more romance, what better divorce lawyer to choose than someone who has a touchy-feely, you-*will*-love-again side to him. As well as being reputedly the most ferocious in the business. (I googled him when he rudely got his phone out to avoid talking to me while we were waiting.)

'That's so lovely,' says Sonja. 'Why, then, did you audibly snort in response to Freya's beautiful answer?'

'I felt that it was hollow.' Jake speaks so affably that it takes a moment for the words to achieve their full impact.

When they do, Sonja gasps.

And I clench my jaw, purse my lips and narrow my eyes.

Until I remember that I don't want to disappoint my readers, and plaster a big smile back onto my face. The whole point of my job is to make people happy. My readers do not want to witness me getting *really* irritated by this man. They want to know that I'm a happy, nice, kind, unlucky-in-love-but-will-eventually-find-my-soulmate woman, just like my heroines. Which I *am*, I hope, except for the eventually finding my soulmate bit. No soulmate exists for me.

I smile some more, going for chin *and* warmth projection.

It's working. Sonja's returning my smile like she can't help herself. We're going to forget about the *hollow* comment and move on.

I open my mouth to elaborate on believing in love, and then Jake leans towards me, and speaks quietly, so quietly that it almost certainly won't be picked up by either Sonja or the microphones. 'I saw that,' he says. 'The eye narrowing.'

I freeze for a second long moment, and then apply an enormous effort not to react to how *incredibly* rude and annoying he is, breathe deeply, and do not narrow my eyes again.

Instead, I carry on smiling and pretend that he said absolutely nothing.

'Hollow?' asks Sonja, raising an eyebrow in Jake's direction. Dammit.

'Ms Cassidy doesn't seem particularly convincing about believing in love,' Jake explains.

I turn to stare at him. What the actual? Is he trying to ruin my entire career? I *have* to appear to believe in love. And I *do*. For some people. Just not for myself. Well, not for a lot of people actually. Look at the British divorce statistics. Which Jake, of all people, should know about.

I decide to laugh, not too much and not too little, before saying, 'Ha, that's funny. I'm not really sure how someone can seem convincing about believing in love. Of *course* I believe in love. It's all around us.' It actually is, insofar as the studio is decorated for Valentine's Day with pinkness and fluffiness and hearts galore. I adjust the cerise velvet cushion behind me.

'The thing is.' Jake leans forward again, the way he did before, except this time he isn't lowering his voice, so everything he says is going to be broadcast live to the programme's three million viewers, many of them my readers. 'It's dangerous to peddle false narratives around love.'

'Dangerous?' Sonja queries while I focus very hard on maintaining a quizzical smile and not re-narrowing my eyes at Jake. Or just digging my kitten heel into his foot. (For a fairly low heel, it's very spiky, and would definitely hurt him, and right now that would give me great pleasure, even though I am at all other times extremely pacifist and non-violent.)

His response drags me back from a lovely fantasy about crushing his toes.

'Writers of romance, like Ms Cassidy, peddle dangerous nonsense,' he says, still with that affable air, as though he's chatting about the weather or his views on the latest Italian restaurant, rather than being incredibly insulting and also possibly costing me a *lot* of sales. 'They give people – often women – unreasonable expectations.'

'You mean they expect their other halves to be like the heroes and heroines of romance books and are disappointed?' Sonja checks.

'Exactly,' Jake confirms.

As Sonja, to my horror, begins to nod, I leap in with, 'I think that it might be a bit of a stretch to suggest that someone reads about a lovely hero or heroine, looks at their spouse and thinks *hmm, they don't bear much of a resemblance to that hero, oh, I know, I'll divorce him.*'

'Sadly,' says Jake, 'it happens all too often.'

'What?' I ask. I'm *really* annoyed now. 'It can't. It just *can't.*' I mean, really? How likely is that? Not at all. Surely.

'You'd be surprised,' Jake tells me.

'Yes, I would,' I agree. I suddenly think of something. 'Especially since my protagonists are all people with flaws, not models of perfection.' I smile, probably a little smugly, if I'm honest, because I feel that's an *excellent* argument.

Jake shakes his head. 'That's like that clichéd interview question – what's your biggest fault – isn't it? No-one ever says, "Well, I'm always late, I'm careless and I can't write reports to save my life." They say things like: "I'm too much of a perfectionist because I'm *sooo* keen to do the job well." And your protagonists don't have *bad* flaws, do they? They don't say nasty things about people; they aren't huge, infestation-inducing slobs; they don't torture insects.'

As a divorce lawyer, he must hear about some very bad behaviour, I reflect, before I focus on the matter in hand, i.e. beating him in this argument.

'*Obviously,*' I say with dignity, 'my characters don't have those particular flaws. They actually have worse flaws.'

As I pause to gather my thoughts, Jake says sarcastically, 'Oh, they're murderers or thieves?'

'Far worse,' I say, ignoring his childish interjection, 'I mean they have flaws that have often been developed by their life experiences. For example, if a person has had several disastrous romances, they might find it difficult to commit to a relationship.'

'Bad argument,' Jake replies triumphantly. 'That person might be incredibly *nice*; they've just encountered some unpleasant partners.' He is so annoying.

Because he is of course right, in that of *course* the protagonists in romances have to be people that most readers will like, because if the readers *weren't* rooting for them they probably wouldn't enjoy the books.

I need to regroup. I look at the studio audience – a sea of avid faces – and then at the cameras trained on us, which are sending live footage of this conversation directly into people's houses all round the country. (Hello Maud!) It does not matter what Jake Stone thinks of me. It *does* matter what the viewers think of me.

I produce a pleasant smile and say, 'I would suggest that someone finding their partner lacking when compared to a fictional romantic hero is a *symptom* rather than a *cause* of their relationship breakdown.'

'While that is to some extent true,' Jake says, not missing a beat, 'it is also the case that most relationships – romantic or otherwise – go through difficult patches, and it is better to work at them than to be told by the book you're reading or the film you're watching that your partner is lacking.'

I open my mouth to say that that's ridiculous and how suggestible does he think people *are*, and then close it again on the off chance that they *are* that suggestible and I'd be insulting those people.

'Have you read any of Freya's books?' asks Sonja into the pause left by me not replying.

'No,' Jake says, 'but I know a woman who did read a lot of them.'

'And who is that?' I ask, not sure that I'll like his answer.

'My ex-wife,' he says, like he's playing the trump card to end all trump cards.

'Ooh,' says Sonja, looking delighted. 'Was she the one who instigated the divorce and did she cite Freya's books?'

'I...'

For the first time, Jake looks a little uncomfortable, and I realise that he was goaded into saying something he now regrets, and that he – obviously – doesn't want to talk about the circumstances of his *own* divorce on national television.

And, despite his nasty (and also correct) cynicism about my views on love, I do actually feel a bit sorry for him, so I give him a little helping hand and move the conversation away from the details of his divorce, asking, 'And yet you still believe in love?'

'Certainly,' he says. 'And that one sentence there demonstrates to me that I don't think you *do*. Your use of the word "yet".'

'Nonsense.' I cannot *believe* I was trying to help him. I also cannot believe that, courtesy of him, I seem to be digging an unforeseen hole for myself. I do not want to alienate or upset my lovely readers.

Suddenly, though, something occurs to me. Maybe Jake Stone is doing me a *favour*. It's very hard work constantly pretending that I think I'm going to find my own true love one day. As time goes on, I get more and more questions about it and they're more and more difficult to answer. And people like honesty, don't they. And I *do* believe in love, I really do. Just not for myself.

I sit and blink for a couple of seconds. Then I come to a snap decision.

I'm going to go for it. I didn't expect to, but I am. I'm going to do it now. Admit the truth.

'I do, very much, believe in love,' I say. 'I mean, as we've said, look around us. Figuratively. We all know many people who are clearly deeply in love, in wonderfully satisfying, passionate relationships. Adorable couples. I don't think anyone could sensibly suggest that love is not a thing, or that *forever* love is not a thing. It is merely that I, personally, don't think forever love is for *me*.'

'Oh my goodness,' breathes Sonja. 'Freya!'

'Hunh,' says Jake, slightly frowning, looking satisfyingly wind-out-of-sails.

'I love your honesty,' Sonja says. 'Is this—' she lowers her voice, as though we aren't on national TV but are sharing confidences in one of our kitchens over a glass of wine '—the first time you've admitted this?'

'Yes.' I'm really not sure now whether this was a good idea.

'So... you've been *pretending* all this time?' she continues.

'Well, I...' I'm trying to think really fast. Would it be bad for me to own up to a teensy pretence that really hasn't hurt anyone? I mean, the whole of fiction is *pretending*, isn't it? In that it's made up. And fiction is *great*, because books and films make people happy. I mean, obviously not if they cause people to get divorced, but that clearly isn't actually true.

Sonja's been studying me while I've been thinking. Now she gives a decisive nod, and I realise that, oh crap, she's made up her mind about me, and it might be good, but also it might be bad.

I try for an innocent, helpless little smile.

'So you've been pulling the wool over your readers' eyes by pretending to believe in happy-ever-after love in order to sell more books?' asks Jake. He's such a weasel.

I shake my head, speechless. I actually want to kill him. Is he *trying* to upset people and ruin my career?

'No, I don't think so,' Sonja pronounces. 'I think Freya has just felt unable to admit to her feelings about her own love life because she cares so much about her readers, and didn't want them to feel bad for her.'

Oh my goodness, the *relief* that she seems to have come down on my side. I could kiss her.

'*Exactly*,' I say with great emphasis.

'I think it's *great* that you've finally felt able to admit the truth, and that we helped you do that,' coos Sonja. 'I think it's incredibly brave of you. Because these are private feelings.'

Yes, they are private. I should *not* have come on national TV with someone as famously probing as Sonja. She's such a dog with a bone. But you don't realise initially. She lulls you into a false sense of security, like at first she's like a cute, cuddly labradoodle chasing a fake bone, and then she morphs into a terrifying Rottweiler trying to eat you.

'Private feelings of... lying?' Jake snarks.

'No,' says Sonja while I bristle internally. 'Private feelings of loneliness, which she didn't want to burden her readers with. But now I think your readers are ready. We're here to support you, Freya.'

'Thank you, Sonja.' I'm quite confused, if I'm honest. I don't really know how we got to this point. I do know that I'm *very* happily single and need no support whatsoever. But if Sonja wants to play it that I need support, that's totally fine with me: it's a lot better than being criticised by Jake in front of the nation.

'We're also here to help you.' Sonja's pressing her earpiece, nodding and smiling so much that I'm beginning to feel slightly alarmed. What are her producers saying to her that's making her look so excited? She turns to Jake. 'Would you say that Freya is the exact opposite of you, Jake?'

'I, well, yeah, yep.' Jake does look as though he's almost squirming – insofar as a large, handsome, overconfident-looking man can look squirmy. I'm guessing that he's also alarmed about the direction in which Sonja's taking the conversation.

'So to clarify—' Sonja picks up a pen from the coffee table in front of her and points it in our direction '—Freya you write romance for a living, but you don't believe romance is for *you*, and Jake you're a divorced divorce lawyer who *does* believe in romance, and you believe there's a happy romantic ending out there for you?'

We both nod. Me, quite happily, relieved that Sonja doesn't seem to have anything sinister in mind after all; Jake, not looking so happy (ha, serves him right).

'Well.' Sonja presses her ear again and then nods again. 'Great. Great! It's been brilliant to meet you both. Thank you so much.'

And suddenly the two of us are being ushered off and back down the corridor, even though it didn't really feel (to me, anyway) as though we'd properly concluded the interview. But maybe that's TV for you. Or maybe we got off-topic and took up too much time.

Soraya meets us in the corridor and tells us we were both fantastic, before we're shown out of the building. I realise as we leave that I didn't manage to get Sonja's autograph. I'll have to email someone and ask.

'It was *great* to meet you,' I tell Jake sarcastically as we part ways.

'Oh, likewise.' His sneer is so impressive that I laugh out loud. He's getting to me a lot less now that we're done and never going to see each other again. In fact, I'm going to put having met him to good use. He can feature looks-wise as a hero in my next book, and personality-wise as a villain.

'Bye,' I say cheerily as I hop into another paid-for-by-the-show cab. It is *so* nice to have the interview – and my brief acquaintance with Jake – done and dusted.

4

JAKE

Following my frustrating appearance on TV, I have a busy day with back-to-back client meetings and calls.

In my last meeting of the afternoon, a new female client tells me that the last straw for her in her marriage was going home after having been to the cinema to watch a romcom with girlfriends (who afterwards all gushed about their own partners). Her husband had forgotten she was out and had locked the front door and nodded off in front of the TV. When she'd finally got inside, she'd looked at him squinting at her, with one sleep-crumpled cheek and his shirt hanging out over his slightly squidgy belly (her words). She'd done the comparison with the hero in the film she'd just watched and her husband had not matched up. She decided then and there to walk.

I would *so much* like Freya Cassidy to have heard about this.

Freya would probably have done one of her perfect little smiles (all cute and misleadingly sweet and innocent-looking) and trotted out her symptom-rather-than-cause line again. And, while that is of course a valid point, I really do think that a lot of people, when vulnerable, can be misled into thinking that their relationship is lacking when really they just need to work at it.

People getting their heads filled with fake romantic nonsense is not great.

And it's mind-blowing that a woman peddling such ridiculous and dangerous fiction doesn't believe in love herself. Taking the whole do-as-I-say-and-not-as-I-do thing to great heights.

I blink, realising that my client has spoken and I didn't hear what she said. I am *never* distracted like this.

I apologise profusely and focus very hard on her until the meeting concludes.

I find myself thinking again about Freya Cassidy as I pack some papers together to take home to work on this evening. It's annoying to be left with the feeling that someone whose work you thoroughly despise has in some way bested you. I shake my head. It doesn't matter. I'm never going to see her again and I'm never going to agree to appear on morning television again.

* * *

By the time I've got home from work and parked the e-bike I picked up outside my office, my head is clear, and this morning seems a long way in the past. I'm going to go to the gym, do some more work and then head to the pub for a quick pint with Minuk, a friend who lives round the corner, and my day will end much more enjoyably than it began.

I pull out my phone to text him and, wow. The phone's alight with many dozens of messages from friends and family. I feel extreme worry for a second or two until I realise that nothing seriously bad has happened to anyone I know.

What *has* happened is that everyone I know has left work and seen that the argument between Freya Cassidy and me has blown up.

There are videos of us arguing. They're obviously edited for highlights, I see when I watch the first couple, but at the same time they are actually quite representative of what did happen. We *did* thoroughly dislike each other (well, I thoroughly disliked her, or at least her work, and I'm guessing she didn't love me from the way things panned out) and we *did* argue. And apparently millions of people watched us and a lot of them rewatched us and lot of people who did not originally see us now have.

There are also already actual memes of us, and apparently (according to my friend Affan) they're multiplying by the literal second.

I don't do social media at all; it's a whole other world that operates in complete parallel to my – real-life – world. It's odd to think that without anyone telling me, all of this could have been happening online without me ever having found out, just passed me by. It has not passed a lot of people by, though. It's crazy.

Yeah. Wow, basically.

I send brief replies to everyone who's messaged me (no small job), before getting changed for the gym. Hopefully this will all have blown over in a couple of hours' time.

Nope, I discover when I emerge from the gym. That was total social media naivety. I have a lot more messages, many of them from people I haven't heard from in quite a while, some of whom should surely not even have my number. It seems like everyone I've ever met has seen the clips. Freya and I have 'gone massively viral' in the words of my cousin's thirteen-year-old daughter.

I really have no way to respond other than to hunker down – sparing the odd brief thought for Freya and wondering whether she's experiencing the same – and *not* go for a pint this evening after all. We can go tomorrow; this is bound to blow over soon, I'm sure. Another five-second wonder story will come along.

* * *

My phone *is* a lot quieter in the morning; it seems that everyone saw the clips yesterday and it's already blowing over. Good news.

If I had Freya's number, I think, as I grab a bagel and a banana from my kitchen on my way out for work, I'd almost be tempted to text her to see how she is. I can't imagine she's experienced something like this before either; if she weren't one of the most annoying people I've ever met, I'd quite like to discuss our mutual weird experience with her.

Fortunately, I obviously don't have her number, so I can't message her. And that's that. I'm off to work and by the end of the day this will all just be an anecdote for future dinner parties.

* * *

Except.

Mid-morning, Veronica, my PA, tells me she has a Very Important Caller on the line. She's behaving a little oddly, if I'm honest. Eyes rounded, almost popping out of her head, and mouthing something indecipherable at me. She's been working for me for over two years and *never* in that time has she referred to someone as a 'very important caller'. Even when the callers *are* very important. I'm wondering if the caller is *royalty*. (Veronica is an ardent royalist.) Is this breaking news? Another royal divorce?

Oh. As soon as she puts the caller through I realise what has happened. It's bloody Sonja.

She sounds a little breathless.

'Jake. I only have a minute while the ads are on. I know that Freya's on board. Your chemistry together. The way you argued. Viral. It was already kicking off even *as* you were on yesterday. We'd love to set the two of you a challenge and then have you back on the show.'

'No,' I say immediately. I'm not stupid; lesson learnt.

'Jake, darling, I know you'll agree. We'll meet for a drink later to discuss.'

And then she's gone.

She's as crazy as the whole viral thing. I will not be meeting her for a drink.

Except (again)...

She messages me during what I'm guessing is the next ad break. It seems that she isn't above a bit of outright blackmail.

She's suggesting (commanding) that the three of us get together this evening in the bar at the Savoy to hammer out the details of our challenge. (What does she mean by *challenge*?) And she says:

> Don't forget that millions of people have seen the clip of the two of you, and some of those are prospective clients, or the friends of prospective clients (it's a small world). Did I tell you that my friend Laura Darke mentioned you the other day and is planning to get in touch?

Right.

Laura Darke was one half of Britain's now-ex-favourite TV couple before they announced they were having difficulties in their marriage. I would very much like to represent Laura in the divorce that the nation knows is coming.

I stare at my phone and shake my head as I think.

Sonja is a sneaky woman.

Laura Darke. I would *really* like to represent her.

It's very likely that Sonja knows her. So it seems quite possible that whether or not I agree to meet her and Freya for a drink this evening could influence whether or not I get to work with Laura.

Fine. *Fine.* I'll meet them. I will not, however, be participating in any kind of a challenge.

5

FREYA

Six evenings after the TV interview, I'm on my way into London's Savoy hotel, to meet Jake and Sonja in the bar here. I wasn't that keen to come – I really didn't want to see Jake again and I really don't want to join in with whatever challenge Sonja's talking about – but she promised me the autograph for Maud if I did come. So here I am. Once I have the autograph, I will politely decline the challenge and leave.

I think Jake was quite obstructive when it came to finding a date for this meeting; it's nine o'clock on a Tuesday evening, a time when I would definitely rather be watching a box set or meeting a friend locally. But here we are.

They've both already arrived before me, I see when I enter the bar. Jake's looking drop-dead, suck-your-breath-in-on-sight-of-him gorgeous in dark jeans and a navy crew-neck jumper, and Sonja's a vision in a fluffy long lilac dress, which she pulls off amazingly.

Sonja hugs me at arm's length (I'm guessing she doesn't want to crease the dress) and aims dramatic air kisses in my direction.

Jake nods, says, 'Hello,' and does not get up from his stool to greet me.

'Bubbles to celebrate the beginning of the challenge,' Sonja says. 'Champagne.' She peers at the wine list. 'God, that's expensive. TV production budgets aren't what they were. We'll have the house prosecco.'

Soon we're all sipping prosecco. I do love prosecco. Jake, however, looks as though he's wishing his was a beer.

'I hope you both had lovely weekends,' Sonja says, before carrying straight on with: 'So. The challenge. Exciting!'

I decide that I need to get the autograph before I decline to join in with whatever the challenge might be, and open my bag to take out Maud's autograph book.

'Later.' Sonja waves her hand dismissively in the direction of the book. 'Now. Credit where credit is due. It was Mandy, our producer, who came up with the fantastic idea of the challenge. Just so that you know that everyone on the show is behind it.'

Oh-kay. I *know* that I will not want to do this challenge. I glance at Jake and see that he's glancing at me too and looking very frowny.

'So basically—' Sonja takes a long slug of her prosecco '—the challenge is like a wager. You bet each other that you'll win, prove the other wrong. You have three months. And, obviously, report back, come back on the show. We're announcing it on the show tomorrow, exactly a week after you came on.'

'What?' Jake asks.

Sonja's beaming. 'You have to prove to Freya that there *is* romance for her. And she has to prove to you that...' She looks at both of us and then continues, 'Well, not to be too harsh, but that romance is just a fairy tale.'

Jake shakes his head, like he's stunned. 'Why would we do that?'

He's right (for once). Why *would* we do that? I did not enjoy going on TV last week. It's one thing doing a nice quick chat about one of my books; it's entirely another talking about my views on things, and myself. I do not want to be interviewed on air by Sonja again.

Although... my editor and agent have both told me that appearing on the show was a good thing. It caused a big spike in sales, which currently isn't showing any sign of tailing off. I can hear both their voices in my ear now: *No publicity is bad publicity.*

Hmmm.

'I'll give you the autograph after you've agreed,' Sonja tells me.

I gasp.

'Yes.' She nods, very seriously, like she's making an acceptable point. '*That's* how much we believe in this.'

As in, she believes in it *so* much she'll stoop to blackmail? Lovely.

'Ridiculous,' says Jake, very decisively.

As though he has the right to reply on my behalf as well as his own, speak for me as well as himself. Arrogant. Annoying. Irritating.

'Are you worried about losing?' I hear myself asking, widening my eyes in fake innocence as I speak. If nothing else, I would *love* to prove Jake wrong.

'Certainly not,' he says.

There's a long pause, into which Sonja, to my confusion, says, 'Laura Darke.'

There's another long pause, and then Jake – looking as though he's just agreed to have teeth extracted without an anaesthetic – says, 'Fine. I'm in. Under duress.'

'Great. It'll be fun!' Sonja's beaming and it wouldn't surprise me if she clapped her hands in glee any minute now. 'How exciting! We've thought of prizes too for the winner.'

I nod, a little miserably, because, even though I know my agent would advise me to do it, I strongly doubt that I'm going to enjoy whatever's in store for us. 'Yay, yes. Exciting!'

Jake shoots me an if-looks-could-kill glare, which immediately cheers me up.

'So. We have a legal contract.' Sonja's voice is suddenly steely.

Jake lifts a lawyerly eyebrow and Sonja says, 'We have witnesses.' She points at the table nearest to the bar, and the two people there both wave at us. Jake and I both gasp. 'We all know what happens when things go viral. I wouldn't like to think what would happen to your reputations if the nation thought you'd reneged. Jake, I'll let Laura know how much I like you. Freya, I'll sign that autograph in a minute.'

'Yeah, I might be too busy to join in.' Jake's lips have gone very straight and a muscle is twitching in his jaw area.

'Mr Stone,' I say, just because I can't resist. 'Are you *scared*?'

'Of...?' he asks, and I realise, because he did this during the interview too, that this is a thing he does. Encourages you to finish your own sentence and often land yourself in a quagmire.

'Of losing,' I say, not – I am pleased to say – in any kind of a quagmire. I'm beginning to feel like I don't really mind if we do the challenge or not. The downside would be having to speak to Jake again. The upside would be more publicity. And beating him.

And I do *know* that I will win. I've lived through every romance trope under the sun and it just isn't happening for me. I used to be a hopeless romantic but now I know better. It's probably something about me, if I'm honest. My parents got divorced when I was twelve. There was no amicable conscious uncoupling; it was full-on hatred (which persisted beyond my father's funeral); and they both had several further disastrous relationships before ending up alone. I feel like it's a genetic thing, like I'm not *capable* of a happy romantic relationship. I'm not lovable and I don't fall in love with people properly either.

And I'm pretty sure that I can convince Jake that romance isn't for him. My mind's already whirring with the possibilities of all the awful dates I can set him up on. I can go through every single trope for him (can I actually organise an enemies-to-lovers snow-in for him? Hmm) and then he'll have to admit defeat.

It would be a lot of effort, though. Practically speaking, it would be a lot easier to walk away and never see this man again and say goodbye to the extra publicity.

'I think you're going to have to do it,' says Sonja. 'Because if you don't, it might become known who pulled out, and why.'

'I won't pull out,' I rush to say (pathetically, I know, but threats do scare me, and I'm worried that my pulling out would go down badly with my readers).

'Outrageous,' says Jake.

Sonja smiles at him.

He glares at both of us and then, after a very long pause, says, 'Well, fun times. When do we start?'

'We need some rules first.' Sonja takes her phone out of her bag and consults it. 'Here we go. To clarify: Freya, your task is to prove to Jake that he's never going to find lasting love.' She ignores my audible choke at how mean that sounds. 'And Jake, your task is to prove to Freya that she *is* going to find love. To further clarify: you do both have to join in, in good faith. We considered sending cameras with you on each date, but we don't want this to look too much like reality TV, so you're going to take selfie videos during the dates and send them over, and we'll do ninety-second montages once or twice a week on the show to keep viewers up to date with how things are going. We'll send written instructions but basically we'll need to see footage of the venue, footage of you and your date, if they consent, otherwise just you, and a debrief from you afterwards.'

She finally pauses for breath, while we both stare at her, speechless, before continuing, 'Now, prizes. Freya, if you win, Jake will spend a weekend on a learn-to-write-romance course. He will then come back on the show to read us his romantic short story. Jake, if you win, Freya will spend a weekend on a love-therapy-for-singles course. She will then come back on the show to tell us what she's learnt. If it's a draw, you spend a weekend together on a team-building weekend to try to overcome the mutual antipathy the nation has seen you fall into. There might be camera crews involved on the final weekend.'

She smiles at us while we both continue to stare slightly open-mouthed at her, before continuing, 'The production team and I have discussed and we think the best way is for you to spend one evening a week on this. You take it in turns to set the other up on a date or do whatever it takes to prove your point. And you do both have to be honest.'

She looks me hard in the eye, and I nod, feeling about six years old. Then she switches her gimlet gaze to Jake, who also nods.

'Wonderful, then.' Sonja slaps her card on top of the bar, signals to the bartender, downs the rest of her glass, refills it, waves her card over the paying machine, and downs her second glass, all in the space of about a minute and a half. 'Excellent.' She slides off her bar stool. 'Enjoy your evening. I'll be checking in with you regularly.'

And off she goes. Leaving me to realise just after she's disappeared out of the door in a lilac whirl that I still don't have the autograph. Well, next time.

I can't actually believe that two grown adults have just been manoeuvred into accepting a ridiculous challenge. It's such a bizarre turn of events.

At least I know I'm going to win. There is no possibility that anyone can convince me there's romance out there for me.

6

JAKE

'Well, fuck me,' I say eventually.

'No, thank you,' says Freya extremely politely, which to my surprise makes me smile.

Freya doesn't smile; she just rolls her eyes slightly.

We sit there in silence for a long beat, and then Freya says, 'So. Taking it in turns. We should decide who gets to go first in choosing the date.'

'Toss a coin?' I suggest. Usually, I'd be polite and ask if she'd like to go first, but politeness has no place in a serious contest.

Freya nods and I pull my wallet out.

'Got no coins,' I say, a moment later.

'Me neither.'

I ask the bartender if he has one.

'Only if you buy something else,' he tells me. 'Can't open the till otherwise.'

'Honestly,' says Freya. 'Everything about this situation is ridiculous, including the fact that apparently it's really hard for two adults to find a coin.'

'What about using a nut instead of a coin?' The bartender picks one up from a little bowl on the bar and puts his hands behind his back. 'Which hand?' he asks Freya.

'Right.'

'Left. Sorry.' He puts the nut back in the bowl and licks his hand. I glance at

Freya to see how she's reacted to the lack of hygiene and see that she's just staring at him.

I snigger a little internally and then say, 'Well, thank you. I guess I won, then.'

Freya drags her gaze from the nut bowl and says, 'Enjoy this tiny victory while it lasts.' Then she smiles. I don't like that smile. It's too confident. I don't want Freya to be confident about this. Although... with confidence does often come failure, so... yeah, maybe this is good.

I return her smile, and then realise that I have absolutely no idea how I'm going to get Freya to fall in love with someone. I need time to prepare.

'As the winner of the nut-hand choosing—' I do a confident smile of my own '—I'll allow you to go first.'

'You'll *allow* me?'

'Yep.'

'How *extremely* kind of you.' Freya stretches a hand out in the direction of the nut bowl before obviously recalling what the waiter did and withdrawing her hand. She smiles at me. I'd have to describe it as a complacent smile. 'You have *no* idea what to do next, have you?' She's obviously right, which annoys me.

I do my best scornful laugh. 'I have *every* idea of what to do next. I just want to see what *you're* going to do.'

Freya looks right into my eyes for a moment, and then smiles.

'I'm going to win,' she says. 'And on a more granular level, I'm going to organise an evening out for you next week. Are we thinking the same evening every week, or more random ones?'

'Tuesday every week?' I don't want to give up a Friday or Saturday to this ridiculous challenge. Plus it'll be easier to arrange dates on evenings on which people aren't usually busy. Although. What if one of us finds something like speed-dating to help things along the way? That might be a weekend thing. 'As a general rule. But I'd suggest that we ought to agree that we can change the evening by mutual consent. And that we both – obviously – have to be reasonable. If the other has a very good reason and gives sufficient notice and we're free.'

'Of course.' Freya's laughing, and – irritatingly – I think she's genuinely amused. She has this dimple that appears when she laughs, which makes me think of my friend Dan, a self-confessed sucker for a cheek dimple. Objectively, it's what a lot of people would call very cute. Subjectively, she's *far* too confident about this challenge and it's incredibly annoying.

I decide that I would like to go home. 'Next Tuesday, then? And you'll let me know what time and where?'

'Yep.' She picks up her bag and slides off her bar stool. The way she does it irritates me. It's too obviously graceful, almost like a choreographed slide would be.

'Will you be okay getting home by yourself?' I feel I should ask, even though I really don't want to.

'That's a very kind thought. Thank you.' She's sounding sarcastic again. 'Yes, I will. I'm going to get a cab to Waterloo and then a train. Quicker than a cab all the way, however much I'd like to spend *Wake Up Britain*'s money.'

'Great. I'll wait to hear from you then.' I'm not going to *choose* to spend any more time with her than I have to. 'I'm just going to finish my drink.' I am not. It's far too sweet. I'm going to give her a few minutes and then go home, do another hour's work and then go to bed.

'Okay. Night.' And there's that dimple again. Frankly, I feel she must do it on purpose, to disarm people.

Well, I will not be disarmed.

I watch her walk gracefully across the room and out of the door. Objectively, she looks very attractive in her wide greenish trousers and cream silky shirt. Well, she *is* very (physically) attractive, which is a good thing for my mission. I just need to find someone who only cares about looks and doesn't mind about how *incredibly* annoying she is.

I'm still nursing my oversweet prosecco when I suddenly realise that I've been thinking about this entirely the wrong way. It isn't about finding someone who finds *her* attractive. It's all about *her* falling in love.

Which is fine. Easy. I know who I'm looking for: her perfect romance hero. Except, in practice, how the hell am I going to manage to find that person?

I mean, what's her type? How can I find that out? Can I somehow wangle an invitation to meet her friends and ask them? No. Clearly not.

I down the rest of the prosecco in preparation for leaving, and then wonder why I did that. I could have just left it and had less of an aftertaste. I need to eat something salty (and not those nuts) to clear the sugary sensation.

My mind continues to whir on the subject of the challenge as I make my way through the bar and out of the hotel.

I know that I'm not going to lose the challenge, because Freya cannot possibly convince me that I'm never going to find lasting love. I mean, romance isn't for me right now, because I did not enjoy my divorce and one of the reasons that our marriage fell apart (I think) is that I was working too hard, which I'm still doing. Also, as my parents get older, I need to help them more with my brother, who was seriously injured a few years ago in an accident and can't live alone, and not every woman (certainly not my ex-wife) is up for that, plus again it means I'm even busier. So I'm not currently ready to begin serious dating again. I will be one day, however, I'm sure. And there is no reason that romance will not then turn into lasting love. Freya cannot convince me otherwise.

Freya. I really don't want to have to spend too much time talking to her but I would very much enjoy beating her. I do not want to draw with her.

I step outside the hotel and nod a thanks when a doorman asks if I want a cab. Yes I do, since *Wake Up Britain* are paying. Kind of the least they can do when they're subjecting us to this torture.

How am I going to find love for Freya? Maybe I can introduce her to my single male friends and colleagues. I might – probably will – also need to go down the Tinder route. Although... how? Can I sign up for it on her behalf? I mean, obviously I *can*, but is that legal? As a fairly high-profile lawyer, I really can't be doing illegal stuff, however minor.

'Nice evening?' the taxi driver asks me. 'It's fancy in there.'

'Yes, it is,' I agree politely. 'And yes, great evening, thanks.' Shit evening actually.

I continue to think about the challenge as we make small talk, until I realise something. I think that – just like some of her readers – Freya's fallen in love with her own romantic protagonists to such an extent that no-one in real life matches up.

Okay, so all good: I'm going to win this stupid challenge. I just need to find the right romantic hero personified and introduce her to him. And – brainwave – I just need to read one of Freya's books, get to know the kind of heroes she's created.

And then find a similar man.

I'm going to win.

* * *

I decide that I'd like to get the book out of the way as soon as possible so it isn't hanging over me, so I download her most recent one as soon as I get home. As I buy it, I wonder what proportion of the money will go to Freya. Probably not that much, but any amount is too much, as a matter of principle. I'm paying good money to read a book in a genre of which I thoroughly disapprove, written by a woman who really annoys me. It doesn't feel like money well spent.

She's dedicated the book to her friend Lizzie, 'who's always there for me'. Yeah, whatever. Does Lizzie even exist, given that the 'I believe in love' persona that Freya created for herself was fake?

I begin the first page with great reluctance. I'm *gutted*, frankly, when a laugh is surprised out of me within the first paragraph. A great first paragraph does not a great book make, however.

Okay, it's actually, as it turns out, a great first *page*, insomuch as from my perspective at least it's very well written, it's made me laugh and I do actually want to read on. Just to see exactly how the two main protagonists are going to meet.

When I get to the end of the first chapter, I read on again. I've got to know the female protagonist, and, if I'm honest, I like her. But that's not why I'm reading this book. It's the male protagonist I want to get to know. We've met him, but only through the eyes of the female protagonist. It would be nice to know what *he's* thinking.

By the end of the second chapter, which is written from the male protagonist's perspective, I'm feeling a little gloomy. He's great. I really like him. He's *really* great.

I'm so engrossed in the story that I don't do any of the work I needed to get through this evening; I just carry on reading, until *way* past the time I should have gone to sleep, until I've finished the story.

I love the ending. I love the heroine. And I *really* love the hero. I mean, I don't usually go for men but he's *so* great I think I'm almost in love with him myself. He's tall, dark and handsome (okay, so he's a walking cliché, but I didn't notice that while I was reading him). He's funny. He's a little arrogant and a little hard-hearted to start off with, but in a very understandable way, and underneath he has a huge heart of gold. There's *nothing* he wouldn't do for the heroine. Or his family. Or his friends. Or anyone, frankly.

Yep, okay, so it doesn't *matter* that he's so great. I just need to find someone equally perfect for Freya. There clearly *are* great men out there. Like a lot of my male friends, so no problem. Her hero's a chef, and I don't know a lot of chefs, but that's fine. Freya's obviously creative, being a writer. And chefs are obviously creative and artistic. So that's the kind of man I need to find for her. Not *specifically* a chef. Really no problem. I do have three months after all. I don't need *him* to fall in love with *her*. I just need *her* to fall in love.

It really annoys me that I feel a twinge of guilt – bigger than a twinge actually; a large pang – at the thought of somehow causing someone to fall in love with someone who isn't interested in them. It's ridiculous having to feel guilty about a situation that I did not in any way cause.

She'll be fine, I tell myself firmly. It doesn't seem *that* likely, if I'm honest, that I can tempt her to fall in love with someone, but if I *do*, it's only what I've been asked to do, and she knows that.

* * *

I don't hear from Freya for a couple of days, and begin to hope that she's so horrified by the entire challenge that she's just pretending it isn't happening and isn't going to do anything about it. By late afternoon on Friday, I'm pretty sure that I'm never going to hear from her again.

And then, very disappointingly, just out of a meeting with a potential client so unreasonable that I fully sympathise with his soon-to-be ex-wife and am strongly considering refusing to act for him, I get a message from her:

> I have a plan. Bit of a two birds one stone: forced proximity and literal blind date.

I have no idea what she's talking about. Is this message even for me? Then I get another one:

> See you at In The Dark at 8 p.m. on Tuesday. It's a restaurant – don't eat beforehand. I'll send the address soon.

Oh, okay. The *date* is going to be forced proximity and a literal blind date. Right.

* * *

I work quite late and then have a Friday evening dinner with uni friends, and it's only when I'm on my way home that I think again about the challenge and next Tuesday.

Have I made a strategic error asking Freya to go first? Given her a head start on me?

No. I've just given myself extra planning time, which I should use.

Given that I *do* have extra time, I'm thinking I should use it for extra research.

Yep. I'm going to read a second Freya Cassidy, much as it pains me to add to her sales. I'll listen to one on the way to visit my parents and brother tomorrow.

* * *

I always enjoy the journey out of Central London to Barnes to visit my family. Firstly, the familiar route gives me a kind of comfortable going-home feeling. Secondly, it's nice visually to see the beautifully well-kept pastel terraces of Chelsea give way to the bustle of the Sloane Square end of the King's Road, followed by the always-fascinating array of different shops as I trace the road all the way to the New King's Road and Putney Bridge (thankfully for once not too traffic-ridden) and along the south side of the river to leafy Barnes.

Today, though, my journey is marred by having to listen to my second Freya Cassidy book. I'm frowning within only a few paragraphs. The first chapter of this one is written from the hero's perspective, and at first acquaintance he seems to be completely different from her other hero, but equally lovable.

The second chapter sounds weird to me, because it's from the heroine's perspective and read by a female narrator, and – even though I do not like Freya – I can't help wishing that it's her, and not some stranger, reading her words.

By the end of this chapter, I realise that, yes, the hero *does* seem very different from the other one. And the heroine, also adorable, is different from the other heroine.

And that is a real bugger, because maybe, after all, I'm not gaining any insights into Freya Cassidy, the person behind the author. Or into her perfect man.

No. That can't be true, I think as I pull up outside my parents' house.

There must be some common themes. Like, for example, both her heroines are very optimistic people. And her heroes are both creative (this one's an architect).

It's a relief to spend some time with my family and then drive Max, my brother, out to the Surrey countryside to get a break from obsessing about winning the challenge. I tell Max about it and he laughs so much I actually feel grateful to Sonja for a moment.

* * *

I finish Freya's second book the next morning, Saturday, while on the treadmill in the gym. I have to admit that it's genuinely almost unputdownable (or un-stop-listen-to-able). I find myself really caring about her characters and simultaneously sad to say goodbye to them and happy about the ending. (I don't think it's a spoiler to say that, yes, they do have a happily-ever-after.)

The story was – within the constraints of being another romance – really quite different from the first one. I don't think I've fully got a handle on the perfect hero for Freya yet.

I'm going to have to read a third one.

And – something I would not have credited – it isn't even going to be that much of a hardship if her other books are as well written and as unputdownable as the two I've read.

* * *

By Tuesday, when it's time to head out to meet her and whoever she's set me up with, I've read (almost *inhaled* if I'm honest) another three of her books and have come to the conclusion that she's cleverer than I had previously given her credit for and that her books really *are* quite dangerous. (I'm also wondering why I've never read a romance before; *she* is not great, but her stories *are*.)

Of *course* readers fall in love with her heroes. Of *course* her books are contributing to marriage breakdowns. Real people are rarely going to match up to fictional but well-drawn, believable ones.

I think it's going to be very hard for me to outright win this challenge.

I'm not giving up though.

7

FREYA

As I wait for my friend Charlotte outside the restaurant where she's going to be having dinner with Jake this evening, I grapple again with the ethics of this challenge. I *really* don't like upsetting people. Even people like Jake Stone.

I say *people like* Jake Stone. There are very few people like him. He might be the only one. *The* most annoying person ever born. I've literally never met anyone else who gets under my skin in the exact way he has done on the two occasions we've met. He isn't *overtly* unpleasant (except to me), it's more his *air*. Like he *knows* he's right. Except he isn't. And he isn't loud or brash by demeanour, but people still just *listen* when he speaks, because he has this really irritating air of authority. (As commented on, on social media, by many of the viewers of the show.) And it's incredibly annoying when someone is extremely authoritative and yet wrong.

And he *knows*, it seems, that my books cause relationship break-ups.

I mean, please. Of course they frigging don't.

My thoughts are interrupted by Charlotte's arrival.

'Freya!' She envelops me in her arms and a wave of her gorgeous perfume hits me. I immediately worry that Jake's going to love the scent as much as I do.

Which brings me back to not wanting to upset anyone.

It took a lot of thought deciding who to ask to go on this blind date, given that in any dating situation there's the potential for misery.

I don't want to set Jake up with someone who will fall for him who he will not fall for back. That would be awful.

And I also don't in fact want him to fall for someone who doesn't feel the same way. I don't *like* him, but I don't actually wish ill on him (other than for him to lose this challenge and be forced to apologise to me).

But obviously I'm not going to achieve anything if I introduce Jake to women he would realistically never hit it off with romantically and then he... doesn't hit it off with them. That clearly wouldn't shake his belief in finding love at all.

So I think I need to introduce him to women who are exactly his type and have him discover that he *should* on paper be attracted to them but he is not. And I need to go for every single romance trope I can manage to cover, so that there's no possibility he can think it's the *way* he met them. And while doing all of that I do at all times need to do my best to ensure that the women he meets won't fall for him and get upset. Unless he also falls for them (in which case I will have lost the challenge but at least I won't have caused any misery).

It's a complete minefield.

I realised quickly that I can't set him up with strangers – I have to be able to explain the exact situation to his future dates, to minimise the potential for hurt – so I can't do any Tindering.

So I'm limited to my single friends and acquaintances.

I wasted a lot of good writing time doing some internet research on him to try to work out the type of woman he usually goes for. It was fruitless. He doesn't seem to be on any social media. He *is* on his law firm's website but clearly there are no photos of anyone he's dated on there. I found one photo of him with his ex-wife, a very beautiful brunette. But I'm not sure how much a photo of one ex (however significant) helps. I also think that – assuming he has a physical type – it would be *awful* of me to try to find an ex-wife-lookalike for him.

In the end, I decided that the way forward for this first date was to go for someone who is lovely and attractive, not currently looking for love unless it comes right up and slaps her in the face, so hopefully there's no chance of her getting hurt if and when it doesn't work out, *and* does a job that I *know* Jake hates: romance author.

Charlotte has sold literally millions of Mills & Boons under one pseudonym and also writes non-Mills-and-Boon romcoms under another name. You can't get more *romance author* than that. She's also very good company and a lot of fun, and extremely beautiful in a Marilyn Monroe way, and anyone would be very lucky to date her.

I'm hoping that Jake will start to fall for her and then realise that her job is a deal breaker and that it will be a very good start at shaking his confidence in love.

Will it really, though?

I mean, the thing is, how is this even going to work?

It's a ridiculously flawed concept.

Like, I initially wondered whether I should ask my girlfriends to go on dates with him and be obnoxious and put him off. But what would that achieve? He'd just think yeah, no, not for me but, so what, there are other women.

And he'd be right.

How *can* you prove to someone that they won't ever fall in everlasting love if they're eternally optimistic by nature? The only hope is to bombard him with huge evidence that he won't. But Jake's in his mid-thirties and divorced. He's had a lot of life experience already and he *still* believes there's a happily-ever-after out there for him.

I am so clearly therefore not actually going to win this. It just can't be possible. And, really, I shouldn't try to. I don't *like* Jake, but I don't want to be mean to him. I don't want to depress him. I just want him to understand that he's wrong about romance novels. And that he's smug. And generally very annoying.

Unfortunately, however, Sonja announced on national TV that Jake and I are both joining in with this stupid challenge. So I have no choice but to give it a go, nominally at least.

'You look worried,' Charlotte tells me, pulling out of our hug a little and studying my face. '*I* should be the nervous one.' It turned out that I didn't have to tell her about the challenge because she'd seen it all on TV. (Obviously. Everyone's seen it.)

She's a big believer in love but is fairly newly single and quite cautious right now about leaping into a new relationship, although totally up for some no-strings sex. (I must remind her *very* firmly not to tell me *anything* if they do end up hooking up in any way. I do not want to hear about Jake and sex.) So she's actually an ideal person (insofar as there can be one) in that she's very unlikely to fall for anyone right now but *is* open to love.

'There's no need at all for you to be nervous,' I say. 'I know that *I* found him annoying, but you might find him excellent company. You might adore him. It might be the start of a beautiful relationship.' Gaaah. *If* Jake and Charlotte fall for each other, I would be very pleased for her (assuming he turned out to be a good partner) but I'd be very disappointed to have to be nice to Jake forever if he becomes Charlotte's other half. 'And if it isn't, what's the worst that can happen? Even if he's terrible company, at least you get to have a really interesting experience. I've been wanting to go to this restaurant for months.' It's really hard to get a table here; the TV company had to pull strings.

Charlotte nods and says, 'That *is* true. I hear they operate a several-month-long waiting list.' She's still frowning a little, though. Then, suddenly, her demeanour brightens. 'I *know*. Why don't you come in with us for a bit? Just for the beginning?'

I shake my head, as sorrowfully as I can manage. 'Although I'd love to, I can't, because it's a table for two.' Thank goodness.

Charlotte shakes her own head. 'No, no. I read about it. You spend a little bit of time in the bar first, getting acclimatised to the darkness, before they lead you through to your table. You can come and have a drink with us before we eat.'

It's fully pitch-dark in there, so that you (according to their website) savour both the flavours of your food and your companions' company without getting distracted by visuals. They recommend that you arrive separately so you don't see each other at all beforehand, and you can leave separately too. They have several different entrances for that very reason. I love the concept and will be looking forward to hearing about Charlotte's experience.

I don't want to join them, however; I have no wish to see Jake. I just came to meet Charlotte before she went inside to thank her again and give her more of a personal low-down on things, and check that she's definitely okay about doing it. I can't say no to a drink, though, because she's my friend, she's lovely, and she's basically doing me an enormous favour.

'You can obviously back out if you'd like to,' I say, really hoping that she won't. I don't want to have to organise a different evening this week. Sonja extracted written promises from us that we would do something on a weekly basis with exceptions only for illness, holidays and extreme personal events.

'No, no, I'm here and as you say what's the worst that can happen. Especially since you're coming in with me to start off with. And I *do* think it will be an interesting experience. Plus I saw him on TV and he's *gorgeous*. So smouldery.'

I clamp my lips together to stop myself from correcting her. She's got the wrong 'sm' word. What he actually is, is smug. And smirky as well. Not smelly, I'll give him that. But not smouldery either.

'You'll have a fantastic time,' I say.

'Starting with a lovely drink with you,' she says, and grabs my hand. 'Let's go.'

* * *

The second we get inside, I realise that I am in fact quite pleased that Charlotte brought me in. It's very interesting being in a social situation operated in complete pitch-darkness. It will also be interesting witnessing the first meeting between Charlotte and Jake.

We're being led by the hands by a woman towards the bar.

I'm completely and utterly clueless within seconds about my surroundings. I have no idea how far we've walked or what direction the door we came in is, or... anything.

(Apparently there are lights in the loos – you're led to your fully lit cubicle, released inside and then afterwards taken back to your seat. Charlotte specifically checked about that before she agreed to the date.)

We're both guided onto bar stools (which have backs, luckily, because the darkness seems to affect balance too) and then a deep voice says, 'Hi. I'm Jake,' and I nearly fall off mine.

I hadn't really registered before how very deep his voice is. I was too busy being furious, initially about his disdain for the romance genre, the reading of which makes a *lot* of people *very* happy, and then about his apparent desire to trash my reputation and career.

His voice is *really* deep. Being a romance writer, I'd have to call it gravelly. And if I were one of my own characters, I'd have to mention that it's caused the little hairs on the back of my neck to stand up. I think the reason for that is – even though I did know we were meeting him here – I didn't expect him to have arrived first, so hearing him speak was a bit of a surprise.

'Hi,' says Charlotte. 'I'm Charlotte.'

'And I'm here too,' I say quickly because I suddenly *really* don't want to know what Jake's like in flirt mode. I think it might make me feel sick. 'Freya.'

'Oh, right.' And, yes, his voice has definitely changed, got colder. Clearly he dislikes me as much as I dislike him.

'I thought it would be nice if she came in and introduced us,' Charlotte explains. 'Shared a drink with us at the bar.'

'Great,' says Jake in an unenthusiastic tone.

I glare in the direction of his voice and say nothing.

A silence almost as dense as the darkness begins to envelop us, and then, just as I'm beginning to feel very guilty in case this is awkward for Charlotte, and am considering starting up some basic conversation, there's a bit of shifting around from what I think is her direction, and then she gamely says, 'So, national TV and a challenge. I'm guessing you've entered into this as reluctantly as Freya has?'

Jake laughs (clearly going for fake charm – I've just thought of another 'sm' word for him – smarmy) and says, 'It's certainly a strange one. And I think Freya might have drawn the short straw. Whatever she does, I don't think she's going to be able to convince me that there's no everlasting love in my future. Whereas all I have to do is get her to fall in love.' I don't like his tone. Sarky. He put a lot of emphasis on the word *whatever*. As though he thinks I'm going to go down the setting him up on disastrous dates route on purpose.

Charlotte is not stupid. 'Are you perhaps imagining that Freya thinks there is *no* possibility that you could fall for me?'

'Ha, yes, no,' Jake says. 'Perhaps I worded that badly.'

'Yes, you did,' I inform him. 'Charlotte is one of my best friends. And also very attractive by anyone's standards.'

'Great,' replies Jake, even more sarkily. 'I'm sure we'll hit it off very well then.'

'Frankly,' says Charlotte, 'I'm tempted to walk out at this point, but I'm actually quite interested to experience the restaurant part. Happy to stay with Freya instead of you, though.'

'Sorry,' says Jake. 'I would very much like to spend the evening with you. I, er, just couldn't resist a little – entirely joking – dig at Freya because we had the small disagreement that led up to this challenge.'

I *love* hearing him grovel.

'Are you just saying that because you have to – because of the contract with the production company?' I can't resist asking. I'd be extremely happy to have dinner here with Charlotte in his stead and tell Sonja that he reneged. That would pretty much be a win for me straight off.

'Certainly not,' Jake says, doing something with his voice that makes it sound almost caressing, and makes me want to reach out in the dark and punch him, frankly. 'I'm very much looking forward to getting to know Charlotte.'

'Keep talking,' says Charlotte, apparently having fallen for his caressing tones.

'What would you like to drink?' a voice asks us and I scream slightly.

'It's okay. You're safe,' says Jake, in a *really* sarcastic voice.

'Thank you so much,' I say, not gritting my teeth at all.

There's laughter coming from the direction of the voice (well, I think it's the direction; I now feel that I have no idea where anything or anyone is, even with sound clues).

I choose a mocktail (I feel like I need to keep my wits about me) while Charlotte and Jake both choose margaritas.

'So how do you two know each other?' Jake asks once we've finished choosing.

'Well,' Charlotte begins. 'There's a long version and a short version.'

'I'd love to hear the long version.' Jake has injected a hint of laughter into his voice, which, if I didn't know better, I'd think was bordering on attractive. As it is, I know it's an entirely cynical ploy to make sure he's definitely got Charlotte back on side after his earlier mess-up.

Charlotte starts the story by telling him that she writes romance too.

'Oh, I *see*.' Jake sounds like he's sniggering to himself, and I'm pretty sure that he's immediately realised that one of the reasons I asked Charlotte this evening is that I know he cannot stand romance authors.

As she tells him about us being the only two authors at a conference who got the wrong bus (we went north; we were supposed to go south) from our hotel and ended up at a solar-powered swimming pool makers' conference (which we did not immediately realise), he chuckles in all the appropriate places (Charlotte is a *great* raconteur) and generally behaves like the entirely pleasant companion he is not, all the while giving me the impression that he's seen *right* through me.

This impression is confirmed when his first question following the story is, 'So romance. What books do you write, Charlotte? Do you have a pen name?'

'Ha ha, no, I think it's too soon to tell you that,' Charlotte says. 'I saw your conversation on TV.' She lowers her voice so it's all husky and seductive-sounding. 'If you fall in love with me and prove Freya wrong, I'll tell you then.'

Jake and I both laugh, which is an achievement on Charlotte's part; I can't imagine there's much that Jake and I would both find funny.

'What *kind* of romances do you write?' Jake persists after a moment. I'm quite surprised that he knows there are different kinds; I'd have thought he'd lump romance as a genre all in together.

'All contemporary. Some comedies, some *extremely* spicy, some both funny *and* spicy.' Charlotte doesn't write under her own name and is clearly not going to fall into the trap of telling him anything that will make her easily identifiable.

If I thought there was the slightest chance I could win this challenge, now would be a good time to try to get to know a little bit more about Jake and try to work out what direction I should be going in with these dates.

'So that's me and my career,' Charlotte says. 'What about you? What made you decide to become a divorce lawyer?'

'I suppose it's the combination of law and helping people through a difficult time in their lives.' He says it so glibly that it's obvious he says it every time like that. And of *course* he isn't going to say anything in front of me that would give me any leverage for the challenge.

This is pointless, I decide, and I have stuff to do this evening.

Hopefully – unless she falls in love with Jake and would feel disloyal doing so – Charlotte will fill me in later on anything she learns about him (barring anything physical, I very much hope).

'I should leave you two to it,' I say. 'So you can move on from the why-do-you-do-your-job interview-style questions to your actual date.'

If only it weren't pitch-black and I *could* actually leave. 'Um.' I catch myself pointlessly looking around.

'Are you looking around for someone to help right now even though you can't see?' Jake asks. 'Because I just did that and I'm wondering if I'm the only one who can't adjust fast.'

Okay. No. We don't do pally. He's obviously just trying to make Charlotte think he's a normal, friendly person. I'm not going to be petty though. (Not in front of Charlotte, anyway.)

'Ha,' I say. 'Yep. I did.' I put my hand up and kind of waggle my fingers, and then I clear my throat loudly.

A voice immediately says, 'Can I help you?'

And within a minute I'm on my way out, saying, 'Well, I would hug one of you and blow polite air kisses at the other, but I obviously can't see you, so... I'll just wish you a good evening and look forward to hearing all about it. Have fun!'

As I'm led away, Charlotte says, 'I'll text later.'

And Jake says, 'You're never going to win.'

'In your dreams,' I reply, because childishly I am not going to let him have the last word this evening.

And, *crap*. The more I think about it, the more it's obvious that I can't win because I *cannot* convince him that a happily-ever-after isn't waiting around the corner for him. But, also, *he* can't win, because I know I'm not going to fall in love. Which means – terrible thought – if we're both honest about the outcome of these dates we're both going to be losers on a team-building weekend in Devon.

Torture.

8

JAKE

As I bite into a perfectly cooked rare steak, I admit to myself that I'm actually quite grateful to Freya for choosing this restaurant for my date with Charlotte.

Firstly, it's a fascinating experience. It's absolutely true that when it's pitch-dark all your other senses are heightened. All of them. And that is interesting.

It does make a difference to how you enjoy the food. The restaurant asked about allergies and intolerances in advance, and they haven't told us what we're getting; they just place it in front of us and guide our hands to our cutlery. The food's in bowls, rather than on plates, which makes it a lot easier to find with our knives and forks.

The first thing that hits you is the smell of the food, and then there's a texture clue from how your cutlery goes into it, and then of course the taste. Eating in the dark like this demonstrates how heavily you're influenced by visuals when you have them.

I thought it would also be very instructive not being able to see my companion at all while talking to her, but realised quickly that, once you're opposite each other at a small table, it isn't particularly different from talking to someone over the phone, when you also can't see the other person's facial expressions or body language. (I *will* be interested to see what Charlotte looks like, whenever I get to see her – I trust that I will – because I have of course – as one does – formed a vague idea.)

It also hasn't taken very long to get used to the fact that there are 'helpers' walking around checking that everyone's managing their food properly.

'What are the vegetables?' I ask Charlotte. We established quite quickly that she is better than I am at identifying meal constituents in the dark.

'I think the sweetish, softish chunks are sweet potato, and I think there's some salsify in there. Also some broad beans and some diced tomato.'

I nod even though she can't see me do so. 'Sounds right.'

I like Charlotte. Yes, she's a friend of Freya's, and, yes, she's a romance author, but she's very pleasant company. She has a very pleasant voice, too. She's very pleasant full stop. I'm not feeling any strong attraction, but I wasn't expecting to. Plus the presence of the helpers (whose breathing you can definitely hear at times) would inhibit intimate conversation if one were inclined to engage in it.

'That was delicious,' Charlotte says some time later, after we've finished an excellent dessert that we agree – well, Charlotte told me, and I thought she was right – was plum and almond cake with yoghurt sorbet and prunes. 'Should we...?'

'Yep.'

A helper immediately materialises and asks us if we arrived together and if we'd like to leave together or separately.

'Together?' Charlotte says. 'I feel as though I know exactly what you look like from the TV, and I'd really like to know whether you look the same in real life.'

'Absolutely. I'd like to know whether you look like the idea I've formed of you.'

'A flattering one I trust?' Charlotte's smiling (I think) – you can hear it in her voice – and I laugh.

The helper leads us out of the pitch-dark room and into a dimly lit area, where we blink a lot.

'From what I can see, you *do* look like you.' Charlotte's peering at me.

Charlotte seems to be medium height, blonde and beautiful.

'And you look pretty much as I imagined,' I say.

'Let's both take that as compliments.'

'Good idea.' I grin at her, thinking that I'd like to see her again, but only as friends; she's lovely but I haven't felt a romantic connection. Plus I just don't think I have space in my life for romance right now. It's something for the future.

We then go into a slightly less dimly lit room and so on until we're in regular light. And, yes, Charlotte is indeed blonde, beautiful and medium height.

'Good to meet you,' I say.

'Lovely to meet you too.' She smiles at me. 'Guessing this evening made absolutely no difference whatsoever to your views on happily-ever-afters.'

'None,' I agree.

She laughs. 'I'll let Freya know. I don't think she'll be surprised.' We've already established that she and Freya are very good friends. 'I'm sure she can still win,' she adds loyally. 'Rome wasn't built in a day.'

I shake my head. 'She won't be winning.'

And that's the end of our dinner. It was a perfectly pleasant evening having an interesting experience with a very nice woman and I have not changed my mind about anything.

* * *

In the morning, I pick up my phone to message a friend, and see that Freya is typing a message to me. The typing stops, restarts, and then stops again. I have to say, I do enjoy imagining her being tempted to send me a snarky message and then feeling that she has to restrain herself.

I'd quite like to send *her* a message, pointing out that she cannot possibly win this, because she cannot change my mind. You can't ever prove to someone that something they think *might* be out there doesn't exist.

Whereas I *could* win. You *can* prove to someone that something they don't believe in *is* there. I just need to find someone she falls in love with, and who will from their side fall in love with her to provide that happily-ever-after. Yeah, the latter part might be tricky. Even in the dark Freya was annoying. Plus she's going to be trying *not* to fall in love. Plus I only have three months.

The whole thing is a complete farce. Neither of us is going to win.

I send Sonja two videos from last night, one of me outside the restaurant saying I'm going in, and one afterwards walking along the street saying I had a great time with a lovely woman but that I don't think I've necessarily found true love; but one blind date has not changed my views on the likelihood of me finding love in the future. (I asked the restaurant if they were happy for me to video inside, and, happily, they weren't. Thankfully, Charlotte also declined to be videoed.)

Yep, such a farce.

* * *

After spending far too much time trying to come up with something better than meeting in a regular restaurant for Freya's date, I decide that my best approach is to steal her idea and hope that she doesn't feel any sense of victory as a result. Okay, I think she *will* feel smug about it and that annoys me, but I'm just far too busy to waste any more time on this.

So I ask Sonja if the production company can book the same restaurant for next Tuesday, and message Freya to ask her to meet my friend Minuk there.

Minuk and I met in our first term at uni and have been very good friends ever since (half a lifetime now). He's had the odd serious (ish) relationship but basically goes from short-term fling to short-term fling, always monogamously. He has *no* trouble attracting very attractive women – understandably, because he's great company and objectively good-looking and in good physical shape – and has always said that the reason he never stays with anyone for long is just that he hasn't met the right person yet. He's definitely not averse to longer-term relationships.

He could be the perfect person for Freya. She probably just hasn't met the right person yet either.

I mean, no, who am I kidding? What are the odds? You never know, though. Worth a shot.

Freya does of course gloat about my inability to think of a different meeting place. Her first message in response to my question is *Ha ha ha*. Her second is *Okay. I'll be there.*

And there we go. I can now put the whole challenge out of my mind for a few days. Well, not entirely, because I'm unable to prevent myself watching the *Wake Up Britain* montage of my date. (I'm pleased to see that they only managed to cobble together thirty seconds of footage.) I'm also recognised twice in one morning in the street, which I do not enjoy. And I can't help thinking of Freya and how incredibly annoying she is at least several times a day. But apart from that, all good.

* * *

Minuk messages me at around ten on Tuesday evening to say he and Freya have finished their evening and do I want to meet at our local (we live ten minutes apart on foot and there's a pub exactly equidistant between our houses) for a one-pint debrief. I did offer to meet him before their dinner but he said with great scorn that he's been on a *lot* of first dates before now and he really doesn't need anyone to hold his hand, which was good news for me; I don't want to see Freya more than I have to and I wanted to squeeze a gym visit in this evening.

I set off immediately and as I arrive at the pub I can see him walking down the road towards me. I wave and go inside to order us both a pint.

'So how was it?' I ask as soon as we've slapped each other's shoulders and sat down at a corner table.

'Well, she's lovely. Very nice.'

I nod, make a huge effort and do not correct him by saying no she bloody isn't.

Each to their own, after all.

And, obviously, if they *did* hit it off, great. As long as they don't hit it off so much that I lose one of my best friends to her. Fuck. That would be terrible. What was I *thinking*? I do *not* want Freya in my life as Minuk's plus-one.

'You going to see each other again?' I ask, panicking.

'Yeah, no, maybe. I liked her a lot.' Minuk likes a lot of women a lot, so that isn't too worrying. 'And I think she liked me. We agreed to leave by the same exit, and had a nice chat in the light out of earshot of those helpers. And by the way, that was *such* a weird experience. I'm glad to have been but I don't think I'd go back.'

'Same,' I agree. 'I liked the way that it made you really focus on everything about the food and your companion *except* the way they looked, but having the helpers there was just weird. The way you could hear their breathing from time to time.'

'Exactly.'

'Soooo... what are you thinking about Freya?'

'Ha. You have an extreme one-track mind this evening.'

'Totally,' I agree. 'I need that woman to fall in love.' Although not, in fact, with a good friend of mine, as I have just realised.

'Yeah, I don't think she's going to fall in love with me. I think she *liked* me.'

He's almost certainly right; everyone likes him. 'And I think we could maybe date a little. But I didn't get any I-could-fall-hard-for-you vibes. And I feel like I've reached a stage in life where I don't want to start anything that I know isn't going anywhere.'

I blink. This is not the Minuk I've known for eighteen years. 'Mate.'

'Yep. I know. Apparently it comes to us all. Thirty-six is a serious age, though. Like, blink and we'll be forty. I mean, obviously it's four years away, but that isn't long when you think about meeting someone, dating them for a while, then making a commitment, then having kids. If that's what you want. So there we go. I don't think I'm up any more for relationships that I know are going to be short term before I've even started them.'

'Wow,' I say.

'I know. I'm an adult.'

'Well, congratulations. And also, dammit.' I'm not sure whether I really mean *dammit*, because if Freya begins to date a good friend of mine I will obviously just be swapping one problem for another. I should probably actually be punching the air right now.

'Yeah. Sorry. I mean, Freya's a wonderful woman. Great company, beautiful. Just no spark.'

'Okay. So.' I'm still one-track. 'Did you learn anything about her that would give me a clue about how to find the person she's going to fall in love with?'

Minuk puts his elbow on the table and props his chin in his hand and spends a little time in a thinking pose.

Eventually, he comes up with: 'Nope.'

'Dammit,' I say again.

'Although... I've had an idea.' He pauses for a moment and then nods. 'Yep. I have it. You and she can't stand each other.'

I nod.

'So you need to find a man that you can't stand and she'll probably love them.'

'That's your idea? I find someone I really dislike and she'll fall in love with them? That's ridiculous. I mean, she *really* annoyed me but she isn't *weird*. She isn't going to like mass murderers or fascists, is she?'

'You don't know any mass murderers or fascists,' Minuk points out, like we're having an actual serious conversation.

'And I don't dislike any of my friends. No. This is stupid. I think I need to find someone who shares a lot of her tastes and set them up together. I'm thinking Tinder although I'd have to get her to agree to me putting her on there. Did you find out anything useful about her? Hobbies? Music tastes?'

'She is *not* a massive Swiftie even though she does really like some of Taylor Swift's songs and did go to one of her concerts with a friend and had a great time.' He says it like it's really unusual and not entirely normal for an affluent British woman in her thirties.

'Thanks. Anything else?'

'She likes good food. All global cuisines. She likes playing tennis but hates running. She enjoys going to the cinema. Likes holidays.'

As in, like a significant proportion of the population.

Yeah, this is not going to work. Of *course* I'm not going to find someone she's going to fall in love with.

* * *

Sonja tells Freya and me the next day on our *Love Challenge* WhatsApp chat that she and the production team *adore* the fact we went to the same venue for both our dates, and that's what we'll be doing going forward, and we'll be taking it in turns to choose.

Since Freya chose the *In The Dark* venue, I'll be choosing the next one.

And it can't be a restaurant.

But it's got to be *real* because we are essentially a reality show, Sonja says.

So real that we're being told what to do, I think, not really knowing what she means by *real*.

Anyway.

I need to come up with a venue that I will not mind going to myself and that might be conducive to Freya falling in love.

My mind's a blank, and I'm really busy with work, so it's a good job that Sonja texts a few minutes later to say:

Scrap that, we'll choose. Will revert.

When she comes back to us on the group chat she tells us they'd like us to have the choice because this is *our* challenge. So for the next double-header I can choose between their shortlist of Russian banya baths or feeding alpacas.

And we'll have to do a weekend day, whichever I choose. I'm a little speechless in horror.

Freya is not speechless. She shoots straight back on the chat with:

> Out of those two I would choose the alpaca feeding. A Russian banya sounds great but I'm not comfortable with getting into a swimming costume with a complete stranger. However, I don't have a lot of spare time at the weekends. Are there evening alpaca-feeding options so we can stick to Tuesdays as planned? Otherwise I think we will have to look at alternatives.

I have to acknowledge that that is punchy but fair. I can't bring myself to agree in writing with anything Freya says, but I do thumbs-up her message. Sonja tells us to leave it with her.

Within an impressively short space of time, she gets back to us and tells us that the alpaca farm will open specially for us next Tuesday and that – *brilliant idea! We're switching things up even more!* – we're going to have our dates simultaneously from now on.

I just stare at my phone. Now I'm double-dating with Freya? While I try to set her up with the man of her dreams? And she tries to destroy my faith in happily-ever-afters?

For fuck's sake.

***

I have a very busy week both work-wise and socially, so I don't have a lot of time to think about who to ask to go on this next date with Freya, and – let's face it – I have absolutely no idea who the right person would be so it would probably just be wasted thinking time anyway, so I basically do absolutely nothing about it.

Late on Sunday evening, though, when thinking about the week ahead, I realise that I do need to ask *someone*.

I have no time to try to find a stranger, so I text another good friend, Dan, explaining the situation and telling him I'll owe him his body weight in beers if he will help me out, and he very kindly agrees.

***

And here we are, on Tuesday evening, having travelled for over an hour and a half to somewhere that Sonja pretended was a very short journey away but is in fact quite a long distance into Kent, to meet Freya and whoever my date is, standing at the gates of an alpaca farm. As you do on a Tuesday evening in early March.

'You know what,' says Dan. 'I'm pretty happy to get up close and personal with an alpaca. They look very cute from a distance.'

I nod. That's the upside to this evening. I'm sure it *will* be cool to feed the alpacas and learn about them.

There are downsides though. And there's the big one: Freya, just getting out of a taxi, followed by another woman, who is clearly my date.

She's tall, slim and auburn-haired, with a very nice smile, which she is now directing towards Dan and me. She doesn't really look like someone who's going to convince me that I will never find love again.

Dan steps forward and sticks his hand out.

'I'm Dan.' He shakes Freya's hand and then the other woman's hand in turn. 'I recognise you from the TV, Freya.'

'Hi, Dan. It's lovely to meet you.' Freya bestows a big smile on him, and I see him slightly blossom under the full force of it. Ridiculous. Yes, on the one hand it's movie-star hot, but on the other, can he not tell that it's totally fake? She turns in the direction of her companion, and says, 'This is Lizzie. Lizzie, this is Jake.'

Lizzie and I shake hands and then we all stand there and say that the journey was long but it'll be *great* to meet the alpacas.

I push a buzzer on the gate post, and we're led inside. Dan and Freya walk together, and so do Lizzie and I.

'So how do you and Freya know each other?' I ask Lizzie, more for something to say than because I'm particularly interested.

'We were at uni together. We shared a kitchen and were also on the same course, and just kind of hit it off in the beginning.'

'Oh, that's nice. Dan's a uni friend of mine too. What did you study?' I'm not exactly producing scintillating conversation, but in my defence I don't like blind dates at the best of times, and knowing that this is designed by Freya to put me off dating for life, and doing it as a double date, is not making me happy.

'Economics.'

That's interesting, though.

'And Freya did that too?' I query.

'Yep. The girl can do business stuff *and* write well. She's a very impressive woman.'

'Yeah.' I'm annoyed with myself for being annoyed about the fact I cannot be anything other than impressed by what a great all-rounder Freya appears to be. Albeit an incredibly annoying all-rounder.

'Is she bad at anything?' I ask, because I can't help it.

Lizzie laughs. 'Not that I can think of. Apart from DIY. She can barely change a light bulb. And she wouldn't mind me telling you that.'

We're interrupted by Dan saying, '*Lizzie*. I've just been hearing about what you got up to on New Year's Eve.'

'Freya!' Lizzie gasps.

'Not *everything*,' Freya says. '*Obviously*. Just our outfits.'

'And the dancing on tables,' Dan says.

Freya dismisses that with a wave of the hand, while Lizzie says, 'Phew.'

'I'm intrigued.' Dan will now not let this go, and they *will* eventually tell us. Charming but steely tenacity is one of his most pronounced characteristics, which he uses to particularly good effect in his career (investigative journalism).

He's thwarted for the time being, though, because our alpaca farm host has appeared.

The alpaca host *does* consent to doing a short 'we've just arrived on our double date at the alpaca farm' video for Sonja, commenting that no publicity is bad publicity. Dan and Lizzie do *not* consent, which is a wise decision: in my brief experience any appearance on daytime television can lead to people recognising you in the street and, unless you actively want to be a celebrity, that is not fun.

A lot of alpaca facts are fired at us.

When we're told that they are easily house-trained due to their tendency to use a communal dung pile, and therefore make very good pets, Freya breathes, 'Oh my goodness, I want to *get* one.' She smiles at me and says, 'So much better than getting a man.'

'They're quite *big* for pets,' Lizzie points out.

'Not as big as a man, though,' Freya returns.

'No sex, though,' Lizzie says.

Freya shrugs and says, 'Yeah, no-one *needs* sex.'

Dan looks at me and shrugs too. And I shrug back.

Lizzie laughs at all of us, which makes me smile and Dan grin broadly.

Next, we glean a lot of facts about alpaca fleeces.

Freya is apparently fascinated.

'So their fleeces are hypoallergenic? And non-flammable? And water-resistant?'

'Are you having a business idea?' asks Lizzie.

'Totally.' Freya's looking the most animated I've seen her since she looked at me like she wanted to kill me in the TV studio. 'I mean, it sounds like a no-brainer?'

Lizzie turns to Dan and me. 'Not joking, she'll probably own the most successful alpaca farm in the UK in a year's time. The last time she got this excited about something, it was writing romance. And here we are.'

'Have you had any failed businesses?' I can't help asking.

'A couple,' Freya says.

'Not *failures*,' Lizzie says. 'Just you kind of lost interest.'

'Some businesses are less viable than you think they're going to be,' Freya elaborates. 'Like a vegan cake-making business is a tricky one. I ended up having to stay up all night baking a lot, and worked out that my profit was around one pound fifty an hour.'

'*This* one won't fail, though,' Lizzie says.

'Love a loyal friend,' says Dan. 'What other businesses have you tried?'

I very much like having a wingman to ask all the questions I'd like to ask.

Freya begins to speak but is interrupted by our alpaca farming host telling us that we are now ready to get to know the alpacas a little better.

It's immediately obvious that Freya, Dan and I all like the alpacas but Lizzie *adores* them. Where Freya's basically looking at them with dollars in her eyes, and Dan and I are looking at them with mild fondness in ours, Lizzie's looking at them through hearts.

We feed them – I've got to say that you'd have to have a heart of stone not to fall a little in love with their big, long-eye-lashed eyes as they look at you when you hand them the food (grass, leaves, bark and some broccoli stalks as a treat) – and the way they hum is, as Lizzie says, several times, very cute.

'I *so* much want you to set up an alpaca farm,' she tells Freya after we've said our – reluctant – goodbyes to the alpacas. 'So that I can come and cuddle them. And help you with them, obviously.'

'You could offer alpaca-cuddling experiences,' Dan says, very seriously.

'Exactly.'

'Fancy continuing the alpaca business development discussion over dinner and a drink?' Dan suggests to all of us.

'Definitely,' Lizzie says immediately.

Which basically means that neither Freya nor I can say no.

'Maybe somewhere nearby given that we've got a big journey home afterwards and it's Tuesday and places might not stay open late?' Lizzie sounds very keen for the evening to continue.

And so fifteen minutes later, the four of us are sitting in an Italian restaurant in Sevenoaks, and I'm surreptitiously googling what time the last train home is, while Dan and Lizzie talk nineteen to the dozen and Freya smiles at them both indulgently.

'I have to congratulate you,' she tells me while Dan and Lizzie exclaim loudly over the fact they've incredibly surprisingly found a mutual acquaintance. (It is not surprising; they live round the corner from each other and go to the same gym.) 'I think you might have genuinely engineered a lasting-love-at-first-sight situation.' She smiles. 'Not me, though.'

I'm tired and we're miles from home and I need to be up very early in the morning and I don't want to talk to the only companion available to me right now, Freya, but I really can't actually pull my phone out and start going through my emails. I mean, I would, but I don't want to upset Dan and Lizzie.

I also can't be bothered to try to think of anything sarcastic to say to Freya. She's entirely right about this.

So I just nod and say, 'So near and yet so far.'

9

FREYA

I'm genuinely very pleased for Lizzie about how she and Dan seem to be hitting it off so well. He seems like a nice guy. She's an incurable romantic and she needs a bit of good luck on the dating front, and this could be it.

So I *am* pleased, I really am.

But now? This Tuesday evening? In Sevenoaks? With Jake's very close friend?

Selfishly, I'd have loved this date to have been a lot closer to home and a lot shorter, and – the big thing – not involve Jake.

But it is what it is, and it *is* lovely that Lizzie seems to be having such a good time.

She and Dan have been talking to each other, eyes locked, apparently oblivious to anyone and anything except each other, for a good half hour.

Jake and I, by contrast, have not addressed a single word to each other for a long time, at least five solid minutes, I think. We've each glanced in the other's direction a couple of times, but that's it.

Lizzie and Dan probably won't have noticed the stony silence from our half of the table given how they're gazing into each other's eyes and physically mirroring each other's head tilts and hand gestures and generally looking besotted with each other, but in case they do, I feel as though Jake and I should make some small talk. This could be a memorable evening for Lizzie and Dan, in a good way, and we don't want to introduce any negativity to it.

So I address Jake. 'Great vegetables.'

'Vegetables?'

'The broccoli and carrots. They're very nicely done.'

He raises his eyebrows superciliously and then says, 'Yes, they are.'

'I'm enjoying eating them,' I persist.

'I'm so pleased to hear that.'

I draw a deep breath and remember that I am doing this for Lizzie, my very good friend.

'Are you enjoying yours?' I ask.

'My vegetables?' Jake tilts his head to one side for a moment as though considering, and then says, 'Yes.'

I want to kill him. Why can't he contribute at *all* to the conversation? For the sake of Lizzie and his close friend Dan?

'Great,' I say. 'How's your steak?'

'Not bad.' He looks at me for a long moment while I glare at him, and his lips twitch the tiniest of amounts, which makes me glare even more. 'How's your sea bream?'

'It's very nice, thank you. Cooked just the perfect amount and I like the sauce.'

'Excellent. That is *great* information.' He forks a piece of steak and puts it into his stupidly well-shaped mouth and begins to chew.

I'm really irritated by his chewing. I'm just sitting here watching him, and normally when you watch someone chew they do actually look quite weird and they also usually get quite self-conscious. Not Jake, however. Firstly, he doesn't look at all weird. Secondly, he seems completely fine with me watching him eat. He chews for a while, and I have to admit that it's a good length of time, not too long and not too short, and then he swallows.

'Before you ask—' he cuts another piece and puts it on his fork, together with some broccoli '—that was a very nice mouthful.'

'Great.' I spear some of my fish on my fork and put it into my mouth, and, oh bugger. That was a mistake. I have just given Jake the opportunity to stare openly at me while I eat. And, unlike him, I do not have the ability, it seems, to chew nonchalantly away while someone watches me.

He puts his cutlery down, leans back, folds his arms across his chest and continues to watch me.

I chew a few times while he carries on watching.

I do not like this. I do not like it at all.

I've chewed enough. I'm sure I can swallow now and end this being-watched-while-I-chew misery.

I swallow, and, gaaah, I hadn't chewed enough. I can't... I'm choking... I...

To give Jake his due, it does seem that he doesn't actually want me to *die*, or not right now anyway. Probably because of the hassle of getting my body home from Sevenoaks. Also, maybe he'd get done for manslaughter for staring me into choking. He stands up and takes one big step round the table and gives me a massive slap on the back, and the fish flies out of my mouth and lands exactly halfway between our plates.

While Jake sits back down, I stare at the half-chewed fish mouthful for quite a while, wondering if this day could get any worse. Then I recall that I do not like Jake and should not care what he thinks.

'Thank you.' I take my napkin from my lap and pick up the fish and fold it all up and put it under the side of my plate.

'My pleasure.' Jake's lips are twitching again.

Astonishingly, Dan and Lizzie have not looked even once in our direction.

Jake moves his chair towards the table and then leans in towards me and speaks softly, so that – if they *did* suddenly notice that we still exist and are still right next to them at the same table – Dan and Lizzie would not hear.

'Did I just beat you at your own game?' Jake enquires.

I close my eyes and summon up every single ounce of self-control I have and give a tinkly little laugh.

'Ha.' I don't say anything else, because I would like to be very cool or very cutting, but words have failed me, possibly because there is literally nothing cool or cutting I *could* say at this point.

Jake laughs out loud and I tap my foot under the table in irritation.

I've got a dilemma now. I want to eat the rest of my fish, because it's delicious and I'm still hungry. But I don't want to be stared at while I eat.

It's very, very annoying when you're in a tricky situation and you have only yourself to blame. Although I do also have Jake to blame, because if he hadn't irritated me so much I wouldn't have started this.

He leans in *again*. And says nothing.

'Yes?' I say after a few moments, a little tetchily if I'm honest.

'Shall we...'

'Yes?'

'Both eat without staring at the other?'

'Fine,' I say.

And we do, without speaking at all.

We finish at about the same time – I think we've both been keeping pace with the other kind of on purpose, with sneaky glances across the table – and we then look at each other.

'I hope you enjoyed the rest of your steak,' I say, very, very politely.

'I did, thank you. I hope you enjoyed the rest of your fish.' Jake's demeanour is also that of great politeness.

'I did, thank you.'

'I'm so pleased that you didn't choke again.'

'Thank you.' I do want to kill him.

Dan and Lizzie have also finished. So we should be able to go home soon, thank goodness, and put an end to this torture.

'Desserts?' the waiter asks.

Jake and I both shake our heads and begin to speak, just as Dan says, 'That would be wonderful. Or coffees, at least?'

Yay.

I order a fresh mint tea. Jake orders an espresso.

And Dan and Lizzie order an apple tarte tatin to share, and when the waiter tells them that it will take an extra fifteen minutes to make, they smile and say that that is not a problem at all.

And yay again.

After a couple of minutes of further silence, I feel guilty again in case our blatant not-getting-along might make Dan and Lizzie feel awkward, and say, 'I'm glad they have fresh mint here. Some restaurants only have peppermint tea bags. Which I do like, but I prefer fresh.'

'That is… *fascinating*,' Jake says.

I swivel my eyes towards Dan and Lizzie and mouth, 'Don't want to be obviously silent and miserable.'

'Oh, right,' Jake replies.

'Did you assume that I had an incorrigible desire to talk about food and drink with you?' I ask.

'Nothing to do with me if your conversation runs entirely on fish and tea,' he says.

I smile at him. 'I have thoughts on coffee too.'

'That's wonderful to hear.'

I nod and then look at the other two and then back at Jake.

He looks at Lizzie and Dan, then raises his eyes ceilingward and says, 'I do like espressos.'

We maintain a stilted beverage conversation until our own beverages arrive, and then we both sip slowly until I've finished my tea. Obviously an espresso is small and vanishes quite fast but I have a whole teapot so I drink two and a half cups, as slowly as I can.

By the time I've finally finished, Lizzie and Dan's tarte tatin has arrived, so it feels as though the end is in sight.

'Guessing you might have observations on apple-based desserts?' Jake asks me.

'Many,' I confirm, smiling to indicate to Lizzie and Dan – should they spare the odd second or two to look away from each other in our direction – that Jake and I are getting on very well.

Jake raises his eyebrows, and off I go. Tarts, crumbles, strudels. Jake nods and smiles, clearly having reluctantly bought into the idea of not making the others uncomfortable. Occasionally he makes an apple-based comment himself, but basically he leaves the heavy conversational lifting to me, which I do not appreciate, because I'm getting a very dry throat, and I have no more mint tea and – as I'm slightly losing the will to live – I can't really be bothered to try to attract the waiter's attention to ask for more tap water.

Eventually, thank *goodness*, Lizzie and Dan finish their bloody pudding.

'Wow, it's a lot later than I thought,' Lizzie says, staring at her watch.

Dan's phone is lying right next to him on the table, but he leans over to check Lizzie's watch rather than just turning the phone over. Cute.

'What time's the last train?' asks Jake, clearly pretty much as desperate as I am to get home and wanting to nudge them in the direction of thinking strongly about leaving rather than, for example, spending an eternity cutely drinking coffees together.

'Good point.' Dan checks Lizzie's watch across the table again and then he picks his phone up to check train times. 'We'd better get the bill. I'll order us an Uber to get to the station.' He swipes a bit on his phone and then says, 'There don't seem to be any Ubers available that will take four people, so we'll need to take two.' That sounds like a very transparent ploy to get some time alone with Lizzie. 'I can get one in two minutes and one in maybe ten. Why don't you two take the first one?' He smiles at me and Jake. 'And we'll see you at the station unless you get a train before us.'

After a slightly longer than acceptable pause, Jake says, 'That's very kind, if you're sure.'

'Yes, thank you, if that's definitely okay,' I chime in. We clearly have no choice.

From the way Dan's grinning at Lizzie now, I *very* strongly suspect that it isn't true that there are no Ubers around that would be able to take all of us.

We all hug goodbye (one or both of Dan and Lizzie is *so* clearly planning to miss the train), Dan whispers in my ear that Lizzie has told him the whole New Year's Eve story and I wince (and, no, I'm not sharing it more widely), I dash to the loo (far too much mint tea) and then the first (and perhaps only) Uber arrives and Jake and I climb into the back.

The driver is very chatty and assumes we're a couple.

I begin to correct him and then decide to just let it go and give vague responses to his questions. Jake says nothing at all. I look over at him and see that his stupidly perfect profile is pointed straight ahead and his features are totally unsmiling. That does actually cheer me up a little.

'There you go,' the driver says as he pulls into the station. 'Safe journey and enjoy the rest of your evening.'

'Thank you so much. You too. Good luck with your guitar exam,' I say. He was just telling us how he took up the guitar for his fiftieth birthday and his teacher has him doing exams and he's *loving* it.

I turn round and catch Jake rolling his eyes behind me.

'What?' I say as I wave goodbye to the driver.

Jake just shakes his head.

The train's delayed by fifteen minutes. I decide that I've had enough of Jake for this evening so I go and sit on a bench by myself. Within about twenty seconds I realise that there are greater evils than sitting on the same bench as him; there's a big group of drunk men about ten feet away from me, who aren't holding back on the shouted arsehole-letchy comments.

I'm actually – to my extreme annoyance – pleased when Jake comes and sits down next to me and gives them the evil eye and they shut up.

'Thank you,' I mutter.

'Please don't thank me. They're stupid dicks and I'm not specifically being helpful to you, I'm just ashamed of the world we live in and the way some men behave.'

'Okay. Well, good.'

'Yeah. If it makes you feel any better, it *really* wasn't personal. Like, we both know that I wouldn't do *you* a favour.' He's making a rare fair point.

I nod.

Then we sit in silence.

'No sign of Dan and Lizzie,' Jake observes as the train pulls in.

'No,' I agree. 'And this is the last train and it's delayed.' I wonder whether they've already found themselves a hotel for the night.

Jake follows me into the same carriage and sits diagonally opposite me in a four-group of seats, and I don't object, because, given those drunk men, his company is obviously the least of the evils that could befall me right now, especially if we don't talk.

Jake, however, *is* speaking.

'Still don't believe in love?' he enquires. 'After seeing such a blatant case?'

'Love?' I'm delighted to be on very sure footing for once. He's so clearly wrong and I'm so clearly right on this. 'That wasn't love. That was mutual *lust* at first sight. Which might totally turn into lifelong love, definitely. But right now, it's just lust.'

Jake nods, a hint of a smug look that I don't like on his face. 'Absolutely. But there's definitely the potential for it to turn into love, isn't there?'

Seriously. He cannot possibly think I'm going to fall for this argument.

I shake my head sorrowfully. 'Yes, there is. For *Lizzie and Dan*. Not for me. *I'm* not going to meet anyone. You aren't here to prove that *people* fall in love. We all know they do. You're here to prove that *I* will fall in love. Which I won't. So you cannot win.'

A small frown furrows Jake's handsome brow for a moment, before he says, in a suspiciously friendly voice, 'Why is it that you don't think love is for you?'

I sit back in my seat. 'Interesting change of tack,' I observe.

'Sorry?' He's still doing the friendly voice.

'Trying to see whether I just have a nebulous "I don't think love is for me" feeling or whether there's a concrete reason for me saying I won't be meeting anyone, which you might be able to talk me out of.'

To give Jake his due (which I do not like doing), he laughs.

Then he says, 'But how can you say never? I mean... surely never say never?'

'I just can.'

'Fine.' He drops the friendliness and leans back against the seat and closes his eyes.

I *had* warmed to him very, very momentarily, but there's something about the extreme self-confidence of someone prepared to snooze, or at least have a very serious rest, in public that really annoys me. I mean, to be fair, when *other* people look as though they're preparing to sleep on a train, I don't really mind. When Jake does it, however... it's extremely irritating. Is he not worried that he might dribble? Or snore a tiny bit? Or just look ridiculous?

Oh. Maybe he just really, really doesn't care what I think of him.

Or maybe he's pretending, to avoid me striking up another inane beverage- or fish-related conversation.

I should be grateful, not annoyed.

As the train pulls out of the station, I'm sure that Dan and Lizzie haven't arrived and caught it; I think we would have seen them.

At least *someone's* enjoyed this evening.

Actually, I did too, in part. The alpaca part. And now I'm going to put this train journey to good use by googling the different variables that would be involved in setting up an alpaca farm, and then thinking about the plot of my next book.

I can't concentrate, though.

I really want to know what Jake's thinking about Lizzie and Dan. It's so sweet. I genuinely think it *could* turn into a relationship. From Lizzie's side, anyway. What about Dan, though? Is he likely to treat Lizzie well?

She's had some very bad luck romantically, and been very hurt. It's rare that when one of your best friends meets someone you have the opportunity to ask a close friend of the person they've met what their intentions are... I really don't want to give Jake the opportunity to be rude to me *again*. But I feel that I would be letting Lizzie down if I don't at least attempt to ask him about Dan.

I'm just going to come straight out with it.

'Jake.' I wonder whether he's genuinely asleep. His chest is rising and falling slowly, like a fit person's would be when they were asleep, but he could obviously be pretending, to avoid speaking to me. 'Jake?' I give his foot a little nudge with mine.

'Freya?' He doesn't open his eyes, which annoys me.

'Lizzie is a lovely, kind, wonderful person,' I begin.

Jake does not respond.

'Jake?'

'Great,' he says, eyes still closed.

I pause, wanting to choose my words carefully, because obviously he can and might repeat anything I say to Dan, so I should only say things that Lizzie would be happy for Dan to know.

'She's been hurt before, and I don't want her to get hurt again,' I say, after a bit of thought.

Jake *finally* has the courtesy to open his eyes.

'Dan is also a great person and I don't think would ever intentionally hurt someone,' he tells me. 'I don't think he would have a one-night stand, should that happen, with someone he thinks wanted more if he didn't think he wanted more too.'

'Okay. Well, good.' I hope Dan *realised* that Lizzie looked (to my eyes) as though she was tumbling head over heels on the spot.

Jake closes his eyes again, and there's something about the way he hasn't even twitched during this little conversation, apart from the eye opening and closing, that suddenly makes me *furious*.

'This evening—' I nudge his foot again because I want him to hear what I'm saying '—and this whole situation, it's all your fault.'

Jake opens his eyes for a second before closing them *again*.

'That is incorrect,' he says a moment later.

'No, it bloody isn't. If you hadn't been so bloody rude on TV *none* of this would have happened. We'd have gone our separate ways and never seen each other again.'

He opens his eyes. 'And no-one would ever have called you out on writing such dangerous nonsense.'

'Oh, please. Literary snobs, broadsheets rounding up "books of the year", crime writers, I mean, *so many* people are rude about romance novels and romance writers. You are not the first. You *are* the first to explicitly tell me that my books cause divorces.'

'Yeah, well there you go. Good thing that I said it.'

'What do you *mean*, it's a good thing?' I think my head might explode. 'I'm going to carry on writing my books. I *like* writing them and I *like* my readers and I *like* the fact that my stories and their happily-ever-afters make people happy. People write to me to tell me that my stories have brightened their day, which is particularly important in the world we currently live in. I like all of that. And *nothing* you have said has convinced me that *anyone* would split up from their partner because of a romance that they'd read. And therefore the only result of what you said to me is this. This stupid, annoying, ridiculous, time-wasting challenge.'

Jake is frowning slightly.

I press on, because I have stuff to say and I *really want to say it*. 'You cannot convince me and I cannot convince you. Neither of us is going to win. We're going to be subjected to *dreadful* double dates every Tuesday and then in just under three months' time we're going to be going on a bloody weekend away doing our stupid, torturous team-building for two, because *neither of us can win*.'

Jake frowns more, which – obviously – just annoys me more.

'I mean this is *so* pointless,' I continue. 'Totally, completely, utterly, absolutely pointless. The best we can hope for is that we continue to provide a dating service for our friends. I mean, it's *ludicrous*. We are in a really, really, really stupid situation. And it is *all your fault*.'

'What about we admit defeat now? Both of us?'

I open my mouth to continue my rant and then register his actual words. 'What?'

'We could tell Sonja right now that we've completed the challenge because we have each agreed that we cannot win.'

'We'd still have to go on the weekend, I think.' My mind's whirring. I do think Jake is (finally) making a good point. We *could* just give up now. 'I personally do not want the British public to think I'm a quitter or a reneger.'

'Yep, I think we do both have to do the weekend,' Jake agrees. 'But there will presumably be other people there too. We can do our own thing, come back, do the reappearance on the show, and then it will all be over.'

I nod slowly and say, 'Finally you're talking sense.'

He raises an eyebrow. 'I always talk sense.'

'Agree to differ.'

We do though obviously finally agree on something: that we want to minimise the amount of crap we have to go through before Sonja deems this challenge completed.

'I'm happy to put a message to this effect on the chat tomorrow,' Jake continues.

'I will put a strongly worded agreement to your message on there.'

'She might not agree to it, of course.'

I consider. 'Yep, maybe not. I wish we could in good conscience throw Lizzie and Dan to the wolves. That would make a good story.'

'I mean, no it wouldn't? Boy meets girl and they get on well?'

'Kind of an ironic finish to the challenge, though? And, some would say, quite a sweet one? Made for TV?'

Jake does a sceptical little sneer, I'd have to call it, and then says, 'Well, to be fair to you—' I mouth *wow* and he rolls his eyes at me '—who knows *what* the TV people will like. We clearly aren't going to mention anything about Dan and Lizzie though?'

'No, of course not!' I'm insulted by him *again*. Like I'd throw *anyone*, let alone a very close friend under a bus like that. 'Unless they have an insane urge to get on daytime TV by *any* means, that would be awful for them.'

'Agreed.' Jake looks at me, his mouth kind of quirked up at the corner, like he's thinking *and there's a first*. To be fair, I am also thinking that.

'Anyway. We have a plan. Good news.' And then he – frankly very rudely – closes his eyes again, and I glare at him for a few seconds before beginning to google alpaca farming again.

10

JAKE

I planned to message Sonja on our group chat as soon as I got up in the morning, to pre-empt anything she might have to say to us, but I see when I crawl out of bed that she's pre-pre-empted me, saying that she wants *all the deets from last night, hope there was some ACTION*. Also, with no further pretence that anyone wants to give either Freya or me any choice in the matter, she continues with:

> Exciting news! We've decided on next week's double date! Karaoke!! Yay! Can't wait to hear all about that one too!

I write:

> Wow, that would have been great, but Freya and I have discussed and we've agreed that neither of us can win. I remain convinced that true love is out there for me. And Freya remains convinced that, for her, it is not.

I take a moment to wonder again, as I did last night on the train, *why* Freya is so convinced of that, and then remember that I've already reminded myself that it is no concern of mine. I continue with:

> And we both know that neither of us will change our minds. And therefore we both have to concede the challenge now.

Freya and Sonja are both online.

Freya responds with a *Yes, agreed* message.

And Sonja responds with a *What!!! No?!?!?!?!?!* message.

Freya elaborates with:

> We know that neither of us can either win or lose, so we think we should just cut to the chase and go on our bonding weekend now, should you still wish us to do that.

Sonja does some stop-start typing for a while and then nothing, so I get in the shower, trusting that she's speaking to her producers to okay our excellent idea.

Nope, I discover when I get out; she's insisting that we do the karaoke because it's all arranged and it's going to be *amazing*. We're going to love it! We're going to laugh until our sides hurt! It's going to shake up both our views on love! Because it's a *love*-themed karaoke!

Freya's reply came immediately afterwards, while I was showering, reiterating that yesterday evening we managed to prove exactly nothing and exactly everything (grudgingly I do have to admit to myself that I like that phrase), and that we have discussed and are both certain that the other will not budge in their opinions.

And then Sonja pointed out that we have a contract, *end of*, and told us that the karaoke will be *F.U.N!!!!!*

Freya asks if we can please re-evaluate after the karaoke, because we both *know* that neither of us can win, and when we go back on and they show the montage it's going to be ridiculous. And, she says, really, maybe our suggestion will be *better* TV.

Sonja says that on that subject could we send our videos from last night over, and with regard to our disappointing straight-to-the-team-building-weekend-after-karaoke proposal she will revert.

I guess we'll be doing karaoke next Tuesday, then, and I'll have to find another long-suffering friend to take. In the meantime, I send over the video of us at the beginning of yesterday evening and one of myself afterwards walking home from the train station saying almost word for word exactly the same as I said last time.

* * *

I pitch up at the karaoke bar the following Tuesday with my friend Pete. We met through playing squash about ten years ago. He's great, always up for any kind of night out, a very good friend, and, crucially, he loves his karaoke: *someone* might as well get a good evening out of this. And, who knows, maybe he'll be the person Freya didn't realise she was looking for all this time.

Pete, unlike my wiser friends Minuk and Dan, agrees to be in my 'and here we are about to start the next date' video.

'Are you sure?' I check. 'You know there's every chance people might recognise you afterwards in the street?'

'Ready for a new experience,' he tells me. 'Also, they won't? They'll show max ten seconds of me?'

'Well, unless you and Freya fall in love.'

'I'll take that risk.'

'Hello!' We've been interrupted by Freya and another woman, obviously my date for the evening.

We do the introductions, and I learn that my date is called Sarra.

'Freya and I were neighbours for a couple of years in our mid-twenties. We met during a small house fire due to a defective toaster and got on *like* a house on fire – and yes I do *always* make that joke and yes I *always* amuse myself if no-one else – and here we are today.' Sarra is immediately likeable *and* shows no signs (yet, at least) of falling for Pete, so I'm cheering up; I think this could genuinely be a perfectly pleasant evening during which I have someone to talk to other than Freya.

'You've been booked into two separate tables.' The woman on reception is frowning at her computer screen. 'There must have been a mistake. Give me two minutes and we'll have a table for four ready for you.'

We all look at each other and then we all thank her. Apparently none of us want to say no, we're supposed to be on *dates*, plus I'm guessing Pete and Sarra would rather a four, because, really, does anyone actually *enjoy* blind dates, especially when they're as orchestrated as this? I also would prefer a four; I won't need to spend much time talking to Freya given that Pete and Sarra don't look as though they're immediately smitten in the way that Dan and Lizzie were, and I'm not up for a blind date situation either.

'So I watched the little montages they did of you,' Sarra says once we've been seated and they've poured tap water for us all, telling us that we'll need a *lot* of water, so that we don't get dry throats from all the singing we'll be doing.

'As did I,' says Pete.

'And I know from that that we're all better off treating this as a nice evening out, rather than actual dates,' twinkles Sarra. 'Clearly, I think, neither of you is *up* for having your views changed.'

'You know what,' says Freya. 'It's *perfect* that you said that. If we tell Sonja that that's what the montages show, she might agree that this whole thing is pointless.'

'Other than getting free evenings out.' Pete raises his glass and we all join him in a toast to the production company.

Our conversation is interrupted by us being instructed quite forcefully to make some song choices and join in, and it becomes apparent very quickly that this is an excellent venue if you don't want to spend too much time talking to your companions. The karaoke is constant, and we have to be involved one way or the other most of the time.

I already know that Pete has a fantastic voice. We establish pretty quickly that Sarra and I both have perfectly fine but nothing special voices. And that Freya – by her own admission – can't hold a tune to save her life. Weirdly, though, while she rarely (never, really) hits the right notes, her voice itself is really nice, as in it has a very nice tone. So basically she'd be amazing singing in the shower.

As we all sing along to Ed Sheeran, I find myself wondering idly whether she *does* sing in the shower, and am then horrified and drag my mind straight back to the words of 'Perfect', because I certainly don't want to be thinking about Freya and showers. I really don't know what happened to me there.

A server comes over to take our dessert orders, and we choose as a group; we're going to share four different ones. It occurs to me that Sonja and her producers did not think this one through very well. Karaoke is bringing our little group together as friends, rather than anything approaching lovers. I mean, right now, as long as I don't look in her direction too often, I don't even dislike Freya that much, because

I've barely heard a word she's said all evening. If you came here on a real first date, I feel that you'd have fun with someone if you already liked them, but you wouldn't fall in love with them for the first time. There's no time to talk, for a start, and even if there were, it's so loud that you can barely hear yourself speak. Not to show my age.

'That was so much fun.' Freya's almost hiccupping with laughter as we emerge onto the pavement outside the club later on.

We all agree (extraordinary that I am agreeing with her on something) and then Sarra looks at her watch and squeals, 'Oh my gosh, it's *midnight*. On a Tuesday. And we're in Central London. I need a cab right now or I'm going to *die* at work tomorrow.'

I have no idea what job she does, I realise, because as soon as we arrived we just got straight on with the singing and didn't bother with any mundane small talk. I'm not going to enquire; once this fiasco is over Freya and I will not be in each other's lives any more and there is therefore unlikely to be any point in getting to know each other's friends.

'Quick after-video first?' I ask.

The others all nod and I hold my phone in front of us and start recording.

'Loved it.' Pete grins into the phone camera.

'He's an amazing singer,' Sarra says.

'So much fun,' Freya chimes in.

'Yeah, it was a good evening for a friends' night out,' I agree, before stopping the video, and saying goodbye to the others before Freya and Sarra get in one taxi, and Pete and I get in another.

That's one thing I'll give Sonja; they aren't being tight on the taxis.

I do a solo video outside my house, in which I repeat words to the effect of what I said at the end of the last two dates and also repeat Sarra's words about what she gleaned from watching the montages. And that's another wrap, as I feel they might say in the world of TV production.

* * *

As I watch the montage they put together of us for their next Thursday morning sixty-second catch-up on our challenge, I have to admit that I do enjoy Freya saying, very sunnily, 'I had a *great* time but I didn't fall in love, and I do not believe I'm going to.'

It occurs to me that this week we haven't yet heard from Sonja about what our next challenge is going to be.

And bang on cue, a message comes in from her.

> Jake, Freya, thank you for your videos. This challenge is obviously a rolling process, informed by our rolling data. The real-time data shows that our viewers love your dynamic – the two of you together – and want to see more of you. The data also shows that no-one thinks either of you can win this challenge. But we don't want to end this now. So we're sending you on an experience – just the two of you, no dates required – on Tuesday, to create some more of that TV gold, and then you're going on your bonding weekend asap, where we'll take a lot of footage. Poll attached to see which weekends you can do. And details on your Tuesday evening date to follow.

Thank fuck for that is all I can say. Obviously I could do without a one-on-one experience with Freya, and I don't like Sonja's use of the word *date*, and I imagine Freya feels the same way, but at least this will be the last Tuesday. The team-building thing was always going to happen, and – as Freya pointed out – we can easily each do our own thing that weekend. And then it will all be over, thank fuck.

* * *

I'm thanking my fucks less when Sonja messages us on Monday.

> So we wracked our brains to think of the best evening out for two people who blatantly thoroughly disliked each other when they met lolll. We came up with an embroidery class. With a twist! You'll be drawing portraits of each other and then sewing them. While drinking champagne! What could be more fun?

What? The woman's a lunatic. I mean, what? That sounds like utter torture. I can't draw and I can't sew and I have no particular desire to learn to do either.

A message comes through from Freya:

> Hahahahaha

And then another one:

> I cannot imagine anyone less likely than you to enjoy
> that. Correct me if I'm wrong.

She isn't wrong.

* * *

Twenty-four hours later, Freya and I are in an upstairs room in a pub just outside a train station in Wandsworth, with glasses of champagne in front of us, pencils and canvases at the ready.

'Right.' Petra, the very jolly woman leading our class beams at us all. 'Everyone has their drinks, I see. Perfect. Since this is an extra-long session we're going to have two breaks. You might want to order food in the first one to eat during the second one.'

Freya and I both smile politely. The other ten people in the class (nine women and one man) all say how great/ amazing/ wonderful that sounds. They're basically full of positive hyperbole about every single thing Petra says.

I, by contrast, am very unhappy about what's coming up in the next hour. We're going to begin by learning some basics of drawing faces – which, to be fair, will be very interesting, I imagine – and then each of us is going to draw our partner's face on paper, before transferring that as well as we can to our embroidery canvases.

Before we draw our partner, each of us must study their face in great detail. I'm not looking forward to that bit. I don't think I'd particularly enjoy doing that with anyone, but it's got to be a truly special torture mutually staring hard at each other's faces for an extended period when you really don't like each other but have been forced into a stupid series of activities together.

'Jake and Freya? Ready?' Petra calls. Clearly, we haven't sounded enthusiastic enough.

'I can't wait.' Freya does an incredibly false smile. I'm pretty sure I know what her genuine ones are like because I think she enjoyed the karaoke evening as much as the rest of us, and she was smiling a lot then (not in my direction, obviously).

Her real smiles produce that (objectively very cute) dimple and reach her eyes. This one does neither.

'I also can't wait.' I smile too; I don't want to upset anyone.

Petra's a good teacher. I was not a natural at art at school, and I am not a natural now, but I'm enjoying learning how to draw a face way more than I ever enjoyed school art lessons. She has some really interesting tips for us, and at one point it genuinely crosses my mind that if I'm ever at a huge loss as to how to spend my days, attending art classes wouldn't be the worst thing I could do.

As predicted, things are not so good once we move on to the phase where we're studying each other's faces.

At the risk of sounding like a toddler, I just don't *want* to look at all the details of Freya's face.

We have a checklist. Apparently we would certainly not have a checklist if we weren't total novices, but we do, which does kind of make it better, in that we don't just have to sit with our eyes roaming across each other's faces aimlessly.

I realise as I go through it that there's something interesting about Freya's face: she is – objectively – beautiful, but none of her individual features are particularly remarkable. Well, her eyes are an objectively lovely brown, very deep and chocolatey, which is a nice contrast with her dark-blonde hair. And her mouth is beautifully wide and full, and there's something objectively very attractive about the way she constantly looks as though she's about to smile or laugh. Other than when she's sneering at me, obviously.

As I continue down the checklist looking at all the constituent parts of her face I try to work out what it is that does make her so beautiful. She has very symmetrical features – maybe that's it. And her face is round but not *too* round. I don't know what it is. Maybe it's just the unique way it all goes together.

She's beginning to laugh now, and – to my annoyance, because this frequently happens to me when she laughs, even though I am often very irritated by the reason that she's laughing – my own mouth is widening in response.

'What?' I ask.

'It's just... This is so ridiculous. I mean, Sonja. The producers. *Oh, you two really didn't seem to hit it off, so we're going to force you to stare at each other for several minutes and complete checklists about each other's faces.* It's insane. Why did we agree to this? Why are we here?'

I nod. 'For once, you make a very good point.'

She looks at me for a long moment. I'm pretty sure I know what's coming.

And, yes, she says, 'I feel like this is the last time I'm going to say this, but this is all your bloody fault.'

'Moot point,' I say, really just for the sake of it. 'You wrote the books. If you hadn't written them I would not have said it.'

'Oh please.' She looks like she's saying it just for the sake of it too. 'If the possibly fictitious clients of yours hadn't married the wrong people and then pretended that my books were the catalysts for their inevitable separations, you wouldn't have had your rant at me on national television and we wouldn't be in this position.'

'Not fictitious. I had to say it.'

Freya glares at me. 'And *again*, and I hope for the last time, I am not going to stop writing my books because they are *not* in fact dangerous; they *make people happy*.'

'I...' I don't finish my sentence because I'm remembering that I did in fact very much enjoy her books and if I had to analyse my emotional state after reading them I would have to apply the description *feel-good* to them. I did not, however, feel good after my ex-wife compared me unfavourably to the hero in one of Freya's books. Having read several, I don't know which hero she was comparing me to. Maybe all of them.

Freya smiles at me, and I don't like that smile. It's far too smug. Complacent.

'Would you say,' she asks, 'that on an *average* basis, as in a *for-the-greater-good* basis, if a book made one hundred people happy, and one person sad, it would overall be a good thing?'

'That's a stupid question,' I point out. 'You have to define the sadness. How bad is it? You wouldn't want someone you care about to do an activity with a five per cent mortality rate, would you, no matter how much the ones who survive enjoy it.'

'That's different,' she splutters.

I shake my head. 'If for every one hundred people who read a book ninety-nine come away happy and the hundredth goes through an utterly horrific divorce as a result of it, and the divorce is *so* horrific that overall the average is net misery, should we not ban that book?'

'You *cannot* ban all romances. That's beyond ridiculous.'

I frown. That *is* ridiculous; she's right.

A smile begins to spread slowly but widely across Freya's face, and in check-list mode, I'm forced to acknowledge that she does have very good teeth. Even better because they *aren't* exactly perfect; her front two bottom teeth cross just a tiny amount, and it's... *cute*; that's the word.

'You think I'm right, don't you?' she asks.

Really, really maturely, I decline to answer and decide to roll my eyes instead.

'Toddler,' she says, very conversationally. And then she laughs. A lot. And I find myself laughing too.

Yeah, odd.

'Have we all finished our checklists?' asks Petra. 'Time to draw. Paper first.'

I actually quite enjoy the drawing. The result isn't *amazing*, but surely no-one's will be.

'Now show your partners,' Petra commands.

'No way.' I'm genuinely astonished by Freya's picture. I have to be honest. 'That's really good *and* really bad. It doesn't look like me in the slightest. But it really does look like a person. Like *really* like a person. It's amazing.' It's really, really good. Except not, given that it was supposed to be me.

'Now yours?' She's trying to peer over the top of my easel.

I take the drawing off and show her.

She takes her hands and covers her face with them.

I'm a little alarmed. Yes, she's inherently really annoying, but, no, that does not mean I should be drawing pictures of her that upset her.

'Are you okay?' I ask.

She nods, and then I see her shoulders shaking.

After a few moments, she takes her hands away from her face, and says, 'It's *great*. Also not a *very* faithful likeness, but this is clearly difficult.'

'I've never seen you being so polite before.'

'Not polite, just truthful.' She's put her hands over her face again. Then she takes them down. 'I'm sorry. It's very good. Really. I mean, *really* good. Honestly. Truthfully. It's just... there's just something a tiny bit funny about the very unusually large nostrils you've given me.'

I look again at my picture. Yeah, it's terrible, and the nostrils *are* gigantic. I look around the room, and, wow, everyone else is a *genius*.

'They're all so good,' I say.

Freya is also looking around the room, and pressing her lips together very hard.

Annoyingly, I almost like her when she's clearly trying very hard to be nice to me.

I look back at my huge-nostrilled person and I find myself laughing, and then *really* laughing. Freya joins me, looking like it's a big relief to be able to laugh openly.

'Sorry,' she says when we're both calm again.

'If I'm honest, you'd be weird if you *didn't* laugh.'

'On a different subject,' she says, 'has Dan said anything about Lizzie?'

'You can't ask me to betray my friend's confidence,' I say, pleased for things to get back to normal, i.e. minor mutual hostility.

'That is true,' she concedes. 'I can't. What I meant was do you think Dan's intentions are good? I care a lot about Lizzie, and she's a little vulnerable at the moment, and I asked her to go on the date, so I feel responsible. I wouldn't have asked her to go if I'd thought for a moment that she would actually fall for...' She leaves it hanging and I laugh.

'You thought her date was me,' I say, 'and you couldn't imagine anyone falling for me.'

'Not *anyone*.' She exaggeratedly bats her eyelids at me, and I can't decide whether it's cute or annoying. 'Just Lizzie. Anyway, back to my question, which I do not think is unreasonable. I know I asked you this before but now it looks as though things could be getting serious. Is Dan going to treat Lizzie well? Is he going to stick around?'

'It's been two weeks. Who knows whether *either* of them is going to stick around. But, yes, he will treat her well.'

'Good.'

'Time for a break,' Petra says. 'Go and order your food from the bar, stretch your legs, take a toilet break if you need one. See you back here in fifteen.'

I look at Freya, whose face I now know extremely well, in a very strange way, and decide that this has all been very odd, and that I would now benefit from a little break from her rather than a further fifteen-minute one on one.

'I have some work emails to go through,' I say. 'I'll catch you back here at the end of the break.'

'Great.' She's immediately on her feet and heading off in the direction of the stairs.

I frown as I watch her go. Is she... slightly... likeable?

11

FREYA

I spend a good five minutes choosing my meal – I go for fish and chips in the end – because it's *way* better deliberating over a pub menu than it is having my head full of Jake. For a moment there, I borderline liked him. And then he turned back into the total shit that he is, telling me that my books cause *horrific* divorces. But then he looked as though he was actually, possibly, slightly taking on board my points. And then he was marginally nicer than his usual self when I asked about Dan and Lizzie, before making it very clear that he didn't want to talk to me during the break.

Thank heavens there'll be other people there on the team-building weekend.

I do the 'during the date' video that Sonja asked for, describing what we've been doing so far, and then go back upstairs.

Redrawing our pictures onto the embroidery canvas is slightly boring. I don't *love* art, and we've already drawn each other once. I *am*, though, looking forward to seeing what Jake does with my nostrils.

We all (including Jake and me) work in more or less silence until Petra thinks we should all have finished.

'Great work, Jake,' she says enthusiastically – *so* enthusiastically that either she is *besotted* with him or it is *not* great – as she walks around looking at everyone's work. She finishes looking and then claps. 'Time for the mini reveal before the big one later on when the embroidery is finished. Show your partners!'

'You first,' Jake says.

Mine's fine. It does pretty much look like a real person. It doesn't look like Jake, but it's slightly more like him than my first one was. I'm not amazing at art, although I did enjoy it at school, but it's actually really easy to look like you've attempted to sketch Jake without having made that much effort, because he's *so* classically ruggedly handsome that you just have to aim for a very classically good-looking man with dark hair and you *will* look like you've tried to draw him.

'Not bad.' He looks down at his own and then up again, and his lips twitch, which makes me worry that I'm very rudely going to want to laugh again. 'Are you ready?'

I nod. I. Must. Not. Laugh. He's often annoying, sometimes *incredibly* so, but no-one should ever be laughed at for a slight lack of artistic ability.

He turns it round, and I almost gasp out loud. It's... well, way more like a... well... I don't know what. Not really an animal. Maybe an alien. *Or* a first-draft Picasso maybe. At best.

I fight an emerging snigger, and when I'm sure that I'm going to be polite and definitely not laugh, I say, 'The nostrils are a great size.'

Jake looks me right in the eye and laughs out loud.

I fight some more, and manage again not to laugh. I do have to look down at my lap, though, and hold my lips clamped really tightly together.

'Well done,' he murmurs across the table. 'Excellent no-laughing.'

'Thank you,' I say, with *still* not even a tremor of laughter in my voice. I am *good*.

'Time to begin the embroidery,' Petra says. She's an incredibly enthusiastic woman, which is of course great, because we are here to learn, and no-one likes an unenthusiastic teacher.

We both waste valuable embroidering time trying over and over again to thread our needles, so we both have absolutely no idea what we're supposed to be doing stitch-wise when we do eventually have them threaded, and Petra has to come over to give us an individual lesson on how to do cross-stitching.

'I find this quite often with couples,' she says. 'The drawing each other's faces is so intense when you're with someone you love that you're so wrapped up in each other for the rest of the evening you keep missing things.'

'Not a couple,' Jake says very firmly. 'Just two single people who are all thumbs when it comes to needle-threading.'

'*Really.*' Petra stands back and looks at us both. 'Well... there you go. I must be wrong. I sensed a lot of passion between you. Tension.'

'Ha,' I say. 'No. We're just...' We aren't friends. 'Colleagues.'

Petra looks at us in turn again and then says, 'Interesting. Do keep me updated.' She looks *again*. 'I feel as though I recognise you both. Are you famous?'

'Nope.' Jake shakes his head.

I shake mine too. Then I worry that she'll see us on the show and feel misled.

'It's just that we ended up on TV together on *Wake Up Britain*, and, long story short, ended up doing a series of... evenings out... together,' I say. 'This is one of those.'

'*Oh*. Maybe that explains everything.' She peers very intently at Jake and then me, and then says, 'I'd still like an update on how everything pans out between you.'

'We can give you that update right now,' Jake tells her. 'We're just temporary colleagues, as Freya said, and then we probably won't see each other again.'

Petra frowns.

'He's right. But not in a bad way,' I lie. 'Just... we're both busy people, you know.'

'Yeah, no, I actually see something between you,' she says. 'Anyway. Time to sew.'

We all kind of hover there, as you do at the end of a slightly off conversation, and then Jake breaks the awkward silence.

'I'm *really* sorry to ask.' He presents Petra with a gleaming smile. 'But could you possibly just give me a quick recap on how to do that stitch again?'

'Of course.' Petra's return smile is suddenly so flirty I'm surprised she hasn't written her number on his arm.

Which makes sense actually; what she was saying before about there being some kind of tension between us was kind of weirding me out a little, but I now realise that she must just have been trying to establish whether there was anything between us before making a move on Jake. If he finds true love with her, I'd be quite happy, actually. I'd have lost the challenge, but I'd rather go on a love therapy weekend by myself than the team-building one with him.

Jake does not show a natural talent with a needle, so Petra is forced to keep coming over to help him. I say *forced*; she seems more than happy to spend lots of very tactile time with him.

I find it slightly annoying, actually. I mean, it's hardly professional, is it?

At the beginning of the second break, we're all asked whether we'd rather eat at tables on the other side of the room, or continue to embroider through the break. Jake and I both elect to sew while we eat; having snuck glances at some of the others' canvases, we know we're way behind everyone else.

'I think it was because it took us so long to thread our needles.' I realise that I've been staring so hard at my canvas, trying to get my stitches right, that my vision's gone slightly blurry.

'Yeah.' Jake's staring at his own canvas. 'How is everyone else so good at that? And also why is it not hurting anyone else's fingers?'

'You aren't supposed to keep poking yourself.' I look more closely at his hands. 'Have you smeared blood on your canvas?'

'Might have done. But not to worry. I'm going to sew over it.'

'Delightful.'

He nods very seriously. 'It doesn't matter if you mess up, it's how you recover that counts. Always sew over your blood.'

'You're so right. Why didn't Petra tell us that?'

Our freakishly civilised and friendly little exchange is terminated by the arrival of our food, and then we're both busy juggling cutlery and needles until our embroidery companions retake their seats, and then everyone continues in near-silence, because this is, frankly, a ridiculously challenging task to be completed in the time available (or, indeed, at all).

When we finish, Petra does her clapping thing and then says, 'Okay, so it's time for the big reveal.'

'Would you like to go first?' Jake says.

'Love to.' I turn mine towards him and his eyes widen.

'Wow,' he says. 'You have a genuine talent there. I mean, it slightly looks like me and it fully looks like a person. It's... amazing. I'm genuinely impressed. It's as though you – the prolific author – are naturally creative.'

'Why thank you.' I'm a little stunned by Jake being *nice*. Maybe he's just doing it to impress Petra. 'Now yours?' Petra leant over him a *lot* while he was doing it; maybe she helped and it's actually going to be very good.

'Here we go.' He moves it from side to side in a building-suspense fashion, and then suddenly turns it round.

And then we both just laugh.

When we eventually wipe our eyes, I say nothing. There are in fact no words for how bad it is. If you had to guess the age of the person who did it, you'd probably say five or six.

I lean forward. I've just noticed something. 'Did you spill some of your curry on it? As well as the blood.' I indicate the browny splatters to the top left of it.

'Yep.'

'No time to sew over it?'

'Yeah, there's only so much genius I can produce in one evening.'

'It *is* genius,' I say.

'I know.' Jake turns the canvas back towards him and shakes his head. 'Three hours of my life gone doing this.'

Petra claps. 'Well done everyone. I'm proud of *all* of you, every single one of you.' She looks long and meaningfully at Jake, and I catch sight of his right foot doing a little backwards and forwards circle, and wonder whether it's due to slight sexual attraction or discomfort over the (what I would call) OTT flirting. 'Now. It is of course your choice as to what you do with your finished embroideries, but one suggestion is to make a present to each other of them. A lovely memento of this evening. *Or* you can keep them, as a lovely embroidered memento portrait of each other.'

We look at each other for a long moment, during which I think no thank you very much, I do not want a memento of Jake. He clearly thinks the same thing, because we suddenly, as one, shoot our arms out and exchange them.

Which, frankly, doesn't make any difference because it's still a memento, just one of *his* work rather than *my* work. To be fair, his work has actually given me a lot of pleasure. You don't cry with laughter every day.

I put his embroidery into my tote and slide my arms into my coat. 'I'm genuinely going to enjoy having this memento of what has turned out to be a *way* more enjoyable evening than I was expecting.'

'Are you saying that you take pleasure in the failures of others?'

I shake my head. 'There was no failure, Jake. Just an unusual representation of what you were seeing.'

'Modern embroidery if you will?' he suggests.

'Exactly. And I will cherish your modern embroidery because laughter is good for the soul.'

Jake pulls his own jacket on and begins to stand.

'Jake.' Petra has practically sprinted across the room. 'Are you leaving?'

'Work tomorrow,' he says.

'What job do you do?' she purrs. There's really no need for her to place her hand on his arm, but she does so anyway. And not his forearm, but his bicep, which is, frankly, *very* unprofessional and verging on sexual harassment.

'Lawyer.'

'*Lawyer*. I *love* lawyers.'

'Great.'

I'm in danger of laughing again, because the way Jake's backing away from her is very funny.

He lifts his jacket to look at a watch that is not in fact on his wrist, and then pulls his phone out of his pocket. 'My taxi's right outside,' he says. 'Goodnight. Freya? You coming?'

'Er, yes. Thank you so much, Petra.'

* * *

'Where's the taxi?' I ask when we get outside.

'No taxi,' he says. 'Just thought it wise to escape.'

'Oh my goodness. Have you, perhaps, learnt from Petra that you will never find love? Have I won?'

'No. I've learnt from Petra that I don't believe I will find love with *her*.'

'That's reminded me that we should do our video,' I say. 'Shall we show the nation our finished results?'

'I actually think we should. I mean, not yours. Yours is just a bog-standard very impressively good piece of embroidery art for your first time. Mine, though, could be of genuine public service if it makes other people laugh as much as it made us laugh.'

'Maybe you had to be there, though?' I take it out of my bag and we both look at it and start laughing again. 'Yeah, no, definite genuine public service.'

Jake takes his phone and angles it at us from above and we take it in turns to describe the evening – neither of us mentioning Petra – and then Jake shows my embroidery and says that he was impressed by my natural talent, and then he does jazz hands and then I show *his* embroidery and say that I was impressed too.

'Impressed by my natural talent?' he checks.

'Absolutely,' I say, and he stops the video.

And then we say goodnight to each other as friendlily as we ever have and get in separate Ubers and take our embroidery mementos home.

* * *

It has quickly become a way of life waiting for Sonja's unpredictably timed bombshells following each Tuesday date. Will she insist that we go back to setting each other up on blind dates, single or double-dating, the two of us doing activities together, or will we be sent on our weekend as our next activity, and when will that be?

What I do not expect is for a *lot* of my friends to text me on Thursday morning while I'm still thinking about getting out of bed, to ask if I've seen Jake's newspaper interview in which he *massively* disses romance and links it to the rising divorce rate. *Obviously* the article references me, because the whole reason they chose to write the piece on Jake in the first place was his 'hot lawyer' look on TV with me.

What?

I google quickly and read it. And, honestly, I want to kill him. What a *weasel*. Either he laughed away during embroidery with me knowing that he'd done this interview, or he did it *after* the embroidery. Either way, *so* two-faced.

I begin to type out a message telling him what an arse he is, and then stop. I'm going to try really hard to be mature about this. I'm going to ignore it. Or at least not text for a few hours. Or not until I've had my shower anyway.

Or... No. I can't wait.

I pick up my phone and send a text saying *You weasel*, before stomping off to the bathroom for my shower.

Yep, I've been a naïve idiot. I was not expecting that.

I further do not expect Lizzie to message me a couple of hours later asking perfunctorily how the embroidery went and going straight on to say that yesterday was her and Dan's two-week anniversary and right now she's on the Tube to work from his place, *very* late for work – she's never late for *anything*, especially her high-powered City job – and she already keeps a toothbrush there and she thinks she's in love *and* she really wants to invite me and Jake over for dinner with her and Dan this weekend.

I stare at my phone, imagining Lizzie *marrying* Dan, and me having to be friends with Jake *forever*.

I do not want to do that. Every so often he's pleasant – like he was about his embroidery – and you get lulled into a false sense of security, and then off he goes again being an arse.

But Lizzie is a very good friend and she's had a lot of bad luck and if Dan is a nice person (although *can* he be, when he's a good friend of Jake's?) I should be very pleased for her.

But. Jake. I loathe him.

I settle on replying:

> Did you see the newspaper article about him?

Lizzie replies:

> Yep, nothing new there. Can you do Saturday evening by any chance? If not, let's go Sunday? For dinner.

What? What does she mean nothing new there? Yes it's new. We were being *nice* to each other and he's just reiterated his anti-romance-novel stance but in *writing*. In a national tabloid.

Very, very annoyingly, I don't think I can say no to her dinner suggestion. Fortunately, I have an evening with girlfriends arranged on Saturday, trying out the new Lebanese restaurant that's opened down the road from my house, so I'm not lying when I say I can only do Sunday. There's no way I'd waste a Saturday on Jake by choice.

I've barely finished typing a reluctant *Sunday would be great*, when Sonja messages to ask me if I can meet her one on one asap.

* * *

Two days later, I'm in a café near my house waiting for Sonja to have brunch with her. It's Saturday late morning and Sonja lives on the other side of London but was happy to come my way, she said, so she must *really* want to speak to me.

I'm wondering whether she'll vanish straight after saying whatever she needs to say, but going by her order of smashed avo with chilli oil on toast plus turmeric tea she's planning to stay for a while.

I've had a healthy week food-wise and they have *really* nice pancakes with berries and maple syrup in here, so I've ordered that, as well as a hot chocolate, which I'll be working off this afternoon on a long walk with my friend Charlotte.

'You should drink turmeric tea.' Sonja takes a sip of hers and screws up her face. 'God, that's disgusting. Incredibly health-giving, though.'

'I'll add turmeric to the next curry I cook,' I promise.

'Hmm.' Sonja takes another sip and shudders before waving at the server. 'Could we get some sparkling water, please? And an espresso.' She pushes her teacup away from her. 'One-night stand last night. Got no sleep. Feeling like shit. Can't deal with no sleep due to menopause but at least I haven't lost my libido.'

I blink. That's a lot of information from someone I do not know at *all*.

'I feel like we're friends,' she tells me. 'I like you.'

'Thank you,' I say. 'Likewise.' I *do* like her despite her punchiness but I will *not*, in reality, be telling Sonja anything personal about myself.

'I love your nail varnish,' Sonja says. 'Every time I've seen you your nails are looking amazing.'

'Thank you. I do them myself,' I tell her. 'I've got one of those gel dryers. Yours look fab too.'

Sonja looks at her own very well-manicured fingers, tipped with translucent varnish. 'I think I should try some bolder colours. You're inspiring me.' She turns her attention back to me. 'Your hair's looking gorgeous as well. It has so much body.'

'Thank you. *You* have amazing hair. Gorgeous colour.' I find it *really* hard to just thank someone for a compliment without giving them one back, but this is getting ridiculous.

'Thank you.' Sonja pats her hair and takes a large slurp of the espresso that has just been placed next to her. 'That's better. Sooooo...'

I smile at her, not certain I want to hear what's coming next.

She shifts a little towards me on our corner banquette. 'Jake. Gorgeous, no?'

'I mean, yes, if that's your type?'

'Is he *your* type is the question?'

I stare at her. Was she not paying any attention at all when we met? 'No? He definitely isn't?'

'I thought there was a lot of tension between you. Sexual tension.'

What? First Petra, now Sonja. *So* bizarre.

I shake my head. 'Definitely not.'

Sonja tilts her head to one side and looks into the distance as though she's forgotten I'm there. 'He *is* very, very attractive. I mean, if there's genuinely nothing between you...' She arches an eyebrow.

What? Does this happen to Jake all the time?

'You are incredibly welcome to go ahead,' I say.

Sonja smiles. (It's quite scary, actually.) 'Thank you. First, though, I think you and Jake need to explore what *might* be between you.'

I frown and wait. I don't feel as though I want to give Sonja any kind of ammunition, and I'm not even sure what that ammunition would be for, so I'm not going to be venturing any new thoughts whatsoever.

'So as I said we're not going to do any more of the dates,' she continues, 'but because viewers have responded so incredibly well to the two of you together – arguably as a couple – we're going to send you as soon as possible on your weekend away, accompanied by cameras, and we'll then continue for a few weeks with the montages, longer ones than we've been doing so far, before having you back on to explain how you both feel at the end of the challenge.'

I smile while I consider for a second what she's just said. I think it's good, actually. We were always going to end up on the team-building weekend together – clearly neither of us can win the challenge – and this way it's just going to be sooner, which is a good thing, because then it won't be hanging over us.

'Great,' I say.

'Wonderful.' Sonja looks up at the approaching server and gives her a big smile, before consenting to have a selfie. 'Occupational hazard,' she says when they've finished. 'Now. What are your preferences for what types of bonding weekend you go on? What types of activities do you like and not like?'

'Um.' That's a tricky one to answer off the top of my head. There's no type of bonding weekend I want to go on.

'Okay. Let's begin with what you *don't* like. Do you have any phobias?'

'Just heights. And snakes.' I hate that word. 'And being stampeded by a herd of cows, obviously. And cheese fondue. I really, really can't stand it. All that stringiness.'

'You have quite a lot of phobias.' Sonja sounds impressed.

'Well, yes and no. They really don't impact on my life at all. I don't have an *extreme* fear of heights, more just your usual, the kind that quite a lot of people have. The... reptile one and the cow one and, actually, the cheese fondue one, are stronger, but living in London it's really easy to avoid reptiles, herds of cows and Alpine après-ski food.'

Sonja laughs. 'I'm glad for you that they aren't too much of an issue. What kind of activities do you like? Nights out, daytime hobbies? Or things you hate?'

'Um. I'm pretty easy recently.'

Sonja persists until she has discovered that when it comes to physical activity I hate running but like tennis and the sport I would least like to play is rugby because of all the mud. She then moves on to evening activities, best and worst holidays, favourite and least favourite clothes.

'Maybe,' I say eventually for the umpteenth time. I really do not enjoy being interrogated and she is *thorough*. It's horrible, actually. Like I'm being interviewed for MI6 or something.

'Well, that was delicious,' she says abruptly, when she's finally dragged my all-time favourite and most hated drinks out of me, and signals for the bill, and within under two minutes we're outside the restaurant (even though I hadn't actually finished eating) and she's mwah-mwahing me goodbye and saying she'll be in touch about a weekend that I'll *love*.

Hmm. It might be lots of activities that I enjoy, but it's still going to involve Jake.

12

JAKE

Seriously, I think, as I sit down in the corner of the café at the end of my road. I work hard all week, and half the weekend, and my reward is to meet Sonja for a Saturday afternoon coffee and then Freya for Sunday dinner with Dan and Lizzie.

At least the café does excellent coffee.

'Jake.' Sonja is a vision in head-to-toe electric blue today.

I stand to greet her and she pulls me into a particularly close perfume-infused hug and plants actual kisses onto my cheeks rather than the distant air ones I would have expected.

I kiss the air rather than her and say, 'Hello, Sonja.'

'How *are* you?' She releases me and sits down with a big swish. A further wave of strongly perfumed scent hits me.

I'm still trying to work out what it reminds me of when she asks, 'Have you spoken to Freya today?'

'Nope.' Freya and I are not on friendly text-chat terms. Especially since she sent me a message earlier in the week calling me a weasel and I didn't reply. It was obviously a reaction to the newspaper article that ran that day reiterating my thoughts on romance, which happened to name-check Freya (them not me, but it might as well have been me). The interview actually happened the day after the TV show but they only ran it this week (without telling me that they were doing it then; I presume they were waiting to see whether the challenge took off with the public). I was only reiterating exactly what I said on the show, no more no less, and I do want to explain that, plus the timing, to Freya, but I've had an insanely busy week so I thought it would be best just to tell her when I see her tomorrow with Dan and Lizzie.

'I'll fill you in, then.' Sonja waves her menu at the man behind the counter. 'We're going to send you on your bonding weekend sooner rather than later and I'd love to know all your personal likes and dislikes so we can give you the best weekend we possibly can.'

She's interrupted by the waiter, who's ready to take our order, which gives me a moment to think.

I have the strong impression that Sonja puts Sonja's interests first at all times. She's looking for good television, not trying to give Freya and me a lovely weekend away together. I wouldn't put it past her to try to give us a terrible weekend because surely that would make better television.

I think I would like Sonja to know as little about me as possible.

I spend the next fifteen minutes batting all her questions away while I drink a latte and she alternates between taking reluctant sips of kale and carrot juice and gulping down hot chocolate as though it's the nectar to end all nectars.

Eventually, she gets visibly irritated.

'Jake. Are you being deliberately obstructive?'

'Not at all,' I lie. 'I just don't really *have* strong preferences either way. I'm very busy. I work very long hours. No real time for anything else.'

'Right.' She bites her lower lip and bats her eyelids and I blink. 'Am I right in thinking there's nothing at all between you and Freya?'

I nod, slightly alarmed by the way she's reaching across the table now and clasping my arm.

'In that case, when you get back from your weekend away, maybe we could meet one evening, and I could try to help you *develop* some preferences.'

'That would be *great*,' I lie, very heartily. 'If I have time. Definitely.'

For fuck's sake.

No good whatsoever has come of going on that TV show.

* * *

Once I've escaped Sonja's clutches, the rest of Saturday – watching football with a few friends – is good, as is the first part of my Sunday.

I have a rare lie-in and then go over to my parents' to take Max out for a drive. The serious car crash he was involved in a few years ago means he is now in a wheelchair. My parents are wonderful and devoted and very youthful for their age, but are approaching seventy now, and I'm always conscious that I need to be in a position to give Max a home with me when my parents can no longer look after him on a daily basis, which means working as hard as I can to be on the best financial footing I can be.

I also, obviously, have a fairly constant feeling of guilt, a sense of 'how come this awful thing happened to him and not me' accompanied by a determination to live the life I get to have as fully as I can, kind of in honour of Max, and an equally strong wish to do my best to inject as much happiness as I can into his life.

I take him for a drive to Richmond Park, where we go up to King Henry's Mound to look at the views from there, which he always likes. As we go, I tell him the latest on work, the challenge, the frankly weird art-embroidery evening, and how Freya thinks I'm a weasel. I also admit that I do *really* wish I'd just kept my thoughts to myself when we did the TV show, because if I hadn't said anything then none of this would have happened.

'You're an idiot,' Max tells me.

'I think you're right. I'm going to have to complete the challenge, though.'

'Yes. And the upside is that I'm enjoying watching you on TV. The montages are *great*.'

'Ha.' I give his shoulder a gentle punch. 'At least *someone*'s deriving enjoyment from this whole situation.'

'Not just me. A *lot* of people are enjoying watching you. Everyone wants you to get together with Freya.'

'Yeah, no. I do believe in romance. But definitely not with her.' And not now. I don't feel like I'm ready following my divorce, plus I'm just so busy with work and family. Maybe in a year or two.

We enjoy the rest of our trip round the park and it's with reluctance, as always, that I say goodbye to my family when it's time for me to leave.

* * *

It is also with reluctance that I set off for my dinner with Dan, Lizzie and Freya.

We're meeting at a Thai restaurant in Covent Garden. I'm usually pretty punctual for things but decide to arrive a little late so there's no danger of me arriving at the same time as Freya.

I arrive at exactly the same time as her.

Which is fine, actually; I can't remember why I thought it would be bad to arrive at the same time. We exchange hellos – neutral on my side and blatantly frosty on Freya's – and then go inside. We were *always* going to have to say hello. Dan and Lizzie will already be here so there will be no one-on-one time for me and Freya. And if there *were* one-on-one time it would be fine obviously. I really don't know why I minded.

I'll explain about the newspaper article when we have a moment, and Freya will presumably defrost a little. And, frankly, if she doesn't, it really doesn't matter. Soon we'll never have to see each other again.

Oh, okay, it looks as though we're going to have that moment right now, because Dan and Lizzie have not yet arrived, even though Dan is usually one of the most punctual people I know.

We sit opposite each other, Freya with her back to the wall facing out into the room, and me with my back to the room.

Freya smiles at the server who's shown us to our seats and then immediately focuses on her menu.

'Your weasel message,' I begin.

'Mmhmm.' Freya doesn't look up from her menu.

'Yeah, I presume that was due to the newspaper article.' I pause but Freya doesn't say anything. 'So I just wanted to clear that up.'

She finally looks up at me, tilts her head to one side, raises one eyebrow, and says, 'Fascinating.'

'I did the interview literally the day after we were on TV, and reiterated exactly what I'd said to you in person, nothing more. They didn't publish the interview then; they waited to see what would happen with our challenge, and when they saw that the weekly updates and montages are really popular with viewers, they decided to run the article. Without telling me. So I didn't realise it would be out this week. And I didn't realise they would spin it quite so nastily.' I suddenly do actually want to make her believe that I wasn't being gratuitously mean.

'Because no tabloid ever has spun anything nastily before?'

'Yeah, maybe that was naïve. In my defence, I don't think I really cared because I was furious with you at that point.'

Freya replaces her raised-eyebrow look with a frown. 'Are you no longer furious?'

'Apparently not quite so much.'

'Hmm. I *am* a bit furious still. I don't like people attempting to trash my career for no good reason whatsoever.'

'On the upside—' I feel as though I'm somewhat grasping at straws '— according to Sonja you are *very* popular with the viewing public.' Out of curiosity, I really want to ask her if her sales have improved off the back of this publicity but she doesn't have the air of a woman who'd be keen to discuss that kind of detail with me right now.

'Delighted to hear that.' Freya looks the exact opposite of delighted. The frown is only intensifying. 'So back to your explanation of what happened with the newspaper article. Your apparent need to describe in great detail how it arose screams guilty conscience.'

Our hostilities are placed on hold for a moment while a server places a basket of prawn crackers in front of us and we both thank him profusely.

Once he's out of earshot, I say, choosing my words carefully, 'I do wish, with hindsight, that I had kept my thoughts to myself.'

Freya studies me for a long moment, before saying, 'And that would be because you yourself aren't enjoying the challenge?' She takes a cracker.

'I... Yes.'

'Not because you care about the impact on me or feel guilty about that?'

'I obviously don't want to negatively affect your career.' I realise that is true.

'Well, let's hope it hasn't.' She takes quite a vicious bite of the cracker.

'From what I hear, the viewing public love you.'

'Likewise.' She takes another angry bite.

'Great, then?'

'Yes, marvellous.'

I don't love prawn crackers – controversial, I know – but I'd rather eat one than continue this conversation, which feels as though it could easily descend further, into a shouting match, so I smile and take one.

We sit in silence for an uncomfortably long period, until – thank the Lord – Dan and Lizzie arrive.

We all hug and they sit down with Lizzie next to Freya and Dan next to me, and launch into a description of the fire juggler they saw on the way here.

Freya and I join in, and I think we both do a pretty good job of seeming on friendly terms and not ruining the evening in any way for Dan and Lizzie.

The conversation ebbs and flows around all sorts of non-contentious topics and, actually, I reflect, as Freya and I engage in a heated discussion of the rival merits of a fireman's pole from bedroom to kitchen, or a slide instead of stairs in our fantasy ideal house, she can at times be perfectly good company.

'We need to consider the danger aspects,' she says very seriously. 'If you went too fast on a slide you could fly off and hit a wall and break something.'

'I mean, just don't put it somewhere where there's a wall opposite the end of the stairs?' I point out. 'And also, obviously fireman's poles can be dangerous. What if you just let go?'

'Well, you'd be stupid to let go. But, just in case, I feel like you could pad the aperture and the floor below,' Freya muses.

Our debate continues with genuinely only minimal sarcasm and irritation on both sides, until Lizzie asks into a gap in the conversation, 'Have you had any more details about the team-building weekend?'

'Yes, actually,' Freya says. 'I had brunch with Sonja yesterday and she delved *deeply* into my tastes in absolutely everything – I mean, I was surprised she didn't get into sexual preferences – because she wants to make sure we really enjoy it.'

'Did she use the word *enjoy*?' I query.

Freya wrinkles her brow, in trying-to-remember mode. 'I *think* so. I mean, words to that effect. Like she wants us to get as much as we can out of it. Something like that.'

'Sounds surprisingly altruistic from what I've heard,' comments Dan. 'Don't they just want to hook more viewers? Do they *want* you to have a lovely time? Is that good TV?'

'That's what I thought when she tried to grill me yesterday afternoon.' I pour more tap water for us all. 'So I didn't tell her anything at all.'

'Well in that case,' says Freya complacently, 'we'll spend a weekend doing the kind of team-building *I* will enjoy. Fireman's pole rather than staircase slide.'

'*Or*—' Dan pauses to load cucumber, spring onion and crispy duck onto a pancake '—you'll have the weekend from hell and Jake might or might not, depending on how much his tastes coincide with yours.'

'Nonsense,' says Lizzie hastily as Freya's lips form a horrified-looking 'o'. 'Of course they wouldn't do that. They'll want you to enjoy the activities so you can focus on the team-building aspect of the weekend. That's where the great TV will come from. From you two leaving the weekend finally holding the same views on absolutely everything.'

'I'm not *certain* that's true.' I do if I'm honest feel a little guilty about having brought all of this on both of us, and maybe Freya should prepare herself for a bad weekend.

Freya shakes her head. 'It is. Of *course* they wouldn't ask in a cynical way. I mean, they aren't actual sadists.'

'No, but they *do* want to make great TV,' Dan says.

'And it would not make great TV watching me be miserable.' Freya takes a big sip of her wine.

I raise my eyebrows because, er, I imagine it would make *great* TV if she got really miserable.

'Don't do the raised-eyebrow thing,' Freya instructs me.

'Sorry.' I frown exaggeratedly and she rolls her eyes at me.

Then she says, '*Anyway*, enough about our weekend and Sonja. How's your week been?' She looks first at Dan and then at Lizzie.

'It's been a good one.' Lizzie is beaming. 'A busy one. I've been out a lot. Mainly with Dan.'

'Yeah, it's been a good one.' He's grinning too.

And then they tell us some of the dates they've been on together since the alpaca date. Cinema. Ice skating. Cinema again. I think they mention four different restaurants. A pub quiz. And they went for a long walk together earlier today. Am I misremembering or is it not even three weeks since the alpaca date? I've never, ever, in the nearly fifteen years that I've known him, seen Dan be this joined at the hip with anyone.

I can't really work out whether I think it's far too much too soon or they've both just met their soulmate and it's truly lovely and all their friends and family should start expecting wedding invitations.

The conversation doesn't divide in half again; we talk as a four during the remainder of our dinner, until Dan does a cheek-splittingly wide yawn, and Lizzie says, 'Yeah, we should get going. We haven't had that much sleep this week.'

Freya mock-covers her ears with her hands. 'Eeuuw, no, too much information.'

Lizzie and Dan both chuckle in an incredibly smug-couple way, which is bizarrely just sweet and not at all annoying or cringey, and I blink. I have *never* seen Dan like this before.

As we all get our coats on, I'm standing just behind Freya and Lizzie and inadvertently overhear Freya say, 'I've *never* seen you like this before with anyone.'

Lizzie replies, 'I *know*,' and then they hug each other.

Wow.

On my way home, I am so tempted to message Freya to say: *Tell me* now *that you still don't believe in love for* everyone. But I don't. Apart from anything else, Dan's great, and Lizzie seems lovely and perfect for him, and I superstitiously feel like I don't want to jinx anything for them.

I have to say: if this works out for Dan and Lizzie, that will go some way – a long way – to making the rest of the torture worth it. Dan just seems so *happy*. And, selfishly thinking about myself, I'm now finding Freya bearable in small doses, so it wouldn't be a terrible loss on a personal level if I have to see her sometimes in group situations.

And if I'm right about Sonja's not entirely benevolent intentions, I imagine I might derive a certain amount of amusement from seeing Freya at the team-building weekend.

* * *

'You are *kidding* me,' Freya says for at least the fifth time three weeks later.

We arrived in Devon last night for our team-building weekend. We – the participants – were all put up in separate hotels overnight (very reality-TV-like; I do have the sensation that Freya and I have strayed into a strange world where we have become a reality show through essentially no fault of our own). We were brought here at 8 a.m. this morning and have met our hosts, and are now standing in our shared quarters. Quarters is the right word, because our first bonding activity is going to be an army assault course and we're staying in ex-army barracks.

Freya and I are sharing a two-bedroom apartment. We have our own en-suite shower rooms with a shared sitting room.

I've been on a lot of team-building events, and none of them have involved bonding as a team of two. I was very much not envisaging this and I *would* be looking forward to the weekend even less than I already was, if it weren't for the fact that Freya is so incredibly pissed off it's just very funny.

She points at me. 'This is your fault.'

'Are we back on the same argument? That I started it during the TV interview?'

'You *did* start it then and we both know that, but no, I'm not referring to that. I'm referring to the fact that *I* played ball with Sonja and answered her questions, and *you* refused to divulge anything, so this *entire* weekend is based around what *I* don't like. If you'd told her things you don't like it would have been split.' She waves the card on which our weekend schedule is printed out. 'There could not *be* a weekend I would dislike more.'

I just look at her and smile. I'm enjoying this more and more.

She glares at me. 'Oh my *goodness*. Stop smiling. Stop looking *happy*.'

I laugh out loud.

She walks over to the window and looks out at our view of muddy farmland.

'I cannot *believe* Sonja,' she says.

'I feel like you're gearing up to admitting I was right.'

'You were right about this one very specific thing. Not about anything else. And you were probably only right about this because your mind is as devious as Sonja's. If it weren't, it wouldn't have occurred to you that she would do this.'

I laugh again.

'Oh my *goodness*. You're so annoying.' She narrows her eyes. 'Are you going to *enjoy* this?'

'I think I am,' I admit. 'I do like an assault course.'

'I'm so pleased,' she says.

'I'm really sorry to have to mention it—' I am incredibly un-sorry '—but I think we should get changed now or we'll be late for the start. And we're going to be filmed.'

Freya makes a sound like a very small and high-pitched bomb exploding and disappears into her bedroom with what I can only describe as a flounce.

This is by far and away the most enjoyment I've had to date in her presence.

* * *

I'm halfway through the first chapter of John Buchan's *The Thirty-Nine Steps* when Freya finally emerges from her room dressed in army fatigues. They made us give up our phones when we arrived, telling us that we needed to focus on each other, not the outside world, which is why I am, for the second time since I met Freya, reading a new-to-me author, having chosen it from the small selection available on the shelf in the corner of the room. I'm not a big reader in general, so this is a novelty.

I'm enjoying *The Thirty-Nine Steps*, but if I'm honest, I actually enjoyed Freya's books more. I got into them more quickly; it's something about the way she writes.

'John Buchan,' she says. 'Hmm.'

I don't like her *Hmm*, or the look on her face. I sense that she's about to make some very good point that I'm going to struggle to refute.

'Richard Hannay. He's a *great* hero,' she continues. 'Those manly, all-action men, who always save the day. Don't we *all* want one of those in our lives? Wouldn't those of us who are married to a man want someone like that to rescue us from any given situation? Is he *realistic*, though, as in can we really expect that from a real-life person?' She steps forward and whisks the book out of my hands. 'I'm sorry but I don't think you should be reading that. I think it should be banned. I think it might give people ideas and lead to divorce.'

'It's different,' I say.

'Why?'

'Because it isn't specifically a romance.'

'*Oh*,' she says, with great sarcasm. '*Oh*. I'm so sorry. I hadn't realised. I'm obviously wrong in my assumption that people lust after James Bond and Jason Bourne and all those other famous film action heroes.'

I stare at her.

Oh. My. God.

I'm having an epiphany. Oh, fuck. I think I'm going to have to apologise. To one of the most annoying women I've ever met. *The* most annoying woman, actually.

She's so bloody right. I'm an idiot. I've landed us in this entire challenge on a really stupid premise.

'Erm, oh fuck,' I say.

'Do you mean what I think you mean?'

'Yes. I'm sorry. I was an idiot.' I think my vision has been extremely clouded by my divorce and my wife citing Freya's heroes.

'Have you perhaps now understood that you were being *ridiculous*?'

'Erm. Yes.' I wrinkle my face. 'Sorry again?'

'*Sorry*? Because of your *dickheadedness* we're about to do an army assault course that you are going to enjoy and I am going to hate, having also suffered a succession of ridiculous dates, and you're *sorry*?'

'Yep,' I confirm.

'You owe me so fucking big it's beyond belief.'

I nod. 'Yeah.'

She shakes her head and does some more flouncing as she leaves the room ahead of me. If I'm honest, it's a strangely alluring flounce. Those army fatigues suit her bizarrely well, and the way her hair swooshes manically around her head as she tosses it is actually very cute. And, what, *what* am I thinking?

She mutters something, and I lean forward to hear better.

'What?' I ask.

'I said: *Stupid fucking dickhead.*'

'Fair enough.'

* * *

Twenty minutes later, we've been fully briefed by Sonja, who is host-presenting the weekend. The salient points are that we very much have to do this as a pair. And we're up against a clock and against the other couples who are here. The other couples all paid a tenner to enter an apparently very popular competition to join the weekend. Bizarre what people will do in the name of getting a near-freebie. I'm not sure how many people would otherwise sign up in pairs to a weekend comprising an assault course, a getting-to-know reptiles session, followed by a fondue dinner, and then a treetop rope walk tomorrow. Although, saying that, I'll be quite happy with all those things.

The team who come last have to do ice baths.

'I am not fucking doing an ice bath,' Freya says. 'We are fucking beating the others. And if that means you have to carry me, then you're carrying me.' This weekend is making her very sweary.

'Noted,' I say. Good job she isn't very big. Good job for *me* that I quite like an ice bath, so I don't really care whether we win or lose.

'Ready?' roars the man who briefed us.

We all nod, some more happily than others. And we're off.

13

FREYA

It's so muddy. So bloody muddy. That rhymes. Bloody and muddy.

Bloody muddy.

My goodness. I think I'm losing my mind.

This is awful, though. So much mud. It's such hard work running through it.

I really, really, really don't want to do an ice bath.

So I'm somehow going to have to do this course faster than all these super-fit-looking people.

My lungs are on fire. It feels like my head is too. I really can't think.

'Are you okay?' Jake asks me, talking really easily, like he's just out for a stroll around the park, instead of doing the hardest physical challenge I've ever tried.

I can't talk. I can't even shake my head. I just keep on lugging my booted feet through the quagmire below us. I hate, hate, hate, hate, *hate* running.

Eventually, we come to the end of the hideous running bit, thank fuck. We've reached one of those net things you see on TV and we have to crawl under it. So *so* much better than running. A genuine little break.

The other teams are all already under the net, because they all ran faster than I did. It looks quite hard – some of them are getting quite stuck – but it looks *way* less bad than the running was.

'It's very muddy.' Jake speaks very apologetically. He's been fairly apologetic all morning (when he hasn't been laughing) after he realised what an idiot he's been since the moment we met. Apologies are absolutely no good whatsoever to me now, though.

'Don't care,' I pant. 'Rest from running.'

'Okay. I'm going to go slightly ahead of you and I'm going to hold the net up so all you have to do is crawl as fast as you can?' he says. 'How does that sound?'

Well, it kind of sounds patronising. But it also sounds *excellent*.

'Perfect,' I manage to say.

And oh my goodness I'm delighted to say that I am pretty good at crawling through mud. It's *so* much better than running.

And *unbelievably*, when we get out at the other end, it turns out that out of all the six teams we're *first*, because at least one of every other pair has got tangled in the net.

'No time to gloat,' Jake yells. '*Run.*'

Fucking running. I really, really, really fucking hate it.

This run is a relatively short one, though, thank goodness.

However.

Next thing we have to go up and over a *really* high wall thing. We have to get strapped into a nappy-like keep-you-safe-while-you're-climbing-far-too-high ropey device and climb up it using little sticky-out bits like you see people do in the Olympics now.

I do not like heights. I do not like them at all. I need to focus on the wall in front of me, not the fact that I'm going up and up and up.

I need to focus on myself and what I'm doing and not the ground beneath me.

Unfortunately, what I am doing is climbing with the assistance of Jake, which means that he is holding, pushing and pulling various bits of me.

And in focusing on that I am also focusing on the fact that he has what I do have to admit are very nicely muscled arms and legs. And his bottom looks very hard and muscly too. How is that even possible? And there's something about bits of me being in close contact with him that's giving me serious stomach palpitations. Clearly, I need to date a bit more. I'm going mad just because I'm very literally up close and personal (albeit it covered in mud) with a very physi-cally attractive (albeit very annoying) man.

'You're a natural.' Jake's slightly quirky smile makes me want to smile too, and also causes my stomach to dip again.

When I've recovered from the stomach dip, I take stock of our position and realise that he isn't even joking. I genuinely am not bad at this, especially with Jake's lovely muscly help.

And therefore we get to the top way faster than anyone would have expected me to, and faster than the other teams. And given that we were already slightly in the lead following the net, we're *massively* in the lead now.

I feel amazing. This is so cool. I should take up climbing as a sport. I love it.

And then I look down.

'Fuuuuck,' I scream. 'We're so high up.'

'It's fine,' Jake soothes. I want to kick him, frankly.

'No, it isn't,' I screech.

'It *is*. You're all strapped up, remember. And you'll be back on the ground really quickly.'

'What, when I *fall*? And *die*?'

'No. When you've abseiled down.' He says it like it's a regular thing to say.

'Abseil?' I query, because it is *not* in fact a regular thing to say.

'Remember from the briefing what you have to do? Would you like me to go first or stay and help you?'

I wasn't listening at *all* to the briefing; I was too busy panicking about the run we were about to start.

'I don't know. No, I do know. Don't leave me.' I might, if I'm honest, be clutching his arm with my hands shaped into claws.

'Okay. No problem. Shall we go together?'

'Um.' I look down again and do a big intake of breath and tighten my grip on his arm.

To his credit, he winces and glances once at where my nails are definitely digging in *hard* to his flesh, but doesn't say anything.

'It's very high indeed,' I point out.

'You won't fall because you climbed up brilliantly and abseiling down is easier, but if you did it would be *fine*, because you're safely strapped in.'

Okay. Deep breaths. He's right, of course he is. But the ground is *so far away*. It would *really* hurt if we fell.

I hear a sound diagonally below me to my right, and look over my shoulder. Eek, we're about to be overtaken.

I do *not* want to be doing that ice bath.

'Okay.' I'm suddenly decisive. 'Let's do it.'

'Okay. Like this.' Jake shows me and I copy him.

And *then*, he *lets go* and starts bouncing his way down the wall.

He stops after a few bounces and looks up at me. 'Freya?'

'I can't do that,' I state. I mean, he *let go*. I'm just not doing that. It's too high. Far, far too high.

Fortunately, there are sticky-out bits to hold on to on both sides of the wall, so I can climb down the other side using those. I set off.

'Freya? I think abseiling would be a lot faster.' Jake's bouncing his way down again and is nearly at the bottom.

'Don't care.' I'm too warm to talk much. Climbing is hot work. 'Too high.'

A lot of the others bounce their way past me on their way down. I keep on climbing. Eventually, I get to a point – around the height of Jake's head, so maybe six feet up – where I feel confident to abseil, so I let go, bounce once and am on the ground.

'Yesssss,' I yell. That was *so* cool. Maybe I *will* take up climbing. 'Maybe I could abseil from higher up next time.'

'You definitely could,' Jake assures me, and I find myself beaming at him.

I do feel hugely triumphant and full of excellent endorphins, but only one person gets off the wall after me and he's tall and lean and sprints off towards the next obstacle (I have no idea how he fell behind me in the first place), so this is realistically the end of the race for me in terms of not coming last.

I do semi-run to the next obstacle (a parallel bar thing, which is an absolute fiasco when I do it) and then I don't bother running after that, because there's blatantly no chance of us not losing, and I really don't mind walking through mud – the squelchiness of it is quite pleasant when you aren't worrying about getting your clothes and face muddy (I'm already fully mudded up) – and I might as well enjoy myself as much as I can.

I lumber on to the end, and I do enjoy the last obstacle, a raft thing across a stream (I just sit on it feeling muddy and slightly trembly from all the overexertion) while Jake puts his very well (but not too well) developed biceps to good use paddling us and I admire his strength and the whole muscly thing, and the wider view, because now that I can see something other than mud, I realise that it's very pretty here.

And then we walk through the finish line holding hands, because that's what all the other pairs did and it does actually seem natural to do it, and the others all cheer us. (Unless they're mad and would in fact like to do an ice bath they're probably also cheering because *they* haven't lost.)

As we stand there I suddenly become very aware that I'm still holding Jake's hand, and I think he realises the same thing at exactly the same moment because we both all at once just *drop* the other's hand, very much as though we have hot potatoes on the end of our arms. We stand and don't speak for a few moments, and then we both congratulate the other, at once.

There's not too much time to stand around though (well, not for us, anyway, because we came in so far behind the other pairs) before Sonja – who seems to be absolutely everywhere this weekend – tells us that we need to go and have showers asap so we're ready for our ice baths. *Which the other pairs are going to watch.* Like, actual torture.

'Bloody hell,' I say to Jake as we make our way back to our rooms. He isn't the person in life I would choose to discuss *any* of my thoughts with ever, but I obviously have no-one else to talk to right now. 'Sonja has literally taken every single dislike I mentioned and turned them all into a list of activities for this weekend and she's even managed to add in things I hate that I didn't mention. Like she has a superpower that involves guessing the most evil thing she can do to me. I *hate* cold showers.'

'It's an ice *bath*,' Jake says. 'You know that, right? Not just cold and not a shower. Icy. Bath.'

'What?'

'An ice-cold bath. All of you goes into it. At once. Not like a shower. It's good for you. Health-giving. Invigorating.'

'Have you done one?'

'Yep. Several. Quite enjoy them.' Of course he bloody does.

'Fucking hell.'

* * *

It's more insanely unpleasant than I was imagining, I realise when we assemble for our ice baths. There are two ice-water-filled bath-like containers in the middle of a room and space round the sides for the other pairs *and* a fucking TV camera. As in, if we do this with anything other than very good grace our misery will be broadcast to the nation. *My* misery I should say; Jake is not miserable.

We're both wearing T-shirts, shorts and unattractive toe-boot things that they provided us with.

Jake asked me on our way over whether I'd like to go first or second. I opted for first, reasoning that however bad it is, the anticipation will only add to the badness, and I'm not even being selfish given that Jake said he's *liked* it when he's done it before (five or six times, he can't remember how many; I am certain that I will be doing it once and once only).

And this is it. I'm about to go in.

We had a long spiel beforehand that I really struggled to concentrate on (I am not good with boring instructions) but *now* I'm focused, mainly on not reacting *whatever* happens.

I don't react when I get in. I was worried that I'd scream, but I'm too stunned. It's so unbelievably cold. Shockingly so.

Okay. I'm in. I have to stay in for three minutes and then I'm done. It's invigorating, I tell myself, it's good for me, it's amazing, it's wonderful (er *no it is not*), and this torture *will* be over soon, and I am *not* going to react.

And it's over.

'*Fucking* hell,' I say right into the TV camera as I climb out.

'How *was* it?' asks one of the other women participants whose name I haven't yet caught, because we've barely been introduced; they're trying to keep us apart as much as possible apparently, so that we all focus fully on our partner. 'Are you a convert? Do you feel amazing?'

I just stand there for a few seconds, trying to work out how I feel.

'I think I *do* feel good,' I tell the woman. 'But mainly because I'm *out*. I don't feel good enough to make up for having to do it in the first place. Plus, now I know what it's like, the anticipation would make me feel as bad beforehand as the endorphin rush afterwards, so basically, no, I am not a convert.'

She laughs, and then we all turn round because it's Jake's turn.

I have to say: wearing a water-soaked T-shirt does suit a man with a very toned torso. It's just a fact. Like appreciating a great work of art by an amazing painter, you can't really *not* appreciate Jake's physique. Not in an attracted-to-him way (clearly I am *not* attracted to him), just in an 'oh wow yes that's a great painting or great sculpture' kind of way.

Taking an ice bath suits Jake in more than one way. He looks perfectly happy while he's doing it – very cool.

When he gets out, he's grinning and he does not swear into a camera in a manner that the producers obviously *will* decide to broadcast on national television; he just laughs and agrees that, yeah, you do feel good afterwards.

I've been out for several minutes now and I do not feel on any kind of particular high and I fully remember how much I did not like it, and I will not be doing it again. End of.

'You were amazing,' gushes the woman I spoke to before.

'Ha,' says Jake. 'I don't think there's any particular life skill involved in not flinching during or after a cold bath; probably more that I'm too lazy to twitch.'

'Adorable,' the woman says.

I try hard not to roll my eyes. It's ridiculous the effect Jake has on people.

Sonja is clapping her hands. 'Time for lunch before our reptile experience,' she tells us.

I'm not going to think about the reptile thing, I'm just going to focus on the fact that I'm *really* looking forward to lunch; assault courses and ice baths make you hungry, it turns out. Hopefully they'll have laid on something nice for us as a reward.

Nope. Of course they haven't. Except, I do actually think I'm going to enjoy this.

'Lunch is a MasterChef-style challenge,' Sonja tells us. 'We're all going to a large kitchen where we have a worktop for each team and you'll all have the same twenty ingredients, not all of which you have to use, and you'll be competing to make the best meal and also to showcase the best teamwork. Two-thirds of the marks will be for the food, including taste, presentation and skill level, and one-third for teamwork.'

'Couldn't get more clichéd if they tried,' Jake says in my ear as the host draws breath.

'Sounds like fun, though.' I *love* cooking and I *love* opening a fridge and making whatever I can from the ingredients in there.

'The winners will get to make dessert for everyone and the losers will do an ice bath,' the host continues.

'I mean, I'd rather do the ice bath,' Jake says.

'Okay, this is the *only* part of the weekend that's going to be fun for me,' I say, alarmed. 'You *have* to try hard. I don't want to do another ice bath *ever* and I'd love to make dessert for everyone.'

Jake does a very dramatic whole-body sigh while rolling his eyes and then says, '*Fine*. I'll do my best.' He looks at me. 'Do you cook a lot?'

'Yep. Do you?'

'Basically never.' He screws up his face, as though he's in pain, which –

ridiculously – just makes him look very handsome in a different way from normal, rather than weird, like anyone else would if they did that. 'I might have to take your instructions.'

'Ha, *really*?' I'm delighted. 'Finally I have you at my mercy.'

'I mean, not fully. Or not at all, really. Given my preference for an ice bath over baking.'

I raise my eyebrows very sternly.

'Yeah, no, fine, I will do my best,' he says.

'And do exactly as you're told?'

'Yes. I promise.'

'Good.'

We walk together with the other teams over to the kitchen, which, in *Bake Off* fashion, although in a much less picturesque way – it's surrounded by large, concrete sheds – is housed in a giant tent.

A very jovial man called Fred tells us that his partner, Suzanne, is a bona fide Michelin-starred chef. Bugger. Although it really doesn't matter as long as we don't *lose*. I would *like* to win, though.

Fifteen minutes later, we're all at the right workbenches, we've all seen the ingredients that we have, and we're all raring to go (or in Jake's case leaning with elbows on the worktop, chin propped in hand, unenthusiasm personified) when Sonja raises her whistle.

'Three, two, one!' She blows, long and hard.

'Ow.' I shake my head to disperse the ringing in my ears. That was a very high decibel level.

I've been thinking fast and I know what I want us to make: a prawn and leek risotto, with a fennel, tomato and red onion salad to balance the creaminess.

I set Jake to chopping onions first. He begins with the first one by cutting it the opposite way to how most people do and then stares at it.

'Shall I show you how *I* would chop an onion?' I suggest.

'Can I not do it my way?'

'What *is* your way?'

'I'm just working that out.' He pulls his sleeve up and kind of twizzles his knife.

'Okay, I'm going to show you how to do it.'

'What, there's an actual particular way to chop an onion?'

'Of course?' As I demonstrate, it's clear that he's paying about as much attention as I paid to the assault course and ice bath instructions.

When I'm done, he moves in front of the chopping board and... cuts the onion really slowly into big, uneven chunks, totally ignoring how I showed him to do it.

'Okay, no.' I take – seize, if I'm honest – the knife and set to work rescuing the onions. 'Why don't you wash some vegetables and clear up after me? And pass me things? And I'll do all the chopping as fast as I can.'

'Sounds like this is going to be *fun*,' he says with a sarcastic eyebrow raise before he begins wiping around the worktop.

He looks like he's never held a cloth before.

'This is not a moment for sarcasm,' I tell him. 'This is a moment to shut up and do what you're told and make sure I don't have to do a second ice bath in one day.' I say it with a friendly, team-matey smile, because one of Sonja's side-kicks is making her way towards us, notebook and pen at the ready to record her observations of our work. 'Why don't you wash those courgettes?' I'm not planning to include the courgettes in the risotto but I need to keep him busy. And maybe I can get him to peel them into shavings and toss them with oil, garlic and lemon and have them as another side salad. *Or* make little courgette dumplings with them, although maybe that would be too much heaviness for one meal.

'Why? Are we actually using them?'

'No questions; you have to demonstrate great teamwork,' I hiss. With a smile, because in addition to the observer, the bloody TV cameras are here watching us, and I have no wish to look grumpy in public.

'Team members are allowed to question each other,' Jake says, far too loudly.

'Shhh,' I say, extremely smilingly.

'Being an author must be a very solitary occupation,' he says in musing (and still loud) tones. 'Not a lot of teamwork practice.'

'I've had *plenty* of teamwork practice. I used to be a retail manager. I have regular work meetings now. I can work in a team. Just not with someone with literally no relevant skills and a poor attitude.' I am still smiling.

'Er I have a *great* attitude. I'm *very* kindly helping you to try to win this so you don't have another ice bath today.' Jake's still washing three courgettes, splashing far and wide as he does so.

'Thank you. I'm extremely grateful. Don't forget to dry the worktop and floor when you've finished washing those.'

'I would *never* forget such a thing.'

'Good news.' I chop, cook, season as fast as I can, all the while giving Jake occasionally useful and often entertain-the-toddler type tasks to keep him busy, and smiling away for the observers and the cameras.

'That smells really good.' Jake's standing quite close behind me as I taste the dish and then add a little bit more lemon juice. 'And what I *really* like about your addition of that lemon juice is that *I* juiced the lemon and it was *not* a wasted task.'

I try very hard to ignore the fact that for some bizarre reason I'm enjoying the sense of his *largeness* so close to me, and smile when he indicates with his head the washed and not used courgettes and carrots neatly laid out on the side to our right. I asked Jake to slice one courgette with the wide slice bit of the grater and he managed to slice his thumb (and is now sporting a fetching blue plaster), and I didn't have time to do them myself on top of everything else, so I decided that less is more and binned the extra courgette salad idea.

I turn round and, oops, it turns out that he's taken a step closer and I'm now very much chest to chest with him.

I take a step to my right, just as he takes a step to his left. And then I try one to my left, just as he tries one to his right. And we are still very close to each other.

'So.' Eek, my voice has gone weird. 'I was just going to get a little bit of pepper.'

'Of course.' His voice sounds a bit odd too.

Which is not surprising, because there *is* something very odd about standing this near to someone. It makes you extremely aware of... well... everything about them.

Jake's chest and shoulders are very wide. But not too wide. Just the right amount of wideness. He's tall. But not too tall. Just the right amount of height. And when he smiles, it's just the right amount, so that you want to smile too.

My goodness. Why do I just keep thinking *just the right amount*? Just the right amount for *what*?

'Can I taste our cooking?' His lovely deep voice is just the right amount of gravelly. Just the right amount for *something*. That something – right now – might be causing me to feel butterflies in my stomach.

'Of course.' We're still standing facing each other, very close together. I can see the rise and fall of his chest, the beginnings of his beard shadow. 'So I'm going to step to my right now and take a teaspoon and give it to you so that you can do the tasting.' I described it like that to avoid any more of the weird side-stepping at the same time, but I think I might just have sounded *very* odd.

'Great.' He sounds odd too.

And then we both kind of hover until I take the step to my right while Jake stands there, very strangely still, his arms just kind of hanging by his sides, which is unusual, because Jake is normally very relaxed.

Anyway. Odd. I move over to the counter and the drawer where the cutlery is, take a teaspoon and turn round to hand it to him. He reaches for it at the exact same moment and our hands bang, and that just feels *weird*.

We say, 'Sorry,' simultaneously and then we laugh simultaneously, and, honestly, I feel as though I'm losing my mind a little. As in, I am just not me in this moment.

I'm not sure who I am instead.

All just very peculiar.

14

JAKE

Well, that was weird.

I think I just forgot that Freya is *Freya*. The woman who drives me insane. Well, she's still been driving me insane, but in a very different way.

Anyway. What was I supposed to be doing?

Tasting her risotto. With the teaspoon she just gave me. Got it.

So.

I take a little bit on the teaspoon, wave it around a bit to cool it, and then taste it.

'Wow. That's delicious.' I'm not joking; it's very, very good. 'I'd more than happily eat a giant bowl of that.'

'Thank you.' Freya looks extremely pretty when someone's been genuinely nice to her and she's genuinely pleased. Her smile is – objectively – gorgeous in this moment. Her eyes swivel to the right and I realise that one of the observers is there. 'We worked *brilliantly* as a team,' Freya says.

'Yeah, we did,' I agree, because firstly we kind of *did*, in that she told me what to do (mainly pointless tasks) and I did them, and secondly because you can't help warming to someone who's had to do several activities that they genuinely hate and has done them with a very good grace, laughing at themselves the whole way; and I do think it would be a little unfortunate for Freya if she had to do another ice bath.

I look at the observer out of the corner of my eye and see that she's writing on a piece of paper on a clipboard.

'I think we played very well to our individual strengths,' I say for the observer's benefit.

'Two minutes to go,' announces Sonja. 'Plating up time.'

'Okay, I genuinely think I can competently ladle risotto onto a plate,' I tell Freya.

She gives me a look.

I nod. 'Okay, yeah, no ladling. Just tell me what to do.'

In the end, I hold the large pan that she cooked the risotto in while she very carefully spoons it onto a flat bowl and sprinkles herbs (maybe parsley; I'm really not sure – green, anyway) over the top, and then I watch while she arranges the salad on a plate, and places both the bowl and the plate onto a tray.

'Why don't you carry the tray?' she suggests.

'Very happy to,' I say, aiming to sound like the happiest teammate ever.

Looking around at the other participants, I see that the pair that includes the professional chef (Fred and Suzanne) have produced a very cheffy-looking dish. Of the others, I'd say that ours definitely looks the best.

'Now.' Sonja looks directly into one of the TV cameras. 'Our competitors don't know this but we have three very famous judges to taste our dishes.' She puts her arm out to the side and three people troop out from a door in the side of the tent.

A hum of chatter begins from around the tent, because, yes, they are famous.

One is a chef who I vaguely recognise and who Freya tells me is a judge on *MasterChef: The Professionals*.

One is a woman who Freya tells me is one of the regular *British Bake Off* judges.

And one is a (very well-known apparently) comedian who I do not know.

They all say that they're incredibly excited to be tasting our food.

They don't look particularly excited; clearly the production company has paid them well for this and that is the only reason that they're here.

Freya's practically hopping on the spot as our (her) food is tasted, as though she can't bear the anticipation.

The chef judge, who has been appointed spokesperson for the three of them, tells us that, while it's a little simpler than one or two of the other dishes, it did require some skill and, importantly, it's been executed and seasoned to perfection and we should be very proud of ourselves. We also, apparently, plated it up perfectly.

Freya shifts from foot to foot some more as they deliberate about how many marks they're going to give us and then just beams when we're told that we have the second highest mark for both skill and presentation and joint highest for taste, with Fred and Suzanne overall winners.

'And now to teamwork.' Sonja waves her clipboard at us. 'As you know, we observed you all closely throughout. There was one team, we noticed, where one of the pair did not cook a single thing. He basically just washed vegetables and tidied and carried things when asked.'

'Oh fuck,' Freya breathes. 'That's us. We're in those baths again.'

'I'm going to give that team their mark last.' Sonja smiles directly at us. It's always a little alarming when she does that. We both smile weakly back. I'm feeling genuinely sorry for Freya at this point.

The other teams get quite varying marks for teamwork. Crucially, the ones with the worst food had the best teamwork, and Sonja announces that, once the overall scores are totted up, the ice bath situation entirely depends on *our* team-work mark.

'I refer you to my earlier remarks about this team.' She smiles directly into the camera again. 'So, if you remember, this pair displayed very differing skill levels. And, arguably, enthusiasm levels.'

Next to me Freya heaves a big sigh as Sonja smiles at us and looks round the room.

'However,' Sonja continues, 'what we all thought was great was the way Freya and Jake did work together. Freya – while clearly desperate not to do another ice bath – did her best to take the time to involve Jake so he wouldn't feel sidelined. And Jake – who in his day job is a senior lawyer who we don't believe gets asked to wash courgettes very often – did all that was asked of him with a good grace. And where it *was* possible to work together, during the plating up for example, they did so very well. It was a triumph in terms of a lesson in teamwork. Full marks.'

'Oh my *goodness*,' squeals Freya. 'No ice bath.'

'*And*,' says Sonja, 'you'll be baking dessert for us all after discussions with our judges.'

'Oh my goodness, thank you, thank you, thank you.' Freya's squealing even more, and I'm laughing because it's cute how excited she is.

'We'll discuss the dessert-baking now for fifteen minutes, before the ice baths and then the reptile show, after which Jake and Freya will bake and everyone else will go to the sauna.'

'Hooray,' whispers Freya. 'I *hate* saunas.'

'I quite like them,' I say.

'Of course you do.'

I smile at her, because she seems extremely happy about the baking, and you'd have to be incredibly mean-spirited not to be pleased for her that she's got such a treat after her suboptimal morning.

'Just so you know,' I murmur in her ear as people mill around us before we go off to have our discussion with the judges, 'that was terrible teamwork and I was totally sidelined.'

'You absolutely were,' she agrees. She shoots a grin at me and I feel as though it hits me right in the chest.

* * *

We all had to make enough food for six people so that each of us can have a little of each plate for our lunch. We aren't allowed to leave our partner for long, though; there are six tables for two, spaced far apart, set up for us all, and we're all told to sit down at our own tables in our pairs.

We also aren't allowed to choose our own food; we're each given a plate piled high with a small portion of each of the dishes created during the task.

This weekend is such a peculiar experience that it doesn't even seem odd any more to be sitting alone with Freya, or to dissect the events of the day with her.

'How are you going to taste them?' I ask. 'I think I'm going to take a mouthful of each to see which one I like best. On the assumption that the judges' taste buds speak for all of us, I'm going to start with the one that got the lowest marks.'

'Very good plan,' Freya approves.

Six mouthfuls later, I say, 'Yours is *really* good. Way better than all the others except the chef's one, and in my opinion better than that one too.'

'It was *ours*, not just mine,' Freya says. 'And, also, thank you. I'll take that compliment.' She grins at me and I smile too.

And then we both eat little bits of the four less-good dishes to show willing, and all of our portions of Freya's risotto and Suzanne's deconstructed paella.

'I'm looking forward to seeing what you bake this afternoon,' I tell Freya as we finish eating.

'What *we* bake.'

'Of course. You'll be incredibly grateful to have my expertise, actually. I really know my stuff. I once helped my grandmother bake a cherry cake.'

Freya laughs, and, honestly, it's weirdly as though we don't really dislike each other that much any more.

* * *

The conversation with the judges about desserts has me floundering and Freya buzzing.

I try to listen but zone out quite quickly because it's a whole vocab that means absolutely nothing to me. I'm really annoyed with myself for not having been listening when Freya makes the comedian (I've forgotten his name again; he's very famous to the YouTube generation) throw his head back and roar with laughter, and the other two judges snigger, hard, one of them snorting something very unappealing out of his nose as he does so.

'I've got so many ideas,' Freya tells me as we make our way with the other pairs over to the ice bath hut.

'How do you have ideas for your books?' I ask, suddenly curious.

'I don't know really. They just come to me. How do you have ideas about anything?'

'Yeah, I don't know.' I'm not sure that I do have ideas in the way that Freya does. When she was discussing the potential desserts we could make it was like light bulbs kept going off inside her head. I'm not sure I'm a particularly light-bulby person. Well, I'm not. Definitely.

'I think maybe once you start writing, or baking professionally, or whatever it might be, you have more and more ideas, because you get into the way of it and things just pop up in your mind because you're always thinking about that kind of stuff. I imagine. Probably the same with art too,' she says.

I nod, genuinely interested.

We don't have time for more conversation, because it's time to watch Jerome and Anita, one of the other pairs (the word 'couple' keeps popping into my head in relation to this task, and I keep pushing it away because it's so particularly inappropriate in regard to me and Freya), do their ice baths.

'You did *brilliantly*,' Freya tells Anita when she gets out. 'You were so much more stoic than I was.'

This is objectively not true; Freya *was* stoic, other than a bit of swearing when she got out, whereas Anita squeaked throughout.

'Thank you so much.'

The two of them share a hug and then stand back to watch Jerome get in. Jerome gets pretty sweary about the whole thing.

'Turns out you're an actual man of steel,' Freya whispers to me.

'Small sample size,' I say, but if I'm honest I'm weirdly pleased that she's complimented me. Probably just the contrast to how things were before. It actually gets quite wearing being permanently at war with someone.

* * *

Next it's time for the reptile experience.

Freya begins to tense noticeably on the walk over there. She's no longer laughing – even politely – at even my best jokes; she can barely even raise a smile. And she's walking kind of stiffly.

When I ask, 'So you really don't like snakes?' she physically flinches.

'I can't even stand the word,' she tells me.

'What, the word *sn*—'

She cuts me off. 'Exactly.'

'Proper full-blown phobia?' I check. 'Much worse than your fear of heights?'

She hadn't seemed *that* bad with the height thing. Clearly uncomfortable but not to these levels. More your 'I have a very rational dislike of being high up if there's a possibility that I might fall' type fear.

'Yep.'

'It's actually completely unacceptable to force someone to do something they're this uncomfortable with,' I say.

'We're on national television and we signed up to this and what can I do?'

'You didn't actually sign up to this. Neither of us signed anything saying we'd do absolutely anything they required of us and, if we *had*, I really don't think it would stand up in a court of law because it's so ridiculously unreasonable to expect that of anyone and it would effectively have been under duress due to the on-national-television-you-can't-pull-out pressure.'

'Well, maybe it's good for me to face my fears.'

'Well obviously that might be true,' I concede. 'If you *want* to face your fears.' In front of me and lots of people she knows even less. And TV cameras. I feel that your average person would probably rather face their fears in private and either supported by close friends or with complete strangers. This really doesn't seem the best place for it.

Freya doesn't reply; we've nearly reached the tent where the reptiles are and she's just staring at it as we approach – at a snail's pace, her walking having slowed dramatically.

'Come in.' Sonja holds the tent flap door open and we enter, to see a man with a large snake around his neck only a few feet from us.

'Eeuurrrgh.' Freya makes a strange sound next to me. As I turn to her, I see her do a full-body shudder – definitely involuntary rather than for effect – and she covers her face with her hands.

Okay. This is ridiculous.

'Sorry.' I put my arm round Freya's rigid shoulders and draw her back out of the tent.

'Where are you going?' asks Sonja.

'We aren't doing this activity,' I tell her. 'We're going to go for a walk.'

'Sorry, what?' Sonja's smiling (there's a camera behind us) but her tone is pure steel. 'You agreed to do this weekend and you have to participate in every task.'

I shake my head. 'As you will be aware, there is legislation in place to protect people from being bullied and traumatised in the workplace. You *knew* that Freya had a snake phobia. You didn't ask her if she would like to face her fears or do this. From a legal perspective this is completely unacceptable. The production company is not legally able to *make* anyone go into a tent of reptiles if they don't wish to do so. We are going for a walk. Enjoy the reptiles.'

Sonja's mouth has fallen slightly open and she's doing that thing where she presses her ear to hear what her producer is saying.

Freya's seeming quite limp next to me, as though she might faint, so I maintain my grip on her shoulders, nod at Sonja, and wheel Freya round in a one-eighty and march us both off away from the tent.

'Outrageous,' I say as we walk, hoping to divert Freya's mind from the snakes. 'How can she possibly think it's okay not to give people a choice about what they do? That was all recorded as well. I wonder if they'll destroy the evidence in case we make a complaint.'

'Thank you.' She takes a deep breath and shakes her head.

I feel her relax a little as she takes another deep breath.

'Sorry,' she says. 'That was quite ridiculous of me. It's just...'

'Hey, no.' I remove my arm, because she clearly doesn't need any physical support any more and there's no good reason whatsoever for me to be holding her, and the fact that my arm felt so *right* when it was round her is all *wrong*. 'Not ridiculous. A lot of people have phobias. Apparently it's entirely rational to have them and without them the human race might not have survived.' I have no idea whether or not that's true. It sounds very plausible, though. And a lot of phobias *are* rational.

'Hmm.' Freya's sounding much more like her usual self now. 'That can't be true about all phobias. I mean, that one where people get very distressed by holes, like in crumpets and industrial ceiling tiles. But it's true that it makes a lot of sense to be wary round certain creatures unless you're *certain* they're safe.'

'Exactly. And no-one should bully people into doing something that upsets them in any way. Especially not just for a TV show.'

'Jake Stone, I think I agree with absolutely everything you're saying. How did that happen?'

'Sonja happened,' I say.

Freya nods, very seriously. 'Yeah. I really liked it when you went full legal. Was everything you said true?'

'I mean, broadly. I'm not actually au fait with any laws there might be on making people face their fears but clearly there is legislation and best practice in place to prevent people from being bullied or traumatised in the workplace. And this is kind of a workplace for us in that we've been paid for our appearances. I mean, you can't just *make* people do something unreasonable, and that *is* unreasonable, clearly. Also, *maybe* they could say we were in breach of contract, although I doubt it, but who cares? I think it's more in their interests than ours for us to continue with the rest of the weekend.'

'All very true. Although I do want to do the baking thing.'

'More than you didn't want to do the... reptile experience?' I nearly said the *snake* word there; better be careful.

'No. Definitely not.' She gives me the smile that has such an effect on other people, and I *feel* it. 'Thank you.' She looks behind us. 'There are frigging cameras following us.'

'Yeah, we *did* sign up to that. I would suggest a walk but I don't think it would be that great being followed the entire time.'

Freya nods. 'You're right. Maybe we should text Sonja and ask her to call us when it's time for the next activity, and then go back to our rooms.'

'Good plan.' I pull out my phone and send the text, and then we turn round, and, cameraman in tow, set off back towards the accommodation.

'Are you finding it hard to walk normally?' Freya asks me a second later.

'No?'

'Are you not remotely paranoid about the cameras following us?'

'Well I *wasn't*.' I look over my shoulder and yes they are very much focused on us, from about twenty feet away. 'But now I am. Although is footage of two people walking great TV?'

'Yeah, true, probably only if we do something remarkable.'

'Okay, so let's not walk at all remarkably.'

'No problem,' Freya says. 'I can do that. Totally.'

A second later she begins to snigger. 'I can't. I cannot walk normally when I'm thinking about it.'

I take a look at her. 'What are you doing that *isn't* normal, though?'

'I don't know. I just *feel* weird. Because someone has a camera trained on my bottom.'

I can't say the first thing that comes to mind which is that every time I've seen her bottom it looks lovely. I shouldn't even be thinking that.

Freya's *really* sniggering now. 'I keep imagining doing something quite outrageous by mistake that would then get broadcast on national television.'

'How would that happen, though? Like you would just accidentally... what? What outrageous things does *anyone* do when they're walking?'

'I don't know. Okay, not outrageous. But what if we suddenly started pirouetting. Or *really* sprinting. Or stripping to our underwear and throwing our clothes at the camera.'

'Yeah, none of those things are going to happen to me.' I'm laughing too now.

'I don't *think* they're going to happen to me,' Freya says, 'but *what if they did*?'

'Then they might make good TV and be broadcast or they might not.'

She smiles at me. 'Ever rational.' Weirdly, she sounds almost fond, as though she *likes* me.

I kind of like her, I realise. She's good company; she's *nice*. And funny.

Yeah, weird. Never judge a book by its cover, I suppose.

15

FREYA

'Oh my goodness, the relief.' I open the door to our suite and, as Jake closes it behind him, I flop onto the sofa on the far side of our living room. 'What a ridiculous day.'

Jake sits down on the sofa too, in the opposite corner, and smiles at me. Weirdly, the smile looks quite fond. Equally (possibly even more) weirdly, he has, I realise, grown on me today, and I feel almost fond of him too. He didn't *have* to get me away from that reptile experience.

'Do you like reptiles?' I ask, suddenly aware – now I've stopped panicking – that Jake might have been looking forward to seeing them. 'Sorry; that was really selfish of me. Please feel very free to go back to the tent and listen to the talk if you'd like to?'

'No, I'm good, thanks. I don't have any reptile issues and I'm sure it would be moderately interesting, but also I'm totally happy to have a break. It feels like we're on some kind of school activity trip. This is our actual *weekend*.'

'Yep it's very weird.' I put my hand over my mouth as I fail to suppress a huge yawn. 'Sorry. I'm not used to getting up that early or doing assault courses.' I suddenly realise something. 'Oh my goodness. I don't think I've thanked you for saving me from the reptiles. I'm very, very grateful. Thank you.'

'I love the way you say "saving me from the reptiles", like we're characters in a kids' cartoon being pursued by giant mutant toads. But honestly, it was nothing.'

'That sounds like a great premise for a book,' I tell him.

'Have you ever written in any other genre?' he asks.

I think about the two thrillers I've had published under a very secret pseudonym, and remember that really we barely know each other and that only a few hours ago I still thoroughly disliked him, so I say, with great vagueness, 'A bit.'

For all I know, he has something massively against thriller writers too.

More importantly, I don't want anyone to know about the thriller-writing, because not all readers appreciate authors writing in more than one genre, so I've told almost no-one about it. Jake is definitely not someone I trust enough to confide in about that.

'Oh really?' he pursues. 'Which genres?'

'Just... you know... lots of authors dabble in different things until they settle on their preferred genre. It would be a lot of fun to write kids' books, but obviously completely different. Very different lengths and so on. What would *you* write if you wrote a book?'

He looks at me for a long moment, as though he knows that I was babbling because I have something to hide, and then says, 'I don't think I'd be a good writer. I kind of think it's offensive that everyone says, "Oh, yeah, I could *totally* write a book, I just need an idea and I'd be away." I think it's much harder than people think. But if I *could* write *and* had an idea, both of which are very questionable, I'd go for a legal thriller I think.'

'Busman's holiday,' I comment.

'Yeah. Although if I'm honest my day job isn't that thrilling that often...'

I laugh and then we're interrupted by a knock on the door.

'Come in,' we call as one.

We're asked (instructed) to go and do our baking.

'We'll be there in five minutes,' Jake tells the man, forestalling me; I was about to leap to my feet and pathetically do exactly as I was told.

* * *

We both spend those five minutes freshening up (aka in my case lying face down on my bed for four and a half minutes fighting sleep; and probably in Jake's case just being cool, because he's always cool), before wandering over to the kitchen tent together.

We chat the whole way, about nothing really, like you would with a friend.

Obviously we *aren't* friends, but also Jake – when not being a total arse – is kind of okay. Well, he's actually really good company.

I'm *really* laughing at his impression of Sonja (we both now have a very strong distrust of her bordering on serious dislike) as we enter.

*　*　*

We're a lot less snarky with each other now than we were earlier on when we were cooking together. It's like we've settled into something approaching, well, a team.

'What are your thoughts on the berry compote?' I bother to ask Jake as I work out the exact final desserts we're going to make.

'No thoughts,' he tells me. 'We both know you're in charge and it would be better for everyone if I don't think, just do as I'm told.'

I smile. 'Perfect.'

And it is perfect. The three judges are all around, and they keep popping up, separately and together, for food-related chats. I'm an extremely keen home baker (and, obviously, like half the nation, would very much fancy my chances on *Bake Off*) and I'm really enjoying myself.

Jake tells me that he definitely can't do anything as advanced as cracking eggs without getting shell in the egg, and that the idea of keeping a yolk intact blows his mind. He's also never whisked anything before. Since he's already ruined several eggs, I decide he can just wash and grate lemons and carrots and weigh things out.

He's also pretty good at passing stuff to me, it turns out, and we end up working in perfect harmony, very much like two people who do *not* loathe each other. You might almost say that Sonja's team-building weekend is working, although I'm not sure she was intending it to work like *this*; I think she was hoping for arguments, or breakdowns from me over having to do activities I hate, and certainly not for us to begin to get on well through both refusing to do the tasks.

We've made a trio of desserts for everyone: mini lemon possets, mini carrot cakes (little friands) and mini raspberry tarts, with lemon-flavoured crème fraiche (which Jake does in quenelles, which he's very proud of) and the berry compote. It's all very classic and not pushing the boat out flavour-combination or idea-wise, but I'm very proud of it because, although I say it myself, I think it's delicious, and so do all the judges.

'I'd hire you,' Angus, the chef, tells me, and Fenella, the baking judge, agrees. I'm beaming from ear to ear.

The plated-up desserts are carefully put to one side by waiting staff as Jake and I go to join the other pairs in a separated-off part of the tent, which serves as a dining room.

We are all, as we were at lunchtime, seated at separate tables in our pairs, and then we're served cheese fondues, with each table having their own fondue in the middle.

'So, just to clarify,' Jake says after ours has been placed on our table. 'You don't like cheese fondue, and Sonja knows that?'

'Yep. Can't stand it.' I have my face turned away because (OTT, I know, *but...*) stringy melted cheese makes me gag slightly, and the smell is *strong*.

'So, what, you're going to eat dry bread this evening for your main course? This is ridiculous. How do they keep their viewers? How is that good TV? Exciting! Watch now! Woman looks away from fondue and eats bread! I mean, please.'

Out of the corner of my eye, which is trained very much away from the fondue, I see Jake indicate to one of the staff.

When the man comes over to our table, Jake says, 'I'm so sorry, but my companion has a cheese intolerance, so we can't eat this.'

'Sorry, intolerances had to be mentioned beforehand,' the man says.

Jake raises an eyebrow, and the man wilts slightly before our eyes.

'Firstly, it's rare for an entire meal to be cheese,' Jake says, 'and secondly, Sonja was aware that Freya doesn't eat melted cheese. We'd love anything else. We obviously don't want to make any work for anyone; we will happily eat something very basic, some of the leftovers from the lunch task.'

The man asks us to give him one moment, and then shortly afterwards turns up with Sonja.

'I can't eat melted cheese,' I tell her.

'Won't, not can't,' Sonja says.

I shake my head. 'Can't.'

'You told me you don't like it, not that you can't eat it. Are you now self-identifying as dairy intolerant?'

I gasp at the sheer *meanness* of her.

Jake just shakes his head sorrowfully. 'Sonja. There's literally a camera right behind you. You literally just admitted on camera that Freya told you she can't stand melted cheese and then you chose to serve her cheese fondue. I feel as though it doesn't take a lawyer to point out that that isn't acceptable. If you don't have any food available that Freya can eat, we're happy to leave and go to a restaurant. Or get a takeaway.'

Sonja looks at Jake for an unnervingly long time, eyes narrowed, and then smiles (eyes still narrowed). 'Of course. We're very happy to provide you with an alternative. Leave it with us.'

As she walks away and the camera withdraws somewhat, I lean forward to say in an undertone, 'Okay, so now she's going to spit in our food.'

'At best. I feel like she'd *poison* it if she could.'

'Do you think it's bad that we seem to be making an enemy of one of the most powerful women in British television?' I ask. 'Genuinely.'

'Yeah, maybe. Genuinely. Maybe we should play nice now.'

Our food – heated-up leftovers from lunchtime – arrives very quickly. It is, of course, the least popular dishes.

And – one mouthful in – we both know what Sonja has done instead of spitting in our food.

'My goodness,' I croak, when my eyes have stopped watering from the immense amount of chilli that has been added to the fish stew. 'Pure bloody evil.'

'She's like a cartoon character.' Jake lays his cutlery down and reaches for a slice of the bread that was thankfully left on the table when the fondue was taken away. Then he takes another two slices. 'Quick, take a few of these so you won't go hungry before she realises we have it and confiscates it.'

'Before I went on her show,' I muse as I take bread, 'I genuinely bought into the whole Sonja-is-lovely thing. I'm massively re-evaluating now.'

'Next thing, we'll discover that reality TV is *heavily* edited to make viewers think certain things,' says Jake, deadpan.

'Yes, and on that point, *we* are now reality TV,' I say.

'Yep. We need to be *really* nice to Sonja until we can extricate ourselves. Neither of us wants our reputation to be trashed, and obviously she's capable of that.'

'Er, rich from the man who seemed to be trying to trash my entire career the first time we met,' I point out.

Jake winces. 'Yes. Sorry.'

'Oh my goodness.' I swivel my eyes to the right, signalling. 'There's the woman herself. Heading towards us.'

One of the serving staff pulls a chair over for Sonja and places it under her exactly as she sits down.

'That was great choreography,' I say. 'The chair.'

'Thank you.' Sonja is not smiling. 'I thought it would be good for us to chat now. The three of us.' She waves the camera away, pointing at the far end of the tent. 'So. I think we all have the same aim.'

I nod pathetically, feeling as though we've strayed into a medieval court where our monarch has absolute power and might at any moment decide to send us to the Tower. On the other side of the table, Jake is also nodding.

'Our aim.' Sonja jabs the table with her finger. 'Our aim is to make *great* national television and enhance *all* our reputations.' She looks – glares – at each of us in turn. 'Yes?'

'Yes,' we both say. I can't actually believe this is happening. She is honestly terrifying.

'So. What we want is great footage of you two arguing. Or *making up*, if you know what I mean.' She does an enormous and quite terrifying boob shimmy.

I sneak a look at Jake. He has his lips clamped tightly together like he's scared that if he opens them at all he's going to laugh and laugh.

'*Or* one or both of you finally admit that you were wrong. But, basically, we – the nation – just like seeing the two of you interact.'

Jake still has his mouth clamped shut and isn't speaking.

'Okay,' I say on behalf of both of us.

'So we need a plan,' Sonja continues. 'This evening we've decided that we're going to have a salsa dancing lesson for all of you. You will obviously both join in, fully.'

We both nod.

'And tomorrow we have our treetop adventure. I am aware that you aren't particularly fond of heights, Freya, but I expect you to join in. Jake can help you the way he did on the assault course. Which made excellent footage, by the way. Can you confirm that you will join in? Remember: we've *invested* in you two.'

'Yes,' I say.

'Excellent. Then I won't spit in your desserts.' She pushes her chair back and smiles at us, crocodile-like, as she stands up. We both smile back.

When she's out of earshot, I whisper, 'Spit in our desserts? Did she actually just *spit* in our stew? As in her spit is actual chilli-hot venom?'

Jake's nearly choking with laughter.

'I really hope she doesn't spit in our pudding,' I say.

'Me too. I really want to taste it and I'm hungry.'

We're still laughing about Sonja when our puddings arrive and, thank goodness, they seem to be unadulterated.

'That was *good*,' Jake says as he finishes scraping his plate completely clean. 'I'm impressed.'

'Thank you.' I'm more pleased than I would like to admit by Jake's clearly sincere praise.

I'm actually getting congratulations from all directions of the tent, both from the other tables and from the serving staff who've also tasted the food, but Jake's means the most by far. Nearly as much as the judges' praise in fact. I feel as though I *know* him now, and I think praise always means more coming from people you know. But also, it feels particularly huge to have finally impressed someone who was so extremely antagonistic towards me when we first met.

16

JAKE

We're told that we have half an hour to digest our dinner – apparently Sonja doesn't think a group of people doubled up with stomach cramps after doing salsa on fondue-filled stomachs would make great TV – and that we can do whatever we like in that time.

Freya and I look at each other.

'Back to our rooms?' I ask.

She's already on her feet.

We speed-walk the whole way there. Freya giggles so much at how stupid she's sure we both look on camera, especially from behind, that I start laughing too.

We make it back to the apartment very quickly. I've had my key at the ready the whole way, and open the door immediately.

'Oh my goodness, the relief of being away from that woman and the cameras.' She flops down onto our sitting room sofa as I close the door firmly behind us, and I sit down on the other end of the sofa.

We loll there in a nice, companionable silence for a minute or two, both of us spread out over our halves of the sofa, both with our eyes half closed. It's been a tiring day.

Then Freya says, 'Why do you think she's so mean? It's like she's completely amoral.' Obviously she's talking about Sonja. 'Do you think she's had a difficult life? Do you think that's why? Because surely this sadism is not normal.'

'I think it's *her*. At work I obviously meet a lot of people going through very difficult times. Many of them – usually women – have been cheated on by their spouses or treated badly in some other way. Some of them turn into demons in response. But most of them don't. Some people *are* just amoral. Some can *become* tricky in some way. And others just behave amazingly well in the face of awful adversity.'

Freya nods slowly.

And then I hear myself say, 'Like my brother and my parents. My brother had a terrible accident and is in a wheelchair for life, and my parents are his carers, and none of the three of them have ever uttered a word of complaint.'

Where did that come from? Why did I tell her that? It's almost like I *wanted* to, like I want her to understand me, to know that I'm not just about my work and underappreciating romantic fiction. I think it's because I've begun to like and respect her as a friend. I'd like her to feel the same way about me.

'I'm so sorry.' She places a hand on my arm, and it's *nice*. 'That must have been so hard. How long ago did it happen?'

'Twelve years.' Yeah, no, there's a limit. I don't actually want to go into details. 'What about you? What are your family like?'

'Dreadful,' she says, laughing. 'And let me tell you they *do* complain. Did, in the case of my father. We lost him a few years ago. Yep. They had a *bad* divorce and they were *not* polite about each other afterwards. Ever.'

'That sounds hard too,' I say. I reach for her and hug her into me for a long moment, before releasing her slightly when I begin to feel as though I'm enjoying the hug too much.

Something occurs to me – maybe her parents' unamicable split has something to do with her belief that romance is not for her – and I open my mouth to comment, before closing it again. I like her. I feel as though we have a burgeoning friendship and might perhaps even stay in touch after this. I do not however feel as though I'd like to confide further in her about my family, and I therefore should not be asking her more about hers, or what effect it's had on her.

'You know what?' she says. 'It's totally fine. A lot of people have much worse things to deal with. Like your family. I'm good. Plus, I'm a hypocrite. *I'm* complaining about *them*. And, when I think about it, only my mum complains. In a disappointed way. My dad was just plain *rude*. Anyway.' She looks around the room. 'Game of cards?'

'Yeah, good idea.' It seems like we'd both welcome a break from serious conversation.

We decide to play whist, and it's fun. It turns out that Freya has a really, really good memory for cards. I like a card game or two but she absolutely smashes me. Over and over again.

'You're very good at a lot of things,' I observe.

'Er, what? *You're* good at a lot of things.' She really isn't that great at taking compliments without complimenting back the compliment giver. Like she's uncomfortable with being praised. If I wanted to carry on with the amateur psychology I'd wonder whether her parents perhaps were too busy arguing to focus properly on her and make her feel good about herself, and so as an adult she doesn't know what to do with compliments.

I smile at her. 'Let's agree to both be incredibly excellent at many, many things?'

She laughs. 'Sounds good. Who wants to be pleasantly humble?'

'Exactly.'

We sit and smile at each other – kind of almost soppily I'd have to say – and then Freya suddenly says, 'Oh my goodness, we're going to be late for salsa and the evil woman will try to poison our food again. We need to get our skates on.'

'You looking forward to the class?' I ask as we walk back over.

'Yes. I love dancing and I've actually always vaguely wanted to sign up for lessons in either ballroom or Latin or both but I've just never got round to it. So if she's trying to give me the worst weekend of my life, Sonja has really messed up.' Freya's glee makes me laugh.

'Yeah. Good. I'm glad.'

17

FREYA

Jake and I are on fully good terms, it feels like, when we go, along with the others, into the room that's been designated our salsa dancing venue. We're all given classic Latin dancing outfits and shoes to wear. My skirt and top are extremely skimpy, the top little more than a glorified bra, and Jake's satiny trousers are *very* tight around the crotch and bottom area, and his shirt seems to be missing most of its buttons, giving the rest of us an excellent view of his very well-toned chest.

'I'm guessing that Sonja was sniggering as she chose these,' Jake says after we've all emerged from the changing rooms.

I laugh, while I try hard not to stare at his chest and crotch.

'Did you tell them your size?' I ask him, looking around at everyone. Every single person's outfit is exactly the right size (and no-one else's is quite as revealing as mine and Jake's).

'Nope.'

'Me neither.' I ask the same question of the couple of people closest to me, and then everyone, and, no, no-one gave their sizes.

'This seems very sinister,' I whisper to Jake. 'Not only is Sonja someone whose spit contains super-hot chilli, she psychically knows our clothing and shoe sizes.'

'Yeah, or they just noted the sizes when we got kitted up for the assault course.'

'Oh yes.' Dammit. I was almost enjoying feeling that we'd arrived in some kind of Sonja-led dystopia. 'Are you also going to suggest that she does not in fact have chilli spit and just added actual chilli to our food?'

'Sadly, I do think we're going to have to consider that a very real possibility.'

'Well, damn. I don't want her to be a regular mean woman with no magical powers.'

'Yeah, although a mean woman *with* magical powers would be scarier to deal with.'

'Very true.' I bend down to adjust my right shoe and then stand up again, fast, conscious that my skirt is *way* too short for me to be bending over like that. 'Learning salsa is going to be so much fun. I'm now almost grateful to Sonja.'

'Whoa, steady. I feel that we should expect a catch.'

Ten minutes later, I think I've worked out what the catch is. If you've watched *Strictly*, you know what's involved in the salsa. And I have watched *Strictly*, so it should have immediately occurred to me. There's a lot of physical proximity involved. I think I was just still too mind-blown by everything that's already happened this weekend to think about what was going to happen next.

We're learning some basic moves, which involve Jake's hands on my bare waist quite a lot, plus a lot of shimmying side by side.

I'm very, very aware of where his hands touch me, and even the shimmying feels very intimate, because we have to watch each other the whole time so that we move in sync with each other, which means that I'm just looking at (ogling) his (remarkably gorgeous) body, and I can feel his eyes on me.

I'm extremely conscious of his eyes straying quite a lot to my boobs (there's quite a lot of jiggle involved in this dance) and my bare tummy, and even more conscious of the struggle to keep my eyes away from where certain parts of his anatomy are highlighted.

The one good thing about having to think so hard about the moves is that it's a slight distraction from all the *looking* and *feeling*.

Things get worse when we've learnt the basic moves.

Now I have to twirl and shimmy in front of Jake while he lightly holds my waist. Obviously the premise of the dance is that I'm doing it *for* him, and, watching the way his eyes follow my body and he swallows, hard, as I go for a particularly vigorous shimmy, it does *feel* as though I'm putting on a show just for him. And – horrifyingly – I find myself liking it.

As we do our moves side by side, and then he holds my waist as I do my thing, and then he twirls me round before we resume our side-by-side moves, I'm consumed with a definite sense of huge achievement (when the two professional dancers demonstrated the moves for us at the beginning I had a strong I-can't-ever-do-that feeling) but also a definite sense of extreme *lust*. Like... Jake is *hot*. And he's making *me* feel hot.

He's looking at me as though I'm the only person – thing – anything – in the world that he's interested in right now, and it's making me *glow* inside.

I realise – when a tiny part of my brain tries to analyse it as we stop for a moment while our instructors talk to us – that this is maybe a knack he has. Maybe this – not just his ridiculously classical handsomeness – is what causes so many people to blossom in his presence. He just hasn't exercised this particular talent on me until now, because until sometime during the assault course we had our whole mutual loathing thing going.

'Jake and Freya, you two have been doing *verrrrry* well. Why don't you demonstrate this new move for us?' says Vince, one of the instructors.

Eek. I wasn't paying attention at *all*.

'Could you possibly show us one more time?' I ask.

'Of course.' Vince and his partner Rosetta clearly *love* their job; they're more than happy at any given moment to dance, and they're almost falling over themselves to impart as much knowledge as possible to us.

And this is a *real* eek now. Vince is running his hands up and down Rosetta's sides. I'm getting flustered just *imagining* Jake doing that to me.

And, oh, okay, we're up. Here we go.

We do some of the little forwards and backwards steps, feet going diagonally in front and behind each other, next to each other, all good, and then we turn to face each other and Jake pulls me in and does the hands up and down my sides thing and oh my goodness I am *melting*.

Jake's eyes are on mine the whole time, and we maintain that eye contact until I pirouette round in a twirl. When I get back round, he's still looking at me, and I feel something inside me give a gigantic lollop.

When we finish the routine, it feels entirely natural that he pulls me in for a lingering hug. I can feel his heart pumping where our chests are pressed together, and I feel as though I don't ever want him to let go of me.

And that is clearly the power of Latin dancing and the reason for the *Strictly* curse. I mean, of *course* if two people do this day in day out alone in a dance studio the weaker-minded of them might succumb to the obvious physical temptation. It's *intoxicating*.

Rosetta claps. 'That was wonderful, Jake and Freya. And now, everyone all together.'

And now I'm not thinking at all, I'm just *doing*. The moves are coming more naturally; our bodies seem to be working together in perfect harmony. Everyone in the room has a slight sheen of sweat to them, which should be disgusting but actually isn't; it just adds to the atmosphere, and we're doing nothing but dancing, as though we're communicating a story with our bodies. And the only way of interpreting that story is that we're performing for each other and that we're both *loving* it.

We continue with the shimmying, twirling, fast footwork, mutually admiring (*devouring*) looks, and it's one of the most blissful experiences of my life.

'More?' asks Vince when we finish and there's a chorus of *Yes* from all corners of the room.

We continue with the lessons for a while, and then Vince and Rosetta tell us that the rest of the evening will be us improvising. They start their playlist and join us on the floor, and we all dance late into the night, focused almost entirely on our partners, with only minimal interaction with the others.

Eventually, several of us begin to stumble with tiredness, and we decide as a group that we're all going to head to bed.

Our own clothes and shoes have been taken to our rooms by the staff, so there's no need for us to get changed now.

Jake and I are standing with our arms round each other's waists as we finish the last dance, and, somehow, maybe because after such an intense experience we can't just *stop*, we walk like that, still linked, our hips brushing each other, all the way back to our suite.

And when we get inside the door, we're still, basically, entwined.

'That was fun.' Jake pulls me against him in a salsa move and then twizzles me under his arm, round and round, until I'm dizzy and fall against him laughing.

He steadies me with a hand on either side of my waist as I land with my hands planted against his chest.

I look up into his face and see that he's gazing intently down at me.

We're so close, it's as though we're almost one. The way his hands are resting on the bare skin just above my waist, as though they belong there; the way our chests are rising and falling to the same rhythm; the way, as he moistens his lips with his tongue, I do the same.

I feel him move his thumbs very slightly against my lower ribs and it's as though his touch reaches deep inside me. I take a deep, juddering breath as he moves his head closer to mine until our lips are almost touching.

We hover there like that, for a few unbearably long moments. Jake caresses the top of my waist again with his thumbs, and I clench my hands against his chest.

And then, almost as though reflecting the way we seem to have come such a long way from extreme dislike to this... friendship... that we've developed this weekend, we move our heads closer and closer together, but gradually, tilting our heads this way and the other, mirroring each other, as we do, until, finally, Jake's lips brush mine.

It's nice, it's *really* nice, but it isn't enough. I want a proper kiss.

He's drawn back and is studying my face.

I take one of my hands and run it up his chest and slide it round his neck.

He continues to stare at me for a torturous moment longer, before he dips closer and brushes his lips annoyingly lightly against mine again, and then, suddenly, he's kissing me hard, passionately, urgently, and my other arm has reached round his neck and I'm pulling him against me. His hands are continuing to caress my skin, and it's the best kiss I've ever had.

We stay there in the middle of the room for a long time, kissing, and then Jake's hands move a little further up and then somehow we're undressing each other, and then we're on the sofa, and it's truly amazing.

I wake up at some point during the night. Most of me is lovely and warm where Jake is holding me in his sleep, but my legs, which are on top of his are cold. I wriggle so that my legs are on the side and snuggle against him, nearly falling off the sofa.

I stand up, and he stirs, and then wakes fully, smiling up at me.

And, weirdly, because I don't usually like being naked in front of other people, the way Jake's openly admiring me, reaching his arms out to me, just makes me feel *good*.

'Come here.' His voice is hoarse, as though suffused with desire, which I *love*.

'Come *here*,' I say, and lead him through to my bedroom. We make very, very good use of the bed, before falling asleep again in a tangle of limbs and sheets.

Jake wakes me up in the morning, by pulling my hair back from my face and kissing my neck, which is a gorgeous way to be woken up.

I know it's the morning due to the sunlight streaming through the windows where we didn't draw any of the curtains last night. It doesn't feel like morning, though; it feels like the middle of the night. I'm far, far too tired to get out of bed immediately.

'We're going to have to get up,' Jake says, kissing me again. 'I think that having come this far we shouldn't fall at the last hurdle and incur the wrath of Sonja.'

'You're right,' I mumble, too tired and also enjoying the snuggly kissing too much to be able to speak properly.

'Okay,' Jake says after a while, 'I'm going to drag myself out of this bed and go and get into the shower. And obviously I am not in charge of you and it's entirely your choice but I feel that you should maybe do the same.'

'Definitely.' I'm still mumbling.

'Freya? Are you actually fully awake?'

'Totally.'

'Okay.' And off he goes, which does in the moment make me feel bereft because it was *nice* being held in his arms. However, this bed *is* very comfortable and I'm *very* tired, so I'm still very much liking being under this duvet. Jake's right; I should definitely get up and have my shower. Might just close my eyes for five minutes, though.

'Freya!' Someone's calling me. What's happening? I'm... Oh, shit. It's Jake and we have to get up and I went back to sleep.

'How much time have I got?' I sit bolt upright and then realise that I'm naked, and pull the covers up, fast.

Jake's standing in the doorway looking a little wild-eyed.

'We have to go now,' he says. 'For breakfast.'

'I *have* to have a shower,' I tell him. '*Have* to.' I *cannot* have a night of (amazing) sex and then *see* people before I've showered.

'Fair enough. What's the fastest time you can be ready in?'

'Ten minutes?' That's a lie but I think I can do fifteen.

'Okay. I'll go in a minute and cover for you. Say you have a headache or something but you'll be coming soon.'

'Thank you.' I smile at him and he returns my smile and my insides do yet another gigantic leap.

I have no idea what happened last night – well, I do; it was kind of along the lines of the *Strictly* curse without the cheated-on spouses (obviously) – but it was a *lot* of fun. I don't really know whether we're going to do that again, but I do know that Jake is a lot nicer than I initially thought he was.

If I were the kind of person who dated seriously (which I am certainly not) I might almost be having ideas about him.

18

JAKE

As I walk over to the dining tent for breakfast, I wonder if I might be slightly delirious from tiredness. Or from something.

I don't think I've ever revised my opinion of someone so strongly from meeting them to... well, to having mind-blowing sex with them.

It's fair to say that when I met Freya I couldn't stand her.

It's also fair to say that now I... well, right now, I'm missing her, because she isn't next to me. Even though I'm going to see her in a few minutes' time.

That *might* just be a hangover from the out-of-this-world sex.

But the sex wouldn't have *been* so good if there hadn't been some kind of emotional connection between us.

As in, she's very beautiful, obviously, but there are other beautiful women. Although few with such a stunning smile. But her smile isn't the point. The point is how much fun she is. Her sarcasm. Her humour. The way she laughs. How extremely nice she is. How much I love her writing. *Her* basically. All of her. *That* was why the sex was so good. It was because it was with *her*, not just a beautiful woman.

'Jake. Where's Freya?' Sonja's right in front of me, wearing her usual gimlet-eyed look.

'She's on her way. She was just a little tired after yesterday but she'll be here any minute.'

'Good to hear. I wouldn't like to think of her missing breakfast and having to confront her fear of heights on an empty stomach.'

'Same,' I agree. 'Fingers crossed she arrives on time.' I wonder whether Sonja is going to ask for breakfast to be cleared away early just to spite Freya.

I take an enormous pile of food from the buffet so I can save some for Freya if necessary. I catch Sonja looking at me and my plate, so, when she does finally turn her back, I fill a couple of rolls with ham and cheese, wrap them in napkins and sneak them into my pockets.

True to form, Sonja waits for Freya to arrive and then immediately claps her hands and tells everyone that breakfast is over.

'It's okay,' I whisper. 'Got you some food.'

We slip behind some trees for me to hand over the food and for Freya to scoff it as fast as she can. I kiss her a couple of times on the forehead as she does so, because apparently I can't resist.

'Jake. Freya,' calls Sonja. That woman is *everywhere*. 'Time for the treetop activity.'

'I feel like a teenager round the back of the sheds at school smoking,' says Freya, her mouth full.

'I know. I genuinely feel like we're committing a serious misdemeanour right now. It's like we've strayed into some *Big Brother* world run by Sonja.'

'Jake. Freya.' Sonja's openly yelling now.

'I'm done,' Freya says.

I look at her and laugh. 'There's a *lot* of evidence of your crime,' I tell her.

'What?'

'Crumbs, everywhere.' I wipe them away for her carefully with my fingers, and then can't resist kissing her everywhere that I touched.

She's wrapping her arms round my neck when Sonja goes incredible full throttle on the yelling.

'Oh. We should go,' Freya says.

'Yep,' I agree.

'Where have you two been?' asks Sonja.

'Toilet break,' Freya says blandly.

'Together? In the bushes.'

'Both desperate,' Freya says.

'Fucksake,' says Sonja, not quite under her breath.

* * *

'Fuuuuck,' breathes Freya a couple of minutes later. 'That is *high*.'

She isn't wrong. I have no fear whatsoever of heights beyond not wanting to fall from one without any safety equipment, but I'll definitely be keen to check that our harnesses are properly secured.

'I feel like breakfast was a mistake.' Freya does look quite green in the face now.

'Okay. This is going to be *fine*,' I tell her. 'There's no way they're going to let anything bad happen to us on a programme made for *Wake Up Britain*. It would be the end of loads of people's careers. Especially Sonja's. Also, people go on treetop walks all the time.'

'I don't think we're just going to be walking.' Freya's pointing up towards the sky.

I follow the line of her finger and see that there are hoops and parallel bars and other gymnastic equipment along the walk.

'Well, that looks like fun,' I say, weakly. I mean, it *does* look like fun. But not, I'm guessing, if you're scared of heights.

'Yeah, can't wait.'

'Honestly,' I say. 'I *know* that you don't like heights and I really, really get that, but it truly will be fine. And since this is a team-building weekend, I'm guessing we'll be doing it in pairs, in which case I'll be there the whole way and I'll help you.'

'That's true.' Freya's beginning to look just pale rather than ocean-on-a-stormy-day green.

I really want to take her in my arms to try to cheer her up, but I'm certainly not doing that under Sonja's eagle eye. It doesn't take a lot of thought to determine that Sonja is one of the last people in the world we want to know about last night.

* * *

Freya is amazing. She gets tearful once or twice, she mutters, 'Fuck, fuck, fuck,' a lot under her breath, she tells me more than once that she *can't* carry on, but she manages it. I do my best to encourage her but when it comes down to it, it's all her. She's basically amazing.

'I'm so impressed,' I tell her as we finally reach the ground. 'You're brilliant.'

'This is wonderful,' Sonja gushes, having popped out from behind a bush somewhere to our right. She's wearing camo army-style fatigues, and I think there actually was a camouflage purpose to her wearing it. Thank fuck I wasn't hugging Freya in the way I would have liked to. 'The two of you really have bonded. Which is wonderful, because you came last in that task – we timed you – so you'll be doing one final ice bath, but this time you'll be doing it together, in one big bath.'

'Great,' says Freya, very miserably.

* * *

I think Sonja and the producers imagined that being in a bath together might somehow cause something sexual to happen between us, but it's an *ice* bath and there are many onlookers.

I'm pretty sure that they'll have got max a second or two of showable footage from it, because we both just climb in, don't react and then get out again when our time is up, while the others clap.

Sonja rounds us all up, tells us that we've all been wonderful, instructs all twelve of us to set up a group chat to stay in contact, informs Freya and me that she'll be in touch very soon with details about the live show, and finally leaves us.

'Hooray,' says Freya.

I nod.

When we've dutifully set up the chat (to be fair, the whole weekend *was* bonding and the other participants are a really nice group of people), everyone goes off to get their luggage before we reconvene for final goodbyes.

I wait until I'm sure everyone's out of earshot and then say to Freya, 'I drove. Why don't I give you a lift back to London?'

'That would be great,' she replies with no hesitation, 'but should we drive off together?'

'Yeah, no, we shouldn't. What about if you get a taxi to the station and then say you're catching a different train from anyone else, and then say you're going to the loo and sneak back out and I'll pick you up?'

'I feel like I would definitely bump into Sonja,' Freya says. 'But what about if

I say I'm getting a cab to a different station and actually just meet you in the middle of nowhere?'

'Good plan,' I approve.

As we leave, luggage in hand, Freya hugs absolutely everyone, apparently already very close friends with most of them.

* * *

I pick her up twenty minutes later from a water fountain in a nearby village and it isn't an exaggeration to say that when I round the bend of the road and see her standing there, I feel as though my heart swells. Like, again, I was missing her.

'Well, hello,' I say as she climbs into the car. 'Do you come here often?'

'Never,' she says, leaning back against the car seat and closing her eyes. 'I *never* do weekends like that. What the actual fuck happened there? What world did we get sucked into? Sonja's an actual lunatic.'

'Good weekend overall, though?' I ask. I really don't want her to regret the *whole* thing.

She opens her eyes and gives me a slow smile. 'Yeah.' Then she smiles more and says, 'Some of it was amazing.'

I nod, pleased. It *was* amazing.

'I loved the baking,' she says.

Oh. Okay. I nod.

'And I didn't actually *hate* the assault course in some ways. The net bit was fine. I was pleased to discover that I was good with mud. And the whole thing did feel like a big achievement, and who doesn't love to achieve?'

I nod again.

'And the ice bath,' she continues. 'Obviously I hated it and obviously we all know that they're a fad and not genuinely health-giving, but at least I can now say with authority that I've done one. Two, in fact.'

I pause my slight disgruntlement that she still hasn't mentioned our night together. 'What? They *are* health-giving? Well-documentedly?'

She shakes her head. 'Nuh-unh.'

'Hmm. I'll let that pass until I'm not driving and then I will send you some definitive articles on the benefits of ice baths.'

'And I will retaliate with definitive articles on the quackery of the ice-bath movement.'

'Okay, no. I'm going to prove my point as *soon* as I finish driving.' I look both ways before turning off our country lane onto a main road. 'Anything else good about the weekend?'

'The treetop thing this morning. I hated it in the moment. But I have at least proved to myself that I can do things I hate *and* that I'm not wrong when I say that I absolutely hate heights and so I'm not holding myself back unnecessarily from things like bungee jumping because I really would hate them.'

I nod.

'Also I enjoyed you thwarting Sonja on the reptile experience,' she continues.

I nod.

'Also, the salsa dancing was obviously amazing. So much fun.'

I nod.

'Yeah, so I think that's it.'

'Nothing else stands out in your mind?' I enquire.

'I don't think so.' She's leaning back again with her eyes closed, grinning while she does so.

I turn to look at her properly for a moment while we're at traffic lights, and a shot of some strong emotion that I can't quite identify courses through me.

I look back at the road ahead and say, 'Did you get a great night's sleep?'

'Yeah, no, it was too short. Someone really annoyingly kept me up late.'

'Really annoyingly?' I enquire.

'Yeah. He just kept on kissing me. And *other stuff*. And it kept me up late.'

'Wow, that sounds terrible.'

'Well, yes, I'm tired now.' She does a stage yawn, and then says, her tone cheeky, 'It was *good* though.'

'It was?'

'Well... I thought it was.'

I laugh. 'Me too. I thought it was amazing.' I can't think of another time in my life when I would have had a one-night stand with someone (who I previously disliked) and then admit to them what a great night it was for me.

Maybe... maybe it wasn't a one-night stand.

I mean, we're here in the car together and I'm loving *being* with her, and she seemed pretty happy to get a lift even though just getting the train would have been more straightforward and probably quicker.

I'd really like to see her again.

I'd really like to go on an actual date with her, I realise.

I'm not going to mention that now, though. I'm going to enjoy this journey, just chatting, just the two of us, with no threat of Sonja popping out of a bush or a camera zooming in on us.

'It's *such* a relief to be away from Sonja,' Freya says.

'Wow, it's like you read my mind. I was just thinking that.'

'Yeah, I *am*, obviously, psychic. But also I think maybe *anyone* in our position would be ecstatic to get away from there.'

I laugh. 'Very true.'

We chat idly and the journey passes very quickly. Too quickly.

Freya suggests that I drop her near her house, because she lives on a one-way street and it's several extra minutes of driving to get right to her front door.

I insist on taking her to her front door.

'Obviously it's incredibly arduous having to spend another few minutes with you,' I say, 'but I'm willing to take that hit in recognition of the fact that you've had a tiring weekend. Plus it's raining really heavily. And I have no plans for this evening. So I'm genuinely really happy to. Unless you actively don't *want* me to?'

'If you're sure I would actually be very grateful. I'm *tired*. And not totally up for getting soaking wet right now.'

'Very sure.'

Freya's house is a very well-kept-looking terraced cottage painted in a pale shade of green.

'This is lovely,' I say, as I manoeuvre into the space outside.

'Thank you.' She turns to look at me and says, 'Would you like to come in for coffee?'

'I...' Yes. I would. I *really* would. But only if she does actually want me to.

'It's been a long journey,' she says. 'You might want a little break. But also you might want to get back. I'd love to make you a coffee. It's the least I can do. But also I totally understand if you have other things to do this evening.'

'I'd love a coffee.'

'Great!' Her voice has gone a little squeaky. I'm feeling a little... something, I'm not sure what... myself.

'The rain's died down a bit so maybe we should take our chances now.' I get out of the car and walk round to the boot to get her case out.

Her house is as inviting inside as outside. There's a little hall area, with the stairs ahead, and a loo and what looks like a small study behind that, and to the right an open-plan kitchen/ living room. It's all painted in neutral colours, with wooden floors and lime green, purple and bright pink velvet furniture and nice paintings on the walls.

A couple of minutes later, she has a coffee machine whirring away and I'm legs-stretched-out on her (extremely comfortable) big, squishy corner sofa.

'How long have you lived here?' I ask as she comes over and sits on the sofa, nearish to me but not near enough for us to touch without one of us getting up and purposely moving closer.

'Five years. It was a stretch to buy it, so I've done all the decorating myself, and have *loved* buying the cheapest kitchen and bathroom fittings I could find and trying to make them look as good as possible.'

'It looks fantastic. I love all your creativity,' I tell her. 'I wouldn't know where to start.'

She shakes her head. 'I'm sure you would if you really wanted to; maybe it's just that you aren't into that stuff.'

'Yeah, no. Yes, I've always been far too busy, but even if I hadn't been I clearly don't have your talent. The cooking and baking, the interior design. And obviously your writing.'

'Ha.' Freya's doing her unable-to-receive-a-compliment-comfortably thing again. 'You have no idea whether I have a talent for writing. For all you know my books are genuinely terrible.'

'Okay, I have to own up here.' I'm wincing slightly because I feel that I should have mentioned this before. Although in my defence I really, really did not expect yesterday to end the way it did, and today has been busy. And we're both tired.

'Own up?'

'I read a couple of your books.'

'Oh my goodness.' Freya's hands go to her face and she covers her eyes for a moment. 'Er, which ones and what did you think? And *when*? And *why*?'

'At the beginning of the challenge. Because...' This actually does feel a little awkward.

'Because you wanted to... get to know my writing?'

'Kind of.' I wince again. 'Okay. Full disclosure. We obviously don't agree on certain things. Like happily-ever-afters. I developed a theory.' I'm beginning to think I *really* shouldn't have started down this path. I don't like how her eyes are narrowing slightly. Hard to know how I'm going to extricate myself now though without telling her the whole thing.

'Theory?' Freya prompts, eyes still somewhat narrowed.

'Yes, so...' I don't want to say it, I decide. It just sounds rude. 'I mean, it was silly. And, as it turned out, entirely incorrect. And the salient point is that I *loved* your books. Entirely – as you know – despite myself. I couldn't put the first one down, from the first page. Loved it. Loved the writing, the characterisation, the humour, everything. Same with the second. And the third.'

'Three! Which ones?'

'I can't actually remember the titles. But I do remember the stories.' I begin to list them, and realise that I've gone way beyond three. 'Yeah, okay. I think I read seven in total. Couldn't put them down.'

'Wow. Thank you. I am actually very honoured, given your expressed views.'

'Yeah, I was wrong.'

Freya suddenly narrows her eyes again. 'So you said that you read the books to get to know my writing better, *but* when you read them and liked them you still really disliked *me*.'

'Well, kind of,' I concede. 'Because I didn't really know you at all, did I? Just what you *wrote*.'

'I feel like this doesn't make sense. Why did you even want to get to know my writing? When you disliked me so much? It must have been so you could beat me in the challenge?' She pauses, frowning, and, just as I'm floundering for a good answer, gasps. 'Ohhhhh. Were you trying to get to know my *heroes* better so you could find someone similar?'

'Might have been.' I'm really not sure how Freya's going to take this.

'Hmm. What did you conclude?' she asks. Slightly frostily.

'They were all great but all different so it was a pointless exercise but I kept reading because I loved your writing and your stories.'

'Oh! Well, fair enough.' She smiles at me, and it feels like the tension in the room has suddenly defused. 'We were after all in competition. Did you buy all the books?'

'Yep.'

'Did it annoy you that you were adding to my sales?'

'Of course.'

She laughs. 'Pleased to hear it.'

'Did you do any research on me to find out my type?' I immediately regret my question, because the tension's right back. *Obviously*, if she did any research on me she would have found out about my ex-wife. Who I do not wish to talk about. Also, this conversation is straying into the realms of weirdness and over-analysis, given that last night we were very much *each other's* types.

'A little.' She pushes herself off the sofa. 'I think the coffee will be more than ready.'

And, yes, that was a very wise subject change.

That was all too weird. In fact, I should probably leave. Maybe we can meet up another time, when this conversation is safely well behind us.

I have to stay and drink the coffee, though, or I'm creating more awkward-ness where there shouldn't be any.

'How do you like your coffee?' Freya calls.

'Black, please.'

She brings a plate of macarons with the coffee and says, 'No pressure, but home-made by me a couple of days ago.'

'Worked your fingers to the bone, blood, sweat, tears but definitely no pres-sure?' As I take one, I can't help wondering how many people she has back here, given the large number of macarons, and whether any of them are men. I shock myself by feeling, maybe, a little jealousy at that thought.

'Exactly.' Freya takes one too and I find myself ridiculously turned on by watching her bite delicately into it. She looks up and catches me watching and nearly chokes.

I leap up to whack her on the back, or even go full Heimlich, only to realise that she's completely fine, saying, 'Sorry, false alarm. I somehow forgot how to eat for a moment.'

And just like that, we've got over whatever awkwardness I stupidly created, and we're talking again about anything and everything, other than the challenge.

* * *

'It's late,' she says, a long time later, after we've talked and talked. 'Way past dinnertime. Are you hungry? Can I get you something to eat? And for the avoidance of doubt I would like to eat now, and I have food in and can whip something up very quickly and would love you to stay and eat with me but equally totally understand if you'd like to go, so it's entirely up to you.'

'I *should* go,' I begin, not sure where the end of my sentence will finish... 'But I'd love to stay,' I find myself saying. 'Hard to resist your cooking having tasted everything you've made me so far.' And also, I'm loving her conversation and just being with her.

She makes us salmon teriyaki and noodles (with the teriyaki made quickly but properly, from scratch, not out of a jar, unlike any teriyaki that's ever – rarely – been 'made' by me), accompanied by steamed pak choi, and – of course – it's delicious.

When we've finished eating, she asks if I'd like a mint tea, and – of course – I say yes.

Our conversation continues to rove around all over the place, before we begin talking about driving and travel.

'I had one driving lesson and hated it – and I might have had a small crash in which no-one was injured but which made my instructor swear a *lot* – and decided that when you live in London you can manage for life without a licence,' she's telling me as she brings our teas over to the sofa, where I've returned to digest my meal.

I laugh. 'Yeah, you're definitely right. I'm sure it would have been quicker to have taken the train to and from Devon this weekend. I just like driving.'

'What's the first car you owned?' she asks.

As I tell her about the ancient VW Polo that was my pride and joy, and then we move on to talking about our first solo journeys abroad, I think about how, when she asked if I wanted to come in for coffee, I slightly imagined an immediate reprise of last night and wondered if we'd both be up for that (okay, I wondered if *she* would; I knew that I would), but we've just been talking for hours. And it's been good. Very good.

And now it's quite late. I'm sure Freya has work to do tomorrow, and I have an early meeting in the morning; I should go.

I place my mug on the coffee table in front of me and say, 'This has been great. Thank you so much. It's late; I should get going.'

'It's been lovely. Thank *you* for being a lovely dinner companion this evening.'

I stand up and Freya does too.

And then I walk over towards the hallway, and she comes with me.

And then I turn, and she's a couple of feet away from me, standing there with her hands clasped lightly in front of her.

'Thank you,' I say again.

'Nothing to thank me for. It's been lovely. And thank *you* for the lift. And for being so amazing this weekend because Sonja did a spectacular job of forcing me to face my fears and it would have been so much harder without you there.'

'Hey, no, it was all you. *You* were amazing.'

Freya laughs. 'This is a stunning exchange of compliments for *us*.'

'Yeah. Team-building. Maybe there's something in it.'

'Mmm.'

Freya's smiling at me and I'm smiling at her, and neither of us is moving.

I see the way her chest moves as she takes a deep breath and her smile fades as she bites her bottom lip.

I should go home. We both have work to do tomorrow.

Also, we have diametrically opposed views on a lot of things, including romance, and for two people like us it would be so much better to leave things as one glorious one-night stand.

Freya moistens her lips.

I should really, really go now.

I take a step forward at the same time as she does, and then suddenly, I have her crushed against me, and we're kissing like there's no tomorrow.

19

FREYA

'Freya.' Jake's speaking very softly into my ear.

I'm lying on my side and he's bending over me from somewhere above. That's weird.

I make a really big effort and open an eye and squint up at him. He's crouched next to the bed and wearing yesterday's clothes and a very nice, kind of fond smile.

'Time is it?' I manage to ask. My head's very heavy and so are my limbs and I don't think I could get a full sentence out right now. I'm so, so tired. Oh yes, that's because we were up most of the night. Having really, really good sex. I close my eye and sigh in appreciation of the memory and then open it again to see Jake grinning at me.

'Quarter past six,' he says. 'I have a meeting at eight. Got to get home, get showered and changed and into the office.'

'Early,' I mumble.

'Mmm.' He moves my hair away from my face and kisses me gently on the cheek and I sigh again.

'I'll text you.' And then he's off.

I should think about what just happened and I should also set an alarm because I have a lot to do this morning.

I'm sooooo tired.

Obviously I do not set the alarm and only wake up at around eleven when the postman rings the doorbell with a parcel from John Lewis (nothing exciting: a new baking tray and a five-pack of pants).

After I've thanked him, I stagger into the living room and flop down onto the sofa, still feeling extremely bleary-eyed.

Today I need to start planning my new book, plus I have proofreads to do on the one that's coming out next, plus on Monday evenings I teach a class at the local further education college, and I'd like to do some exercise and get some fresh air at some point. And eat something healthy. So I should really get straight into the shower.

I think I need a very strong coffee first, though.

As the machine hums, I clear up last night's dinner, which I didn't do last night because... Jake.

That was a *good* night. He was lovely company and then... well, just, basically, *amazing*.

Eek, though. Firstly, we had a one-night stand, which is not something I really do. Well, I don't. I have short-term romances at times, making sure that my partner knows as well as I do that it's very much short term and won't be leading anywhere, and sometimes that develops into a sexual relationship. But not on the first date, and certainly not before we've even *had* a date.

And now Jake and I have had a two-night stand. Which I blame myself for, because I shouldn't have accepted the lift home, and I shouldn't have teased him with that conversation about what I enjoyed about the weekend.

He said he's going to text me. And I really want him to because I already feel like I miss him.

But I don't want to start a relationship with him. And I know I'm hugely jumping the gun but at some point, obviously, if I were a different person, this could morph from glorious but uncommitted sex into an actual relationship. And then it would end, because my relationships always do, and then I would be bereft, because Jake – when he's being nice – is intoxicating company, and I don't want to go there. I obviously don't want him to get hurt either. So I'd rather not start a relationship at all.

I haul myself onto my feet and go over to pour out my coffee before taking a large slurp (possibly quite loudly – the joys of living alone).

Yep, we shouldn't do this any more, I decide as I get into the shower.

* * *

I feel a lot more awake after my shower, and I do actually manage to get some work done, until I get a message from Jake:

> You free this evening by any chance?

Okay, that's good, because I have an easy no.

> Really sorry but I teach an adult education class for two hours on Monday evenings so am not around this evening.

Even though my fingers are itching to say when I *am* free (like straight after the class ends at nine) I don't write anything further, because I don't want to lead him on.

But he does, of course, reply:

> I didn't realise you taught as well. A woman of many talents. Let me know if you're free another time.

I sit and stare at my phone for literally minutes, wondering what I should say.

And then I remember how kind he was to me all weekend. And the fact that we had two amazing nights together and maybe he's someone who also doesn't usually do that. I feel like I do owe him an explanation. So I write:

> Perhaps a drink later in the week? I'm free tomorrow and Thursday?

We agree to go for a drink tomorrow, at a pub near Waterloo station, so that we can both get home easily afterwards.

And there we go.

* * *

My proofreads go well, because I've been through this manuscript a billion times during edits, so I'm literally just proofreading for typos and any final spots of inconsistencies, but thinking about my new book does not go well, because my hero just becomes Jake.

Or Jake becomes *my* hero.

Or Jake *is* my hero.

Except, he isn't. He can't be. Because there is no hero for me. Things with Jake might have seemed great up to now – they might have *been* great up to now – but they wouldn't continue to be great. We've had two wonderful nights and that's all it should be.

Because I don't want to get hurt.

And I do not want to hurt him either.

* * *

I'm going to tell Jake that we shouldn't see each other again in any kind of dating way, but I have for some inexplicable (okay not at all inexplicable) reason spent *ages* on my make-up and hair and chosen my favourite top and jeans to wear this evening.

I arrive early and decide to wait outside the pub rather than going inside, so that we don't miss each other.

I'm planning to tell Jake straight off what my thoughts are. I don't want to lead him on in any way, and if he doesn't want to see me on a no-possibility-of-sex-or-relationship basis we can just immediately go our separate ways.

I'm *really* not looking forward to the conversation.

I'm so busy limbering up for the awkwardness that is clearly going to ensue that I don't actually notice Jake approach until he's right next to me, beaming from ear to ear.

Smiling really, really suits him. Actually, everything suits him. Stroppiness, happiness, anger, sarcasm, you name it. He wears them all like they're the coolest expression there is and your face immediately wants to do the same thing.

'Hi.' He reaches for me and I kind of turn away so there's no possibility of us kissing or anything.

Jake steps away from me immediately and says, 'Are you okay?'

'Yes, great. Except... I... There's something I need to say.'

He takes a step backwards. 'Of course. Inside?'

I look around. Yes, I think it would be better to be somewhere less noisy and busy. I nod.

We go inside in silence and head for the bar.

I have my phone ready to pay before we've even placed our order, and shake my head when Jake suggests that he pay, before immediately regretting it, because I don't want this to look like a *pity* drink. No, I decide, I'm overthinking things. It's *fine*. It doesn't matter who buys the drinks.

We find a table in a corner, and sit down.

Jake is clearly waiting for me to speak, and expecting what I say to be something of note, because there's none of the chat we had all weekend whenever we were together.

So I'm just going to say it.

'I thought I should say straightaway,' I say, 'that I'm not looking for a relationship. At all. Because I don't want to start anything that I know will end. And all my relationships do end, so I don't ever want to start anything that could get serious from my side. And I'm not sure that I'm someone who can keep on having sex with someone without developing some feelings. And were you to develop feelings I wouldn't want to hurt you. And therefore I don't want to... *do* anything again.'

'Of course,' Jake says immediately. Then he sits and thinks for a moment, his expression very serious. 'Obviously please don't feel you have to answer, but could I ask why? Not why you don't want to do anything with me. Obviously that's your prerogative and entirely understandable. But why do you think any relationship you start will definitely end?'

'Because relationships are not for me.'

'Is there... a reason that you think that?'

'Kind of.' I do feel that I owe him some kind of explanation. 'It's a lifelong thing, really.'

Jake nods slowly, studying me intently, and suddenly it isn't just that I feel I owe him an explanation, it's that I *want* to tell him.

'As I mentioned in Devon, my parents got divorced when I was twelve. They hated each other and they didn't seem to love me very much; they weren't really arguing over who *got* custody so much as who *didn't* get custody. They both had a *lot* of relationships after the divorce, and they were all disastrous. My father was unhappily single when he died, and my mother's unhappily single now. So, you know, it's probably a genetic thing. And I am *really* bad at romance. It *really* isn't for me.' I pause and take a drink.

'Again, I'm so sorry about your parents.'

'Yep, thank you.' I'm very used to people saying they're sorry about my parents. They were objectively not great parents to me. Although they weren't *terrible.* And now I've lost my father. 'They did have some good points. Like, when I used to visit my dad – not that often because he frequently triumphantly played the I-have-to-travel-for-work card – he would, once I was there, remember that he did love me and enjoy my company and we'd have a lot of fun together, and when I left he would wave and wave until my train was out of sight. And my mum is very interested in my life and proud of my successes and supportive whenever I have failures. And a great baker. It *really* wasn't all bad. They were both just terrible at relationships. As am I.'

'What makes you think *you're* terrible at relationships?'

'Well. I used to think there must be someone out there for me and that I'd like to meet him. But there isn't. I've been on a *lot* of dates, with a *lot* of very different men, and I mean—' I shake my head '—as a romance writer I know my tropes and over the years I've encountered pretty much *all* of them, and every single relationship that I've had, short and long, has ended in failure. It's me. They just all end. Clearly it's something about me, like there's something about my parents. Obviously I've been hurt and miserable at times, and I don't like to upset other people, so now I'm just not doing serious romance, and I'm always very transparent about that if I meet someone and we get on and go on a few dates. I'm only up for something casual.'

Basically, I'm not lovable and I don't think I'm capable of loving properly either. I can't say that out loud quite so baldly to Jake, though. It's like I can't admit it in such basic terms.

He shakes his head. 'You know, I feel really angry with the people who've made you feel this way. It isn't about you, it's about them.'

I shake my own head. Jake is wrong. There's very clearly a common thread and I am that thread.

'Look at me,' Jake continues. 'I've been married and it was a disaster. When my ex-wife left me she cited one of your books and said that I didn't match up to the hero. I mean, that's *ridiculous*. My actual wife left me for a fictional hero.'

'You're better than any hero I've ever written.'

'Well, thank you, but that isn't true. I've read your heroes and they are *great*. But my point is...' He pauses for a moment and frowns, clearly having confused himself.

I wait.

He recovers and nods. 'My point is that my marriage just wasn't right. It was both of us. Well, and the fact that she was sleeping with her tennis coach, which I found out afterwards.'

'It wasn't my books then, was it, you muppet. It was that she was having an *affair*.'

'But did she have that affair *because* of your books?'

I shake my head, definitively. 'No. I cannot believe that she did. As I've said before, my view is that thinking you love a fictional character more than you love your partner is a symptom not a cause.'

'Maybe. And I think we've strayed a long way from my point, which was actually that even though I have had a disastrous marriage, I still believe that there's a happy ending out there for me.'

'Okay. Well. Maybe it's about optimism,' I say. 'Or realism. I don't know.'

'You're saying I'm optimistic and you're realistic?'

I shrug. 'Maybe.'

'Realistic or pessimistic?'

I glare at him.

'Sorry,' he says.

'Apology accepted,' I say coldly.

'*Really* sorry?' he wheedles.

'*Fine*. Apology *really* accepted.'

'Good?'

I nod, rolling my eyes.

'Do you fancy fish and chips before we each go home?' he asks. 'Not to change the subject hugely. But I'm hungry and we still need to bitch about Sonja.'

Sonja called me today, and I'm guessing she called Jake too.

I *would* obviously like to eat fish and chips with him. I love being with him and I'm not going to be with him much from now on and I'd like to spend a bit more time with him. And I would really like to get us back on good, friendly terms before we go our separate ways rather than finishing with a conversation like the one we've just had, which did not feel totally amicable at the end. And, yes, we do need to bitch.

'Sounds good,' I decide.

And so we order the fish and chips and Jake moves the conversation on to cooking, which is a lovely, easy thing to talk about, and then he says, 'So, Sonja.'

'Yes. Cannot stand the woman.'

'Same. She told you that they're going to continue with the weekly montages, but longer ones, using footage from the weekend, and then in a few weeks' time we'll be required to go back on the show for a final hour-long live interview?'

'Yep,' I say. 'Torture.'

'Agreed. And I don't think there's really anything we can do other than go along with it and then be ecstatic to walk away. I think she basically holds all the cards.'

'At least we now know that she's properly evil and we should be very wary.'

Jake nods. 'Yeah. I was *mad* to state my thoughts when we went on the first time. I would like to reiterate, for the record, that firstly I know I shouldn't have said that stuff and secondly I do now realise I was wrong. About your books. They're great and of course they don't generally break up marriages.'

'Love the way you put the "generally" in there,' I can't resist pointing out.

'Yeah, there's only so far I can go in admitting I'm wrong.'

I smile at him and say, in my best patronising tone, 'Well, it's good that you realise that.'

'I'm going to ignore the patronisation and agree. It's also good—' He stops himself from finishing his sentence and I assume that he was going to say something about the weekend or us having got to know each other and then thought better of it given our conversation earlier. 'Would you like another glass of wine?'

'That's really kind but I think I'm good with water.' I'm a complete lightweight alcohol-wise and I do not want to give in to the immense temptation I'm feeling right now to tell him I was being ridiculous and invite him home with me so we can have more amazing sex. If he declined the offer that would be mortifying. And if he accepted that would be very bad. So water it is.

I don't want to leave things on the optimism-pessimism slight dispute, so I ask about the weekend in Dublin Jake said he had planned, and from there we begin to chat. It's a little awkward, but I think we're both working at it, aware that we are going to have to meet again from time to time (maybe quite regularly if Lizzie and Dan stay together), and we want it to be as easy an experience as possible.

It isn't *that* easy right now, though. I feel as though I want to drink in every single one of his mannerisms, turns of phrase, facial expressions, store them away so that I can get them out sometimes and revisit them over the coming months during which I *know* I'm going to question myself and what happened here. I also just want to leave so that I can get home and do some wallowing, because over the course of only one weekend Jake has managed to get to me in a way that I can't remember anyone else ever doing.

Eventually our fish and chips are finished, and with it our polite conversation.

It's *so* polite. As the server takes our plates away, we're literally talking about the modules we took at university. It's basically a mundane sharing of not-at-all-sensitive-or-indeed-particularly-interesting trivial information.

We walk – politely – back to Waterloo together, say our – polite – goodbyes, and take our separate Tube (Jake) and train (me) home.

* * *

I do wallow that night, and I don't have as much rest as I would have liked, given how lacking in sleep our weekend was, so when I wake up on Wednesday morning, I feel as though I'm just going to be staggering through the day, desperate for bed again in the evening.

So I'm not *delighted* (which makes me feel guilty) when I get a message from Lizzie in the early afternoon saying that she wants to convene an 'emergency discussion' with me and can I do this evening.

I reply immediately, panicked that something has happened between her and Dan and she's going to be devastated again.

> Are you okay?

Her response is also immediate.

> Yes I am. Are you though?

What? Has there been another newspaper article or something? Or is the latest *Wake Up Britain* montage out and is it unfavourable to me? Lizzie doesn't know anything about our weekend, so she can't be referring to that.

After quite a lot of toing and froing we establish that Lizzie genuinely is fine but that she thinks I am not fine but won't say why. We agree that we'll meet tomorrow evening so that I can get some sleep tonight. I'm so tired I'm practically seeing bunting round the edges of my vision.

* * *

On my way round to Lizzie's flat the next evening, I'm still in two minds about whether or not I'm going to tell her about what happened with Jake. On the one hand I want to talk about it and on the other it's still too raw. When I *do* tell someone, Lizzie's probably the first person I would tell; she's very kind, very sensible, very caring and always discreet.

Maybe another time, though. When I've digested it all a bit further.

Lizzie greets me by holding me by the hands at arm's length and studying my face closely, before pulling me into a long hug, so I'm immediately feeling a little uneasy. (Clearly she's convened this evening to talk about me, not her, but I don't want to talk about me.)

'Okay, we need wine and then you need to tell me everything about the weekend and you and Jake.'

'Erm…'

Lizzie pulls me into her kitchen and over to the table.

'So you and Jake,' she says.

'Erm,' I repeat.

'Dan told me. Jake told him.' Ohhhh.

'What did Jake say?'

'In a nutshell that at the beginning of the weekend you were still quite hostile towards each other but by the end of Saturday you'd started getting on very well. And that then you had two amazing nights together and Jake felt like it could be the start of something big, but you told him you don't want to begin any kind of romance because your relationships never work out and you don't want to get upset when this one finishes.' Lizzie finally pauses for breath, unscrews the lid of a bottle of red wine and fills our (quite large) glasses to the rim.

'Good summary,' I say, weakly.

'What did you mean, though?'

'Exactly what you just said.'

Lizzie frowns. 'Basically that you *know* that every relationship you start *will* finish? So you don't want to start one with Jake because it *will* finish and you'll be upset?'

'Yes?' I really don't know what's not to understand about that.

'But *why* would it finish?'

'Because my relationships *do* finish.'

'But... what?' Lizzie takes a big slurp of her wine and waves her hand in the direction of mine like she's telling me that I need to drink too.

I pick up my wine glass, take a long, slow sip and say nothing. I'm not sure what else there *is* to say.

'So.' Lizzie stands up and turns her oven on. 'We're having lasagne and salad. I made them earlier. Could you clarify what you mean by your relationships *do* finish?'

'Erm. Just that. All my relationships finish. They just do. It's something about me. So I don't want to start one with someone I'd be sad to split up with. And I don't want to start one with someone I already know I wouldn't be sad to split up with because obviously why then would I want to have a relationship with them?'

'So that's why you only ever go on the occasional date? Because if you really like someone you don't want to date them seriously and if you don't really like them you don't want to either?' Lizzie takes a big oblong dish out of the oven and removes foil from the top of it.

'Basically yes?'

'I'm mind-blown. We've been best friends for so many years and you've been carrying all this around inside you. Why have we never talked about this before?' She puts the foil in the bin and sits back down.

'I've always felt that you *know* this. Like it's so obvious? And I don't like talking about it, plus there's nothing much to say.'

'So that's why you've always been so vague whenever I've tried to talk about the end of your relationships? And I suppose also I did have a lot of dating disasters of my own and maybe I've only started to think more clearly about dating in general since I met Dan.'

Lizzie shakes her head and then sits for a long moment, clearly thinking. (She has this actual thinking-woman pose: elbows resting on table, hands propping chin, eyes kind of swivelling around the room.)

I just carry on taking little sips of my wine and watching her and waiting for her to finish thinking.

'Driving tests,' she pronounces finally.

I look at her, confused. Why has she so thoroughly changed the subject?

'Remember how I took my driving test seven times.'

I nod. You couldn't have known Lizzie during her learning-to-drive era and *not* remember that. She became like a woman possessed. She *had* to pass. I don't think she's driven since.

'And how you took yours twice,' she continues.

I nod again.

She looks over at the oven, where the still-heating-up light has just clicked off, and stands up.

As she puts the lasagne in, she says, 'Until we passed our driving tests, we'd only ever failed them.' She sets a timer and sits back down. 'Similarly, until you've had a successful relationship, you've only ever had failed ones. Failed exams don't mean you're never going to pass. Failed relationships don't mean you're never going to have a successful one.'

I frown, confused again, this time because on the one hand what she just said sounds as though it makes perfect sense, but on the other I know it doesn't.

'Not similar,' I state.

'Why, though?'

'One is an exam and the other is a human relationship?'

'So what, though?' She tops up both our glasses.

I just sit and stare at her, while I try to work out how to articulate this.

'Erm,' I say after a bit, as a space filler.

She stands up and gets oil, vinegar and mustard and makes salad dressing.

'Going back to your driving test analogy,' I say eventually, 'everyone's got something they're never going to manage. And most people realise that at some point. Like you might try and try and try to run a four-minute mile but eventually you realise that it's never going to happen and you give up, be it by choice, or by de facto continued failure. For most people, I think there would be a number of driving tests after which they'd say: *do you know what? This is not for me and I'm giving up*. Remember you nearly didn't take your seventh one?'

'But I *did* take it,' she says triumphantly. 'And I passed it.'

'But if you'd failed it, and then you'd failed say another ten, do you not think at some point you'd have said to yourself that driving wasn't for you and given up?'

'Well, yes, maybe.'

'Exactly.' I feel extremely relieved to have made my extremely sensible and valid point, and now hopefully we can have a nice evening talking about anything but this.

But no. 'Continuing with the driving test thing,' Lizzie says, 'there would come a point where you'd taken a certain number of tests and you'd decide that you were never going to succeed. But there would be a catalyst for that. After investing all that time and effort you wouldn't want to just walk away. Maybe the catalyst would just be that you'd failed one test too many. Or maybe something would make you think there was a particular thing about you that meant you personally were never going to be a good driver. What was your catalyst for coming to this realisation about relationships?'

Lizzie is a very, very good friend of mine and that is why I'm humouring her and continuing with this annoying conversation because I really don't like analysing myself.

'Well,' I begin. And then I repeat what I told Jake, about my parents and my past relationships.

The timer for the lasagne goes off just as I finish and Lizzie stands up to take it out of the oven and the salad out of the fridge, before sitting back down.

'You know I love you and respect your wisdom and life choices,' she says. 'But this is silly. It isn't *you*, it's *them*.'

She stands up again and begins to get plates and cutlery out, waving away my offer of help.

'Your parents,' she says as she places the lasagne dish in the middle of the table and hands me a large spoon. 'You know how both my parents are pretty much tone deaf but I can sing?'

I nod. That's an understatement. Her parents really are not at all musical, and she has the voice of an actual angel. She was a professional opera singer for a couple of years but then decided it involved too little money and too much travel for a happy adult life and became an accountant who sings in a very high-level amateur choir and occasionally does recordings for money.

'So.' She pushes the salad towards me. 'I did not inherit my musical tendencies from my parents. Obviously my grandmother was a great singer—' her father's mother was a fairly famous professional opera singer '—and I probably inherited it from her. Things can skip generations. And you are the product of your parents but genes are complicated and you are a completely different person from both your parents, as we all are.'

I nod and pile salad onto my plate before saying, 'I totally agree that people are not carbon copies of their parents, and everyone is unique. But in this instance it's clear from my life experience that I *have* inherited my parents' relationship flaws. Just like it's clear from your life experience that you might not have inherited your voice from your parents but you did inherit your hair from your mother.'

Lizzie and her mum both have the most amazing thick, very curly, auburn hair.

Lizzie says, 'Okay,' and takes a large mouthful. When she's swallowed, she says, 'Soooo. Talk me through your first ever relationship.'

'But you know about it already?'

'Yes, but humour me.'

'Fine but only because you're a very good friend and you're feeding me very delicious lasagne and salad with very nice wine.'

And then I tell her again about how I met my first boyfriend in sixth form and he dumped me two days before I was supposed to be going on holiday with his family and took another girl. Who had been until that moment a friend of mine. I was still a bit of a mess when I arrived at uni a month later, and my new uni friends very much helped pick up the pieces.

'And is he happily married?' Lizzie does know the answer to her question.

'Nope, serial cheater who cheated on the girl he cheated on me with and is already on his third wife.'

'*Exactly.*' Lizzie raises her hands like *Hallelujah*. '*He* is the problem, not you. You are just one of many women he has cheated on over the years. I bet most if not all of the others have not subsequently sworn off romance.'

'Yes *but* the rest of his romance victims probably haven't had a billion *other* relationship fails.'

'Fine. Talk me through your next relationship.'

We spend an uncomfortably long time going through every relationship – short and longer – that I've ever had, in order.

I *really* wouldn't be doing this if Lizzie weren't such a good friend and didn't clearly have my best interests at heart. And, also, in some ways, it's quite good.

Because, each time, Lizzie concludes that it was either him, or *us*, as in *we* just weren't right for each other, or it was the wrong time, or, in fact, a myriad of other reasons, none of which are that my relationship fails were because *I* can't have relationships.

Obviously I *can't*, but it's actually kind of nice to have it pointed out by a straight-talking friend that a lot of the failures I've been carrying with me as *my* failures were in fact someone else's mistakes or downright shittiness, or an '*our* failure' situation, or just one of those things.

'So.' Lizzie takes a long drink of the water we both now have because we finished the bottle of wine and agreed that we do not want hangovers tomorrow and moved on to water. Then she rolls her neck and stretches her shoulders before adjusting her position, curled up in the corner of the sofa, which we moved to about halfway through the analysis of my relationship demises. 'Where have we got to?'

'We've got to the end,' I tell her.

'*Or* the beginning,' she says.

'The beginning of...?'

'The beginning of your realisation that you are totally able to have great relationships. And something I forgot to mention: *you and I* have a great relationship. You have great relationships with all your other girlfriends. I love you. You love me. You are a person who is *so* capable of having great relationships.'

I'm just staring at her because on the one hand everything she's been saying makes perfect sense, but on the other I'm pretty sure she's wrong.

'I love you too,' I say in the end, because I'm not sure what else to say.

Lizzie reaches over and we share a lovely, big, long hug before we settle back into our sofa corners.

'Would you think about all of that?' she asks. 'For me?'

I nod. I feel like I *do* now have stuff to think about.

'And will you come for drinks at the weekend knowing that Jake will also be here? And quite a few other people.'

I nod again. I care about Lizzie too much to make things awkward for her with Dan. Jake and I can totally be polite to each other for a few minutes and then chat to other people. Totally.

20

JAKE

'Jake, are you okay?' Max says. 'You were miles away?'

Shit. I was thinking about Freya, and Dan and Lizzie's drinks this evening. I can't work out whether I'm really looking forward to seeing her or quite the opposite. I've *really* missed her this week. Like... it *hurts* thinking that there's no possibility of seeing her like *that* again. And I don't want to make that hurt worse. But, also, I can't help stupidly hoping that maybe, just maybe, if we spend more time together something *could* happen. And also it would be nice just to see her because I really do miss her.

'Sorry, yes, fine. Just thinking about the weather.' I don't want to upset him; I know that my family have been worried about me since the divorce. 'I've been cycling into work but it isn't great in heavy rain. A lot of thunderstorms have been forecast for next week; have you seen?'

'Are you sure you're okay? Do you usually worry about *weather*?'

'Ha, yeah, no, true.'

I'm an idiot.

I'm also thirty-six years old, not sixteen.

So it's truly ridiculous to firstly be thinking so much about Freya and secondly be making up stupid things so that I don't have to admit it to my own brother.

* * *

The drinks are in Lizzie's flat, which isn't that far from Freya's house.

I'm still in my do-I-want-to-see-her-do-I-not state when I arrive, but actually, there are a good twenty people here, and I don't immediately see her; instead I end up getting engrossed in conversation with some old uni friends who I haven't seen for a while, and when I do catch sight of Freya on the other side of the room I see that she's surrounded by a little group, all talking very animatedly, and decide that actually this is for the best. We won't really interact this evening and that will be that.

A few minutes later, however, my back bumps pretty hard into the back of someone smaller, and when I turn round to apologise, I discover that it's Freya, and that the bump caused her to spill wine down herself.

'It's okay,' she says in response to my apology. 'One of those things. And, also, it wasn't your fault. It was me. I took a step backwards and bumped into you.'

'I also took a step backwards,' I say inanely.

'Mutual fault, then. And you got lucky in being more competent at holding on to your drink than me.' She smiles at me, and I try hard to ignore the fact that it's like I can actually physically feel the smile somewhere inside me. 'Anyway, at least it's white.'

'Sticky, though. Should you maybe try to wash it out?' I try to avert my eyes, without obviously averting them. The wine's making her top cling to her, which is making me remember things from last weekend and think thoughts that are extremely inappropriate given that we definitely won't be doing that kind of thing again.

'Yep, probably. I'll get something from Lizzie.'

'Let me help you,' I say, before remembering that I will certainly *not* be helping her to clean a stain off the chest region of her top. 'Or not. I mean... Obviously you can probably manage yourself. Just offering. But I totally get that you will probably be very happy to do it yourself.' Yep, the social skills of a sixteen-year-old with a serious crush. I need to *stop talking*.

Freya is just laughing at me, and rightly so.

'Very kind, thank you,' she says, still sniggering.

'Why don't I, at the very least, find Lizzie for you?'

'Find me?' says Lizzie, from right next to my elbow.

'I spilt wine on my top and Jake thinks it's his fault but it isn't,' Freya explains.

'I love that top,' Lizzie says. 'We need to rescue it. Let me give you one of mine to wear and we'll put that one straight in the washing machine so we can get the wine out before it dries into a stain.' She takes Freya's hand and pulls her away. 'We'll see you in a minute, Jake.'

And off they go, and that will probably be the last I'll see of Freya this evening. When I did my teenage-style agonising over seeing her, I didn't actually imagine that all I would do would be stare at her chest and babble. But there you go. I really do need to forget about her and move on. Easier said than done, obviously, with Sonja's one-hour live special looming, but I'm an adult; I should just deal with it.

Fucksake. I'm staring in the direction of where they just disappeared. Like a lovesick teenager *again.*

I give myself a shake and move over to speak to some friends.

* * *

A few minutes later, I'm genuinely properly distracted by a story about a truly crazy stag weekend in Wales a couple of weeks ago (so many clichés: a green moustache was painted on the groom in permanent marker; he was tied to a lamp-post naked; he was then found by his mother's female next-door neighbour who panicked and handed him an actual *sock* to cover himself strategically – why not a larger item like a dressing gown or towel?), when up pops Lizzie, holding Freya by the arm.

'We're back!' Lizzie practically thrusts Freya towards me, and then just walks off.

'Hi.' Freya gives the top she's wearing a little tug. At a guess, she's feeling slightly exposed. It's bright red and extremely tight. It looks very nice but it's more revealing than the clothes she usually wears.

I want to reassure her that she looks lovely but I'm pretty sure I could end up in an awkward conversational quagmire if I go down that route, so instead I say, 'We were just hearing about the stag weekend from hell.' And then I repeat the details I just heard, and Freya obviously exclaims, and then she's drawn into the conversation with the other men.

The group we're in expands to include some other women, but it so happens that Freya and I continue to stand next to each other, and somehow end up in a side conversation, just the two of us.

'How did your panel go?' I ask. I know that she was speaking on an online panel about writing romance yesterday evening, and had been feeling a little nervous following the way our TV appearances blew up.

'All good. There was only one slightly tricky question about *Wake Up Britain* – did I learn anything from it – and I batted it away with a plug for the live update show and a comment that doing it and the love challenge has taught me that I still absolutely adore writing romance and am incredibly grateful to my readers.'

'Nice,' I say appreciatively. Then, even though right as I say it I'm aware that it's a stupid question to ask, I continue, 'Do you feel like in reality it did teach you anything? I feel like it taught *me* some stuff. Like... even though Sonja is objectively manipulative and does not have our best interests at heart it was quite good being thrown into some of those situations. Yeah. I think I might just be saying that team-building events *work*.'

'I think *those* team-building events worked but I don't think they always would. Like, if we actually inherently truly hated each other, making me do things that I hated and you loved would not have improved matters.'

Her words give me a bit of hope – because, okay, yes, I really have missed her *incredibly* this week and I'd love to spend more time with her – and on impulse I ask, 'Want to get some air on the balcony?'

Lizzie's flat is a second-floor one, with a small, flower-filled roof garden jutting off the living room. No-one else is out there at the moment (possibly because it isn't that warm), so if we go out there we'll be alone.

Freya hesitates for a moment, and then says, 'Good idea.'

We weave our way through the others and out onto the balcony.

I close the door behind us, and then say, 'Don't want to let cold air in,' in case Freya thinks that I really wanted us to be alone (which if I'm honest I do, so I feel like I've just made up a pathetic little lie).

Freya sits down on the bench that Lizzie has running along one side of the balcony, and I join her.

'Beautiful view,' she says. 'I always love it out here in the summer.'

'How long has Lizzie been living here?' I ask.

Our small talk continues for a while, and it's nice. Nice to know that we can still chat. I really only think about sexual things about once every minute or so: victory. It's good that we're in full view of everyone inside so there can be no temptation whatsoever to do anything stupid like, well, kissing.

I'm careful not to mention anything about the weekend, because it's hard to mention the activities without then thinking about the sex.

And I would really, I realise, like to be able to be friends with Freya, and I can't do that if I'm constantly thinking about that side of things when I'm with her.

Freya's been telling me about the long walk she went on this morning with a neighbour and the baking she did this afternoon. 'How was your day?' she asks.

I hesitate briefly, and then I say, 'I spent the day with my family.' And this time I go on to tell her in detail about Max's accident, and the effect it's had on the rest of us, and how my parents are amazing but obviously getting older and a little more tired. And it feels good to tell her: even if nothing romantic develops between us, I hope we can stay friends; and we've had a huge experience together.

'I'm so sorry again that the accident happened,' she says. 'You obviously have an amazing family, to have drawn together in response.'

I nod. 'Yep. I think families often either crumble or become tighter. I do feel very blessed in that regard. We have wonderful parents.'

'Do you...' She stops for a moment, and then says, 'How are you now about it all?'

'I feel guilty that it wasn't me,' I say reflexively, and am then surprised, because I don't tell people that. I have so much guilt that I feel guilty just thinking about the guilt.

'I thought you might. You know, we're all dealt different hands in life and we can't feel guilty about them. It's what we *make* of the hands we're dealt that counts. And obviously it happened to your brother, but it happened to all the rest of you too. You've lived through terrible trauma seeing that happen to your brother and you haven't crumbled, you've stepped up and been a wonderful support to the rest of your family.'

'I can't crumble.' The least I've been able to do for Max and my parents is stay strong.

'I know.' She inches closer to me and places her hand on mine for a moment. 'Which is a big burden in itself. You have to deal with your own grief over what might have been for your brother. And you have the worry for the future, I'm guessing.'

'Yeah, that's one of the reasons I work such long hours doing this job. I mean, I genuinely think I would have been happier being a carpenter or a tree surgeon. But I need the money, for the future, so that I'll always be able to look after Max.'

'You're wonderful and I think you have to understand and truly accept that you shouldn't feel guilty that it happened to him and not you. It's so destructive to happiness feeling either guilty or jealous. Every single one of us can look around and see people who we love who are on the face of it unluckier than us, and similarly luckier than us. We can't compare or feel guilty or envious; we can only do the best we can with our own circumstances. I hope it doesn't sound insensitive for me to say that things *could* be worse for Max. He could have had the same accident but not had such a wonderful, supportive family. And things *could* be a lot better for you: you could have had a family that didn't experience such terrible trauma.'

I'm frowning and I'm also almost smiling. Somewhere through her speech I've started to feel lighter.

'It's weird,' I say. 'Sometimes you can carry something with you for a long time and just one sentence or short conversation can make you feel differently about things. I think you're right. And I think I'm going to remember this moment forever. I feel... *better*.' I put my arm round her and hug her into me briefly before releasing her. 'Thank you. Really. I'm incredibly grateful.'

She shakes her head. 'You have nothing to thank me for. It's all just true, and you *are* a wonderful person, and your family are lucky to have you, and I'm just glad if something I said helped at all.' She looks at me for a moment, and then says, 'I had a thing with Lizzie on Wednesday. She said some stuff that made me think about things differently too.'

From the way Freya's looking at me, I feel that Lizzie might have said something about her views on romance. I would very much like to ask but I'm really not sure how to frame the question. Given that I do have a vested interest.

So I say, 'Oh?'

For a moment I feel as though Freya's going to say something kind of big, from the way she's pressing her lips together, then relaxing them, and then slightly screwing her face up.

But then she says nothing.

And suddenly, I go for it. 'Going back to our conversation the other day, I wondered what it was that happened to you. What the thing was that made you decide that relationships aren't for you? If that isn't too much of an intrusion.'

'Yeah, no, it isn't an intrusion. And I suppose it's very simple. As you just said, sometimes you have a one-off event or conversation, or hear just one sentence from someone, that makes a huge impact on you and affects the way you see things forever more, or causes you to make a big life decision. And, yep, I do know when it was. It was the day of my father's funeral. And, coincidentally – well, not really coincidentally; it was because of you – I had a similar conversation with Lizzie the other day. She told me that she thinks I'm not rubbish at relationships and talked me through every single one of my many failed romances and pointed out that they weren't *my* failures.'

She pauses and takes a sip of the water she brought outside with her.

'So after that conversation,' she continues, 'which was on Wednesday, I got thinking. And yes, I do know the catalyst for me realising that I can't do relationships. It was after the funeral, at the drinks, and there were a *lot* of bitter exes of my dad's there – one of them my mother – and I wondered why you would go to the funeral of someone you really loathed. And they did definitely loathe him; they weren't holding back. And then I realised that they had all still loved him and had had bad relationships with him. And that it was his fault. And then someone – one of his colleagues – told me that I was very similar to him and I was simultaneously pleased, because I'd kind of always wanted his approval, and not pleased, because of his disastrous relationship history, and the fact that I had a terrible track record too.'

She pauses again, takes another sip, and then concludes with: 'Yes, so that's it. That was the moment.'

'But you haven't left a string of exes who hate you?' I say. 'I mean, obviously I don't know any of your exes.' I actually feel like an ex myself even though we did not have a relationship at all, we just had a weekend of sex. 'But I know you – somewhat, at least – and I find it hard to believe that you've upset people.'

'I've made some people angry,' she says, as though she's sticking up for herself. 'I had a couple of quite controlling boyfriends and they were not pleased when I left them.'

'That isn't you being, horrible, though?' I want to hug her again as she frowns in a very cute manner as she digests my words. 'Going back to something you said, and at great risk of sounding like a complete amateur psychologist quack, and without wishing to criticise your father in any way, if you always wanted your father's approval do you think the facts are that he *was* a difficult man and you were perhaps – in other relationships – seeking reassurance and approval from men similar to him? And you aren't in fact like him? Perhaps when his colleague said you were similar to him they actually meant you *looked* like him? And weren't necessarily particularly like him personality-wise, or temperament-wise, or certainly not relationship-wise?' God, I hope he *did* look like her, otherwise I could just have made matters a lot worse. 'If you do. Did.'

'My goodness.' Freya sniffs. 'You *are* an amateur psychologist.' She sniffs again and wipes a finger under her eyes. 'I think you're a good one. I think you're right.' She puts her glass down and wipes again, with both fingers this time. 'I think this might be a conversation *I* remember forever too.'

I want to ask her right now if she'll go on a date with me.

I'm terrified to, though. I don't want to destroy this, here, what we seem to have now.

So I just say, 'Beautiful evening for big conversations. The sky's so clear.'

'Yep. The stars.'

She isn't looking at the stars, though, she's looking at me. Her lips are slightly parted and I can't take my eyes off them.

There are a lot of her friends and a lot of my friends just on the other side of the balcony doors, though, so us kissing right now would be a really bad idea.

And maybe it would be anyway.

I really, really like Freya. If there's any possibility of us starting a relationship, we should probably spend some time together actually getting to know each other better away from Sonja and her cameras before we leap into bed together again.

'Are you free tomorrow afternoon?' I hear myself asking. 'Would you like to meet for a walk?'

Freya smiles. 'That would be nice.'

We chat a little more, and then we go inside. I feel as though we've had exactly the same thought about resetting things and getting to know each other better before anything else happens, if it does, because at about midnight Freya tells me that she's ordered an Uber and will see me tomorrow for our walk; there's no suggestion of me accompanying her home, which I think is absolutely the right thing.

* * *

When we meet on Wimbledon Common the next afternoon for our walk, I'm pretty sure that my face is split into a foolish grin, and I'm pleased to see Freya beaming at me as we approach each other.

'Hello,' she says.

'Hello.'

We begin to walk, side by side, no hand-holding, and we just chat. We chat a lot. We walk from where we met, next to a large pond in a big open expanse of grass, across the Common to where there's a windmill, with a tea shop. We get tea and cake and talk the whole time. Sometimes it's serious; most of the time it's just chat. We smile, we laugh, we listen. When we've finished our cake, we wander down to another pond and look at the ducks and moorhens, before continuing our walk.

Our arms brush a lot – we're definitely walking more closely together than you would with someone who you thought of as just a friend – and at some point – I'm not even sure how it happens – we begin to hold hands.

It's a great, great walk.

'We've been so lucky with the weather,' Freya observes as we complete our big loop of the Common and end up back where we started.

'Yeah.' I feel a lot luckier about the company than the weather, though.

We decide to go to a nearby pub for a drink, and then we decide that we'd both like fish and chips. Eventually, it's last orders and time has apparently flown.

I walk Freya home, and at her front door we kiss.

It's a long, tender kiss that, certainly on my side, feels full of promise.

It would be so nice to go inside with her, but I feel as though I want to take things slowly, prove to her that she's right in her realisation that it isn't *her*, it's just that her other relationships were bad; she can totally have a great relationship.

I'm very much hoping she feels the same way, though, because in reality I don't think my self-control would actually stand up to her inviting me in.

'I've had a nice day,' Freya says eventually.

'Me too. I should probably get going. Work tomorrow.'

'Yeah.'

And then we share another lingering kiss before I say, 'Goodnight, then.'

'Goodnight.'

* * *

That was Sunday. We meet on Wednesday. And Friday, with friends. And Saturday, with friends. And Sunday, just the two of us.

And then we continue to meet.

We go for walks, to the cinema, out for dinner. We play tennis, we do a pub quiz, we go to Camden Market.

It's nice. Lovely. Wonderful. Perfect.

Three weeks in, Freya comes to my house for dinner on the Saturday evening, with Dan and Lizzie. We agreed that we owe them and we also agreed that we will cook together, with Freya in charge.

She comes over early afternoon; we've agreed that we're going to do most of the dinner prep then (I have no idea what she's talking about but I'm sure it will all become clear), then go for a walk, and then finish off the cooking before the others arrive.

Earlier in the week, I suggested reprising our Sonja *MasterChef* challenge.

Freya said, '*Or* we decide what we're cooking and just buy the right ingredients? For an easier life?'

I said that was a good point and she placed a supermarket order online to be delivered to my house.

So here we are, in my little-used (but very well-equipped; it was refurbished straight before I bought it) kitchen, about to cook.

'Okay.' Freya fishes two navy-and-white-striped aprons out of her bag. 'Do you remember how to chop an onion properly?'

'For a usually very relaxed woman you're very fussy about your vegetable-cutting,' I tell her.

'If you're going to do something, do it properly,' she says severely.

'Harsh,' I say.

'Excuse me.' She nudges me in the ribs and I – obviously – catch her in my arms and plant a kiss in the nape of her neck, and she – obviously – turns and winds her arms around my neck, and I kiss her on the lips, and next thing I have her lifted and sitting on the kitchen counter, her legs round my waist, and from there we do things that should probably never be done in a kitchen. It's a good job I keep almost nothing out on the worktops.

Some time later, I pick her up in my arms and carry her through to the big sofa in the living room next door, and we carry on there.

It's amazing. This is the first time we've had sex since the team-building weekend, and it's even better in some ways, because now we know each other so much better, and this isn't a frenzied one-night stand, pure passion thing; there are – from my side, anyway – definite feelings involved. Okay, it's still quite frenzied, but there's laughter and there are terms of endearment, there's *knowledge* of each other, there's... well, maybe there's something that could definitely turn into love. It's *tender* along with the frenzy.

It's pretty bloody amazing basically.

Eventually, Freya – stark naked (as am I) – sits up from the sofa and then dives back down on top of me (which I'm startled by, because it does not seem particularly amorous, but am not complaining about).

'It's the middle of the day,' she hisses. 'And the curtains are open.'

'Hmm.' I think about the angle of the window and the back of the sofa, and the tree between the window and the road. 'Hopefully no-one will have seen anything.'

'Where are our clothes?' Freya lifts her head and looks around the room.

'I think they might be in the kitchen.'

'Okay. I'm going to crawl to get them.' And she slides off the sofa and commando-crawls naked towards the door before standing up and scuttling into the kitchen. She emerges with her clothes clutched around her. 'Bathroom?'

'Upstairs, first on left.'

And off she dashes, still naked, holding her clothes.

The whole thing is one of the sexiest things I have ever seen in my entire life. Possibly *the* sexiest.

I think I'm in love.

Too soon to mention it, though.

21

FREYA

'Mmm, something smells good,' Lizzie tells me as we hug when she and Dan arrive.

'Thank you!'

We (I) had to improvise quite a lot when it became apparent due to an afternoon of *wonderful* sex that we weren't going to have as much time as we'd thought for the cooking and baking.

Today is the first time we've had sex since the team-building weekend – we've been taking things slowly (by unspoken agreement – I think we both felt the same way) – and it was unbelievable. Like *amazing*. Just... It's definitely ruined me for all sex with all other people for the rest of time, for a start. I just don't think you could have better than that. And if I'm honest, I don't think it was entirely because we do – clearly – gel physically; I think it was also because we now have an emotional connection.

'Freya?' Lizzie's staring at me. Whoops. I'd drifted off into a little thinking-about-sex-with-Jake haze there.

'Sorry. Little bit tired.'

Lizzie is still peering into my face. 'You look very... happy,' she says.

I have to make a really big effort not to swivel my eyes in panic. I am not one of those people who likes to tell everyone (anyone) when they've had sex. I am also not one of those people who believes they can tell when someone *else* has had sex, and I don't really think it's a thing – I think it just happens in books and films – but just in case it *is* a thing, I want to look as normal, non-just-had-after-noon-sex as possible, because I don't want to be on the end of Lizzie wagging her finger and telling me that I clearly just *got some*.

'I've had a nice week,' I say.

Lizzie looks at me for a bit longer, and then says, 'Good! So things are going well with Jake?'

I check over my shoulder that he and Dan are out of earshot and then whisper, 'Yes. It's all amazing. I like him a *lot*.' I actually think I might be falling in love with him but I really cannot say that out loud right now. And if I do tell anyone, if and when I'm sure, obviously Jake would be the first person I should tell. 'It's really good. We've had some great conversations. I think... I think I might have been slightly wrong about relationships. I think you were right.'

'I *was* right. I've been thinking more about it but didn't want to bombard you with my thoughts. But since we're on the subject... I think in all your failed relationships, you've been seeking reassurance and approval, like you never got from your dad. And with Jake it's different. You didn't want his approval at all to start off with, because you loathed him. But he gave it to you anyway, despite his initial loathing for *you*.'

I stare at her. 'I think you might be very clever.'

Lizzie smiles smugly. 'Apparently I am, yes.'

There's no time for further relationship analysis because Jake's poking his head round the kitchen door asking what we'd both like to drink, and very specifically would we like to try the cocktails that he's made, given that in all honesty he contributed nothing of any importance to the meal prep.

'That isn't true,' I protest. 'You...' What *did* he do other than the sex stuff? 'You were great with washing the vegetables. And chopping the onions.' Ish. 'And getting me cups of tea.'

'I did get you tea. And I talked to you while you cooked.' He sends me a crooked smile and it's all I can do not to go over there and throw myself into his arms.

I content myself with saying, 'You were an *amazing* sous-chef,' and smiling at him.

* * *

We drink our cocktails in Jake's small but perfectly formed garden, which is beautifully tended (by a gardener), and then we go inside to the kitchen where my sous-chef and I have laid the table with his very nice (and almost entirely unused) dining ware.

I feel unbelievably contented over dinner (starter, main course, pudding) as our conversation wends its way through topics big and small (yes, we do touch on politics at one point and thankfully feel our way to discovering that we all pretty much agree on all the big points, before Lizzie tells us that in this modern era of high-stakes and high-emotions politics we're playing a high-risk game and could we please now get back to discussing biscuit-making, and Jake replies that if she'd been around earlier when he tried and failed to rub butter into flour he'd know that that is *not* non-contentious). A couple of times we laugh so much that we're almost falling off our chairs. We sympathise with each other on almost everything and challenge each other just the right amount.

It's your basic perfect evening with friends.

Lizzie and Dan stay until nearly two in the morning, before Dan drags Lizzie away.

After we've done our goodbye hugs, as they walk out of the door, Jake's standing behind me with his arms round my waist and his chin resting lightly on my head, and as the door closes he leans down to drop a kiss into my neck. I turn in his arms.

And then – without either of us saying anything about it – I stay the night, and it's very, *very* good.

* * *

It continues to be amazing. I don't want to think too much about the fact that I've never before actually managed a proper, functional relationship for any period of time, because I don't want to jinx it. My conversations with both Lizzie and Jake did make me think – hope – that I can manage a solid relationship, but the strength of my feelings for Jake and the enjoyment I'm deriving from his company make me a little terrified.

We remain suspended in our extremely-close-friends-with-out-of-this-world-benefits bubble until the night before the live show with Sonja.

Jake and I have just finished watching the last instalment of a big Netflix drama (yes, we've got to the point where we stay in sometimes and watch box sets, and, yes, it's *lovely*).

'Live show tomorrow,' Jake says. 'Do you think we should... discuss anything before we go on?'

'Like what?' I ask, alarmed.

'Like what we're going to say about us.'

'Oh, okay.' Phew. I don't know what I thought he was going to say there, but a cold finger of dread had touched my spine for a moment.

'I'm thinking...' He pauses for a long moment, while I say absolutely nothing at all, because I'd very much like to hear his thoughts first. 'I'm thinking it would maybe be better for us *not* to say anything about *us*.'

I nod. 'I feel that way too.'

'Not because I don't want to shout our... friendship from the rooftops,' he clarifies. 'But because I don't want to talk to Sonja about it.'

'Yes, same. It's like everything she touches feels toxic.'

'Exactly. And...' He hesitates again before continuing, 'I would love this to become something longer term. I love you.'

It's like the whole world stops for a moment and then resets itself, exactly right, like everything has suddenly fallen into place.

'I love you too,' I manage to say through lots of smiles and quite a few happy tears.

I pull out of the kissing that ensues to say, 'I'm going to address a little elephant in the room. You might have won our challenge.'

Jake does a mock gasp. 'Freya Cassidy. Romance writer and disbeliever in real-life happy endings. What are you saying?'

'I might be saying that I would also love this to become something longer term.'

Really, really good sex ensues.

And then at one o'clock in the morning Jake leaves my house and gets in an Uber and goes back to his; we've decided that we should obviously travel completely separately to the studio tomorrow morning.

It's going to be weird pretending that there's no romance, or even friendship, between us, but it'll only be for one morning; we'll be fine.

* * *

One of the perks of being an author is that I do not have to get up at the crack of dawn if I don't want to; if I have a lot of work on, I can write in the evenings instead of first thing, or through my lunch. Or both. And I don't have to catch flights at ungodly hours because I can take my holidays at random – cheap – times. All to say that I basically *never* get up early.

When you're appearing on morning television, you *do* have to get up early, because they like you to arrive in very good time so you can do various preparations.

So, when my alarm goes off, I do know that I need to leap straight out of bed, or at least within five minutes, but I just... can't. I'm very, very tired. Okay. I need to. I'll read the news on my phone quickly. That should wake me up.

I get sucked into an article about European royals with very long names. (That's the literal premise of the article: long names; why do I read this crap and very specifically only when I'm tired and struggling to get out of bed?) Then I do Wordle and it's really hard today (and I do possibly nod off in the middle of it and only wake up because I handily mistakenly snoozed my alarm instead of turning it off). I flick through my emails but am too tired to open any of them. Then I rest my eyes for a second and get woken up the second time my alarm snoozes and oh fuck I am *late*.

I finally get myself into the shower and am woken up properly by the water, and get ready as fast as I can, but am obviously still late when I arrive at the studio.

I'm shown into a dressing room and Sonja immediately puts her head round the door and says, 'Morning,' before making a big show of checking her watch to see if it's the afternoon yet before laughing uproariously at her own gag.

'Ha,' I say, already over this.

'You being late has been good, actually.' She comes into the room and closes the door behind her. 'It's given me a chance to chat to Jake one on one, get the low-down.' She winks at me and I have to fight to maintain my smile. What does she *mean*? Has Jake caved and told her anything?

'Great,' I say (croak, actually).

'Would you like a glass of water?' asks Sonja, like the caring person she has demonstrated she certainly is not.

'I have one here, thank you.'

'Soooo... you and Jake?' she says.

I raise an eyebrow. I can totally do this. I've acted before. I was one of the three witches in *Macbeth* in my Year 8 school play. This is just a bit of acting for a couple of minutes.

'Me and Jake?' I repeat in my best guileless tone.

'Exactly,' Sonja says.

I frown innocently. 'You mean us coming on the show today?'

'What have you been up to since the team-building weekend?'

This time I frown thoughtfully, like I'm trying to recall facts. 'I've been *really* busy,' I say. 'Work. Friends. Family. You know. Busy. As we all are.'

'And Jake?'

'I presume he's been busy too,' I say.

Sonja shakes her head. 'Honestly,' she says. And then she gets up and leaves and I sit and worry until the make-up woman barrels into the room and tells me she's going to have her work cut out sorting out the bags under my eyes and says could she suggest that I try to get more sleep.

* * *

I'm reunited with Jake when I'm deemed okay to go on air, hair and make-up-wise. I really want to ask him what he said to Sonja, but I feel that walls might have ears and daren't say anything at all to him.

He clearly feels the same way, because he greets me with a handshake and is now asking, 'How have you been?'

'Great, thanks,' I say. 'You?'

'Yeah, good, thanks.'

And then we sit at opposite ends of our sofa not looking at each other, while Sonja announces us, and then we're ushered on set by Soraya.

Sonja asks how we've been and we do small talk very briefly before she says, 'So let's have a recap.' And she summarises our previous appearance and shows yet another video of us edited to include the most argumentative bits of our dispute. Yay. Then she summarises the challenge and where we got to, with some video footage. Then she talks through the team-building weekend. I'm beginning to relax; it really does seem as though we're here almost just as extras: what's actually happening is that Sonja's showing videos of us doing stuff and she's basically doing a voiceover.

It's actually quite interesting seeing the footage of the weekend. It was well over twenty-four hours of activities, and we were busy most of the time, so by the time they've finished showing it all and we've all agreed that we basically both lost the love challenge, it should be time for us all to smile and say yes the team-building weekend did work reasonably well and we've agreed to differ, shake hands and leave and get on with our Sonja-free lives.

During the extended footage, I'm pleased to say that I look less ridiculous than I thought I might, even during the non-abseiling debacle and the ice bath.

It's all fine.

I'm just thinking that I really shouldn't have wasted time dreading this, when Sonja turns to us both, and says, 'How did you two get *on* that weekend? How did the team-building *go*?'

She looks at me first. I'm suddenly goose-bumpy scared, because we've already covered this, and she's looking at me with gimlet eyes now. What if she knows something? No. She doesn't. And if she does, it doesn't really matter. There's no need to be scared. We just need to stick to our story.

I say, 'Actually not too bad. As you saw, Jake did very kindly help me on the assault course, which was really thoughtful. We basically ended up agreeing to differ and aren't arguing any more.'

'Jake?' Sonja asks.

'Yep, everything Freya said,' he confirms.

'Nothing else?' she asks.

We both shake our heads.

My goose-bump feeling of dread is growing. It's just occurred to me that viewers might not take kindly to us having lied to them about nothing having happened between us. And Sonja's smiling the way she did when she told me what activities we'd be doing during the team-building weekend, kind of slyly, like she has it in for us. I'm beginning to feel very queasy.

'Interesting,' Sonja says. 'Have a look at this.' She points at the screen where all the footage has been shown and a video begins to play.

And oh no. Oh no, no, no.

It's night-time. The camera pans in on a window where two people... oh fuck. Oh fuck, fuck, fuck.

It's unmistakably me and Jake. Kissing, hands everywhere, ripping each other's clothes off...

They have, naturally, edited the footage – in a PG, pre-watershed kind of way – to make it look like we immediately got naked rather than having the lovely long kiss I remember us beginning with.

'Interesting,' says Sonja. She must have been trying to get me to tell her about this when she – clearly – pretended that Jake had told her something.

'Ha, yes, the ultimate in team-building. Yeah. We had a cheeky one-night stand. Not something you want to tell anyone, which is why we... didn't,' says Jake. 'Whoops. Should obviously have closed the curtains.'

I'm very impressed by the way he's risen to the occasion. I nod a lot, judging it better not to say anything at this point.

And, actually, it isn't *that* bad. Just a bit embarrassing. It doesn't *matter* that Sonja and the nation know now that we had sex that weekend. Really, who cares? It means nothing to us that they know. If we stay together forever and, yep, I was completely wrong about relationships, because I do love Jake very much and I really hope that we *do* have a happily-ever-after together, then at some point everyone will know. They can laugh with us about how we got together.

Except... Sonja is shaking her head sorrowfully, and that is terrifying.

'I'm not sure you've been straight with me.' She points at the screen and we all turn to look at it.

And there we see a montage of us in our real lives. Some of the footage is a bit grainy, but it's unmistakably us. Together. Holding hands in the park, kissing, arms wrapped round each other in a cinema foyer. And a delightful shot of me naked on Jake's sofa the first time we had sex again, with pixellated boobs.

'That's completely unacceptable.' Jake's using his hard lawyer voice all of a sudden. 'How did you get that footage? We clearly did not consent to any of that being taken.'

'We did a social media request and our lovely viewers were only too happy to help. And once we realised how big a story this was, the paparazzi wanted to get involved.'

'Because you instructed them,' Jake says. 'Or they would not have known.'

'You've had people *stalking* us,' I say.

'Freya, it's in the public interest,' Sonja tells me, eyes wide and fake-soulful. 'We need our romance authors and our divorce lawyers to be straight with us.'

I *want* to rant at her, because it is not pleasant discovering that you've been followed and videoed so much, but decide that our best bet is to say nothing further.

Jake is also currently silent. His expression is extremely forbidding and I'm glad I'm not the person on the end of it.

Sonja seems unaffected by the stern look.

'How would you say the challenge *actually* went for you?' she asks.

Okay, I am *not* going to announce on national television that I am now if I'm honest hoping to spend the rest of my life with Jake. It's very soon to feel this way, anyway, and I certainly wouldn't want to terrify *him* by saying it now, so I'm not saying it to anyone else.

'Early days,' I say, forcing a laugh. 'We'll have to come back to you on that one.'

Jake nods.

'Oh, really?' Sonja goes all wide-eyed faux-innocent. 'Because you look pretty loved-up to me. Pretty much as though Jake has won the challenge.'

'Listen to this.' She indicates the screen again, and Jake and I both turn to it.

Jake's looking even more tight-lipped and I'm internally panicking big time, my mind on a what-now-what-now-what-*now* loop.

And then she plays us a video, with sound, of us from last night, clearly taken through Jake's window by some stranger, on Jake's sofa, exchanging I-love-yous.

I'm stunned. It's so beyond intrusive it's untrue.

'A little more than early days, wouldn't you say?' Sonja's smiling very widely now.

Jake and I both say nothing.

And then Sonja turns to Jake. 'Have you been straight with Freya, Jake?'

'Yep,' he says, very shortly.

'*Really*?' she says. 'Let's have a look, shall we?'

We all turn to the screen yet again.

I feel very cold and shivery, like flu has suddenly set in. I don't know *what* Sonja's about to show us, but I'm certain it isn't going to be good.

It's footage of Jake talking to his friend Pete. Who of course agreed to be videoed, unlike our other friends. It's from after the karaoke night.

'You could still win,' Pete says. 'Soften her up on the team-building week-end.' There's a bleep during which Sonja mouths 'shag' at me. '—her. Get her to fall in love with you. Then you've won.'

'Yeah, nice,' Jake says.

'Two hundred quid says you can't do it.'

Jake laughs. 'You never know.'

'A serious bet?'

'Sure.' Jake sticks his hand out and they shake.

I myself am now shaking, all over, and my stomach's churning.

I really don't want to throw up here and I also don't want to deal with this now. I just want to get through the rest of this hellish morning and get home and crawl under my duvet.

'That's some seriously misleading editing you've done there.' Jake's looking almost white with what I assume is anger. Anger that he's been found out.

'Not that misleading,' says Sonja, with the air of a woman about to play a gigantic trump card. 'Look at this.'

I don't want to look. I can't bear any more of this. But of course I do look.

And there's a screenshot of a two-hundred-pound donation by J Stone to Battersea Dogs Home.

'Sorry, what? How is *that* legal?' says Jake.

'Fully legal,' Sonja says. 'We consult our lawyers on everything.'

'They're wrong,' Jake says shortly. Like the invasion of his privacy is the most important thing here.

I want to scream at him. Find out more. Find out nothing. Tell him that I trusted him *fully* and how much I'm hurting right now. And scream again.

I can't do any of that now, though. I do not want to do any of it on national television, or in front of Sonja.

I produce a genuine-sounding laugh, and speak over Sonja, who's just begun spouting more of her poison, to say, 'Sonja, congratulations on all your detective work, although I'm not *totally* sure that the British public will think it's appropriate to spy on people in their private lives like that. I'll leave the legal side of things to Jake.'

'Jake won, didn't he?' Sonja says.

I do another excellent laugh (I should have had a way bigger part in *Macbeth*) and say, 'Ha, are we still talking about the challenge? I think we both won; it was a great weekend away and we've had a lovely time since.'

Jake follows my lead and we bat everything that she says away, until eventually the hideous, hideous, hideous stupid live experience draws to an end.

We do platitudes while we're leaving, and then we're finally outside.

'See you this evening?' Jake says, as he begins a speed walk in the direction of a cab, aiming a kiss at my lips.

The kiss misses because I turn my head away, and lands half on my ear, half on my hair.

He stops. 'Freya?'

I don't care who's looking or videoing us now.

'See me this evening? Are you insane? You slept with me for a *bet*.'

'I what? No, I didn't. Obviously.'

'Er, you won two hundred pounds?'

'I didn't *win* two hundred pounds. That was all a joke. But a week or two ago, when Pete realised we were staying over at each other's places a lot and deduced from that that we were having sex, he insisted that I'd won the bet and forced the cash on me, so in the end I gave the money to charity.'

'Fuck you,' I say, very clearly.

And then I wave down a black cab and get into it. 'That stuff was edited very misleadingly,' Jake yells, 'and also *saying* something doesn't mean anything. The bet meant nothing. It was a joke before I got to know you. *I love you*.'

'Fuck you,' I repeat as I slam the door.

My phone rings just as I've given the driver my address.

It's Jake.

'What?' I hiss into the phone.

'Why are you so ready to believe the worst?' he says. 'That footage was heavily edited. Like all the other footage.'

'You know what?' I say. 'You need to give the two hundred pounds back. You've actually lost the challenge. Because you've just proved to me that, yes, all my relationships do fail. Even when I fall in love. There is no happily-ever-after for me.'

'And *you* know what?' he yells. 'I've lost too. Because *you* have just proved to me that there can be no happily-ever-after for me either. Because I'm never going to meet anyone again who I love like I love you, and you've just accepted the word of an evil, amoral, shit-stirring woman over mine, without listening to me at *all*. Goodbye.' And he ends the call.

I sniff all the way home and then when I get there I crawl into bed and just howl.

22

JAKE

I am so pissed off. I raise my golf club and hit the ball as hard as I can. I mis-hit and it goes straight into the net in front of my driving range bay. I swing hard at the next one. That one connects and soars high into the air but far off to the left. I go for another massive hit and completely miss the ball, which never happens to me.

'Mate?' asks Dan from the next bay.

Like a toddler, I pretend I haven't heard, and roll my shoulders to go for my next attempt.

I'm so angry. Or upset. Or let down. Or something.

Freya. Sonja. Freya.

I hit the ball half-heartedly and don't bother to watch where it goes.

I shouldn't have come. It was very kind of Dan to ask me but I think I should actually have stayed at home alone to sort through my thoughts. Or wallow. Or drown my sorrows. Something solitary, anyway. I am not good company right now.

'Fucking Sonja,' I say out loud.

'Yeah,' Dan agrees.

The woman is pure bloody evil. She and her producers obviously completely knew what they were doing when they set us up like that.

With no regard whatsoever for the feelings of the actual humans involved. Freya looked so stricken. And I'm not exactly happy right now either.

Really fucking unpleasant.

Okay, so I have my thoughts clear on Sonja. Unequivocal dislike of her inhuman nastiness.

I take a moment and then hit a good ball.

I hit another good ball before my thoughts resume their circular misery.

Maybe Sonja's actually done me a favour.

Because Freya.

I thought we *knew* each other. We've spent so much time together. We've laughed, we've spent time with other people, we've done stuff together.

We've made love. Well, I thought we were making love. Now I think we were just having great sex.

Because we've also *talked*. And I was open with Freya. I shared my thoughts, hopes, fears, beliefs with her. And I thought she did the same with me. I thought we understood each other.

I do a massive whack of another ball and hit it straight into the ground right in front of me.

I don't know how I feel about Freya. Maybe just *hurt*. She gave me no opportunity whatsoever to explain.

I'm also angry with myself. I should have told her about the bet. Because she and I did talk. In a way that felt as though it was about everything. But I didn't mention it to her.

'I should have told her about the bet,' I say out loud. 'It didn't mean anything, like it wasn't a real bet, and it was made when we still barely knew each other, but I should have told her.'

'Yeah,' says Dan.

Which I kind of don't want him to say, but also, I do, because it's better when friends are straight with each other.

Yep, so he's right, so I should have told her about it weeks ago and so I'm angry with myself.

Why *didn't* I tell her? I suppose... I was ashamed of myself for having been so bigoted about romance books in the first place and for having created the whole challenge situation. And then things were working out so well between us, which was *because* of the challenge, so I was actually grateful to it, but it was like the whole thing was based on my having been a complete arse in the first place and I wanted to skate over that. So I just didn't talk about any of those pre-team-building-weekend things.

I should have mentioned it.

Yeah, so I'm ashamed of myself.

Suddenly I put my club down and pull my phone out of my pocket and send her a text:

> I'm sorry. That bet meant nothing and was made before I even knew you properly, but I should have mentioned it to you. I love you

She reads it immediately, while I'm still holding my phone.

And then she leaves me on read.

Which... I do not love.

And which plays havoc with my next twenty or so shots.

I don't think there was anything wrong with making the bet. I mean, it wasn't even actually a bet and it was Pete who suggested it. It was basically a joke. I never intended to act on it. And I also didn't know Freya properly at the time. I *should* have mentioned it to her, but it was harmless. But also I feel as though she should have given me a chance to explain rather than just immediately believing the worst. It was like she *wanted* to believe bad stuff.

Which brings me back to thinking that maybe I should be very grateful to Sonja because maybe it is for the best. Maybe something would always have broken us up at some point because Freya was just waiting for something to use to wreck our relationship.

Maybe I've had a lucky escape.

Or maybe I don't deserve to be lucky in love. Maybe I've already been lucky enough in life. I mean, look at my life compared to Max's.

I do another half-hearted hit and decide that I should probably just go home and get some sleep rather than wasting my time here.

* * *

I do not sleep well but things improve as the week goes on, basically because I throw myself into my work (not hard – there's always too much to do) until Saturday afternoon, when I go to see my parents and brother.

Max is very sensitive to my moods and I don't want to upset him, so I do my best to do the whole shoulders-squared, best-foot-forward thing as I drive us into Richmond Park.

'What's wrong?' he says, as I squeeze the car into a slightly too-small space between a VW campervan and a Porsche.

Oh. Okay. I need to try harder to seem happy.

'Nothing,' I say.

'You know, you need to stop trying to protect me. You're a real person. Things aren't always going to go amazingly for you. Sometimes bad things will happen. I know that and I love you and I'd be honoured if you would actually confide in me. And then I might confide more in you.'

'I...' I finish parking and turn to stare at him.

'Yes,' he says. 'Disabled physically but not mentally.'

'I...' God. 'Max. I'm so sorry,' I say finally.

'No. Don't be sorry. You're an amazing brother and I know you're always looking out for me. And I love hearing the stuff you do tell me. But don't just tell me the good bits. Tell me the shit bits too. You help me a lot. I'd like to be able to help you too.'

I nod slowly.

'Okay,' I say. And then I tell him how shit my divorce *really* made me feel. And then everything about Freya from start to finish. And how I've been feeling shit all week.

'Do you constantly feel guilty?' asks Max when I finish, surprising me. 'About having had a different life from mine?'

I stare at him again (I'm doing a lot of staring this afternoon) and begin to say no before switching to honesty: 'Yes.'

'And do you feel like you've had so much of what you regard as good luck that you won't deserve more good luck – relationship good luck – until you've earnt it more?'

I'm still staring. 'Kind of,' I say.

'Have you *fought* for Freya or have you just given up?'

Wow. He's right. I did give up very easily. Maybe all of this is what went wrong with my ex-wife too. Although to be fair that *was* a lucky escape.

'Yeah, you've paid your dues,' he says. 'And, also, we all get dealt different cards, you know? And it is what it is. Talk to Freya.'

'I can't talk to her. She aired me.' I *didn't* fight for her, but I don't know whether I have it in me right now.

'Hmmm,' Max says.

'You know what.' I undo my seatbelt. 'Let's get some fresh air. And I'll use this as a learning experience. I'll talk to you for a start, and if and when I start another relationship—' right now I really can't imagine that but you never know; a long time down the line maybe '—I'll open up more with her too.'

Yeah. Maybe I didn't talk to Freya enough. But I feel like that ship has sailed. I can't *beg* her to talk to me, and apparently she doesn't want to.

I get out of the car. 'Let's grab that fresh air.'

23

FREYA

My phone rings with an unknown number as I'm staring at it, wondering whether yet another game of Candy Crush (I'm on an embarrassingly high level now) might kick-start some creative juices. I've been *really* struggling to get to my planned word count each day this week. I'm too... well, downright miserable.

I miss Jake. I love Jake. No, I lov*ed* Jake. But, also, I kind of still love him. But I'm hurt. And I think the trust is gone. I was proved right. Happy-ever-afters are not for me. I *am* my parents' child.

My phone's still ringing.

'Hello?' I'm not exactly disturbing my work if I answer it.

'Hi. This is Max, Jake's brother.'

'Oh my goodness.' My heart's pounding all of a sudden. 'Is he okay?'

'Yes, sorry, yes, everything's fine. Except... It kind of isn't. Could we meet?'

'I...'

'Great. Could you come to my house? Hard for me to go out by myself. I'm disabled following an accident.'

'Erm.' Should I be going to the houses of strange men who *say* they're Jake's brother but might not be? He does sound similar to him, I suppose.

'This afternoon?' he persists.

'Why?' I have the common sense to ask.

'I'm worried about Jake,' he says.

* * *

Two hours later, I'm ringing the doorbell of a double-fronted Victorian house in Barnes and hoping I haven't been really stupid.

The door's opened by a man in a wheelchair, who is nearly as good-looking as Jake and bears quite a strong similarity to him. Actually, he's probably better-looking – he's incredibly classically handsome – but I'm just kind of – if I'm honest – still hung up on Jake and can't really imagine anyone else coming close.

'Hey, Freya.' Max puts his hand out and I shake it. 'I obviously recognise you from *Wake Up Britain*.'

We go into a large, farmhouse-style kitchen, painted a lovely shade of green, and Max makes me a coffee, wheeling his chair adeptly around the room.

We don't talk as he's doing it, and after a long time – a good minute or two – I find myself saying, 'Beautiful weather today.'

'It is,' Max agrees, placing a steaming mug in front of me before going back to get his own. 'Obviously you must be wondering what I have to say to you.'

I nod.

'I love Jake,' he says. 'Obviously I do; he's my brother. But he's an *amazing* brother.'

I nod again.

'So really...' Max looks down and at his coffee and then raises his eyes and looks directly into mine. 'Really I asked you to come here so that I could ask you in person if you could talk to him. Listen to him. He's a good person.'

'I...' I stop as soon as I've begun. I have no idea what my answer to that should be.

'Think about it,' Max says. Then he pauses, before apparently taking pity on me. 'Anyway. Romance writing. What got you into it?'

And then we spend quite a long time talking about my career and, highly unusually, I find myself smiling and not even trying to change the subject.

I think in parallel to our conversation. I wonder why Max didn't push me more to speak to Jake. Perhaps he's just too nice. Or maybe he's going to have a final go when I leave. Maybe he's lulling me into a false sense of security now. No, I don't think he'd act cynically; I think he really is very nice.

Well, whatever his reason for not pushing hard and just casually chatting, I'm enjoying it. He seems like a great person.

'Do you write at all?' I ask out of interest, rather than my usual get-the-conversation-off-me ploy. 'What would be your preferred genre if you wrote a book?'

'I actually do. Thriller. And...' He leans forward, so I do too. 'I've just submitted a manuscript to ten agents.'

'Oh my goodness. *Max*. That's so exciting.' And then I end up telling him about my own thrillers, including my pen name. I rarely tell anyone, but I instinctively trust him.

We continue talking for another hour, until I say with genuine reluctance that I should go.

'I've really enjoyed meeting you,' Max tells me as we say goodbye.

'Me too,' I say as we share a hug. 'You have to let me know how it goes with the agents. I *love* your premise.'

'Talk to Jake and listen to him,' Max calls after me as I walk down the path towards the pavement. His final little push; fair enough.

I don't want to make promises I might not keep, so I say, 'I'll think about it,' as I wave goodbye.

* * *

Maybe I *should* talk to Jake, I muse as I walk down the road. Can it really hurt? It isn't like I'm not dreaming about him and thinking about him far too often.

I didn't give him a chance to explain himself and maybe I should have done. Okay, I *should* have done. Everyone should always – within reason – at least be allowed to explain.

I'll message him tomorrow.

Actually, maybe this evening. Before I go to bed or I'll just dream about him *again*, which always causes me to wake up feeling a bit miserable.

I visualise Max saying *Speak to him*.

Fine. I'll just text him now.

I stop, take my phone out of my bag, send the message, and then turn the sound off and put it at the bottom of my bag so that I won't be waiting for his possible reply.

* * *

I refuse to allow myself to look at my phone during the long bus journey home, and read my Kindle the whole way.

Then, before I get home, I shop for the ingredients for a lasagne I'm planning on making for Maud. I'll make a batch this evening and then freeze it in portions. I pop in to see her on my way into the house – still without having allowed myself to check my phone – and am easily persuaded to stay for a cup of tea with her. She has some new shoes to try on, and then I try them on too (our feet are the same size and I'm always easily persuaded into joining in with the trying-on), and then we spend a good fifteen pleasurable minutes debating which are the nicest. (Maud goes for a silvery woven pair of ballerina pumps. I resist temptation and tell her I'm not taking any of the others; I already have far too many pairs due to a serious lack of willpower on these occasions.)

Eventually, I'm home and it's time to look at my phone.

It turns out that Jake replied to my text about three minutes after I sent it, saying yes he would like to meet. Oops. I now realise that in having felt that it was too huge to check whether or not he'd replied I've inadvertently aired him all day, having been the one to initiate the conversation.

I message straight back:

> Sorry for the late reply. Had a very busy day. When would you like to meet?

He replies immediately:

> Tomorrow evening? If you're free?

I *am* free tomorrow evening, and after a bit of over-polite to-and-froing (no *you* decide, no *you* choose, no whatever works best for *you*), we agree to meet at a pub near Waterloo station that's equidistant between us travel-wise.

My heart's pounding as we finish our extremely polite conversation. I'm going to see him. We're going to have a conversation. He'll probably say something about the bet.

What do I *want* him to say?

I'm not sure.

Do I even really want to see him? I don't think I do. I think I'm just doing this because Max asked me to. I don't want to have my heart broken any more. I clearly *can't* do relationships and I don't want to prolong the agony of the end of this one.

I really wish I hadn't said I'd go now. I can't back out, though.

I'll have to go, listen, and then say a courteous goodbye.

24

JAKE

I don't one hundred per cent know whether I want to be here.

When Freya texted me yesterday, I reflex-action-replied *yes* to her *would you like to meet?* question.

Then she ignored me all day while I pathetically checked my phone obsessively. And then we had an excruciatingly polite text conversation to arrange this meeting.

I nearly pulled out of it today and then decided to message Max for some brotherly input; it genuinely did help talking to him last week, and I totally get his point about wanting to help *me* given the way our relationship has been since his accident. He persuaded me that I had nothing to lose by coming.

So here I am, standing outside the pub we've agreed to meet at. It's three minutes after our agreed meeting time but I don't *think* Freya's going to stand me up; I think she's just slightly late. She probably got engrossed in whatever creative thing she was last doing.

And, yes, here she is, speed-walking up the road. She's wearing wide beigy linen trousers and a short, pinky-orange jumper, and has her hair loose, and she looks *gorgeous*. As she always does. She also, I note, has bluey-green splodges of something on her hands.

'Been painting?' I ask, after she's come to a halt a good metre away from me and we've said hello. (Apparently there will be no physical contact in our greeting.)

'Yep. Downstairs loo. Just needed to finish the second coat. I'm really sorry I'm late.'

I smile, despite the general awkwardness of the situation. I love the fact that she's always doing something creative and that it so often makes her a little late for things and that when it does she's always very apologetic.

'No worries,' I say. 'Shall we go and find a table? What would you like to drink?'

I don't really know how to broach anything I'd like to talk about (i.e. *us*), so when we're sitting down I say, 'So how have you been?'

'Great, thank you. You?'

'Yep, good, thanks.' I'm *really* regretting this now. It's like being in a look-but-don't-touch museum. I'm physically in the same space as Freya, and seeing her is reminding me of how much I like her, thought I was falling in love with her; but we aren't really communicating. Although... she must have a reason for asking me to meet. A stupid part of me is hoping. The rest of me – the sane part – expects it to be something to do with Sonja and the production company. Or some terrible newspaper article that I haven't seen.

'Soooo,' Freya begins, before stopping and chewing her lip.

I wait.

Eventually, she continues, 'When we... after the TV show... I didn't give you a chance to finish explaining.'

I nod, a little warily if I'm honest, because I'm still not sure where we're going with this conversation.

'So... I wondered if you... would *like* to explain. Obviously you might not want to. In which case forget I mentioned it.'

I'm beginning to feel as though I have some kind of chance of resurrecting my relationship with her. If I want to.

'I think I already explained it,' I say. 'Sorry. That sounded kind of rude. But, yep, I think I've already said it. I'm truly sorry for the way I reacted when I met you; I was being ridiculous. I did the newspaper interview in the heat of the moment. The bet was made later, but it wasn't a *real* bet and it was also made before I got to know you properly that weekend. And I didn't want to take the money, but Pete insisted, so I said fine, I'll make a charity donation. And there you go.'

As I conclude, I feel that I might have sounded a little terse, and looking at the closed-off expression on Freya's face, I *know* I have.

'I'm sorry,' I offer. 'I'm sorry you got upset about the interview and the bet and I'm sorry I didn't tell you about it. And I'm sorry that I was so unreasonable about romantic fiction when we first met.'

'Although, as you said at some point, if you hadn't been, the challenge would never have happened, and we'd never have got to know each other any better.' Freya's smile is twisted.

I nod.

And then Freya nods.

And then we both take long sips of our drinks.

And then we look at each other.

And say absolutely nothing.

And there we have it.

I've told Freya I love her. I've explained everything. I think she gets it all. I don't think it's even that huge. I think it's just that when it comes down to it, Freya doesn't do love and at the smallest hint of an excuse she was always going to be off.

'I lost,' I say.

Freya raises both eyebrows in enquiring fashion.

'The challenge. I found out that true love is not for me. I thought I definitely had a happily-ever-after waiting out there for me, but not at the moment. Too busy with lots of other things. And maybe not ready after my divorce. And then I met you and fell in love. And then I discovered that you can't love me back. And I don't think I'm ever going to meet anyone else like you. So, yep, you won. I agree. There is no happily-ever-after for me.'

Freya's been sitting with her hands clasped together on the table in front of her. She shifts so that her elbows are on the table and brings her hands up so they're kind of resting on her mouth. Then she separates her hands and slides them round so she's propping her face up with them. She leans her head forward so she's looking down at the table.

Suddenly, she lifts her head and says, 'I'm sorry.'

That's it? After all that thinking time. She's sorry?

'For what?' I ask, for the sake of it, really. I'd feel too rude walking out before I've finished my drink and I don't want to down it all in one so we kind of have to make conversation until we're done.

I take a long draught of it to speed the process up while Freya starts the whole 'thinking-woman' routine again.

I have my mouth full of beer when she says, 'For not listening sooner,' and I nearly splutter liquid everywhere in surprise. And slight hope.

'The thing is,' she continues, 'I think maybe I was looking for something to go wrong, and I seized on that and didn't think about the realities of it.'

'Oh?' I ask cautiously, not wanting to hope too much, but also, suddenly, *really* hoping.

'Yes,' she replies, very unsatisfyingly. And then she just sits there and sips her wine.

I look at her gorgeous heart-shaped face, her thick hair piled on her head, her delicate frame which belies *huge* strength of character.

And suddenly I just have to go for it one more time. Max was right. I should fight for her.

'I love you,' I say, very loudly. I sense people on the nearest tables turning to see what's happening but I ignore them. I'm focused only on the amazing woman in front of me and whether I can salvage a relationship between us.

Freya swallows.

She looks at me, and I swear I see moisture in her eyes.

But she says nothing.

I've come this far. I need to say more, say as much as I can.

So I plunge in.

'I understand from what you said before that you at some point began to believe that you're unlovable and unlov*ing*,' I begin. 'But... at the risk of sounding know-it-all or patronising, I think you might be wrong.'

Freya is just staring at me, her eyes now looking even damper.

'Lizzie,' I say. 'You can't say you don't love her or she doesn't love you. Charlotte. Sarra.' I start reeling off names of friends she's mentioned. 'To name a few. *Maud*. You're a very loving person. And you're a very lovable person. You are not like your father or mother and there are plenty of people out there who are not like them either.'

A tear rolls down Freya's cheek. I want *so much* to wipe it away, but obviously I can't.

'I'm sorry.' I indicate her tears. More are now falling. 'For making you cry.'

She sniffs, very cutely, and wipes under her eyes with a napkin from the cutlery pot at her elbow.

'Thank you,' she says.

I wait. I'm not sure what she's thanking me for and I want to marshal my thoughts to see if there are any other good arguments I could make. I mean, I'm a lawyer for fuck's sake. Surely I can do better than this. Arguing and winning is my *job*.

'Thank you,' she repeats.

'For...?' I dare to ask.

'For saying nice things.'

'They aren't nice things so much as truths,' I point out. 'Have I mentioned that I love you?'

She nods. I really wish she'd tell me she loves me too but maybe she just... doesn't.

I'm going to give it one last big go.

'I love you and I would very much like to date you – officially – and work at things, like you do in any good relationship... like if we have an argument, not use it as an excuse to leave but assume that we want to work through it. That is what I would like. In an ideal world. Because I love you.'

Freya is *really* crying now. Fuck.

She mumbles something. I really can't work out what she's saying due to the tears.

'I didn't catch that,' I say.

'I said I love you,' she says.

'Oh!' I look at her hands and wonder if it would be acceptable for me to reach across the table and take them in mine. 'I love you too.'

'You actually talk a lot of sense,' she tells me.

'I do?'

'Yep. I think...' She sniffs again and I just want to wrap my arms round her and make sure she never has anything to cry sad tears about ever again. 'I think it's like I always wanted to make my dad love me so I've always sought out men like him, but he was inherently an arse, and so were they, and then they showed their arsey true selves and I walked away, and I've construed that as me being unlovable and unloving but I don't think I fully am unloving because I really, really love you, and you're right: I really love my friends.'

I do take her hands in mine, and squeeze them, hard.

She squeezes mine back.

'Would you... Could we... Shall we date?' I'm so conscious of how extremely important a moment this is in my life (and I hope Freya's too) that I've become remarkably inarticulate.

'Yes, please.' She's smiling through her tears and I feel my heart swell.

'I love you,' I tell her again.

'I love you too.'

And then I lean across the table and kiss her on the lips, and it's perfect.

EPILOGUE
FREYA

Three years later

'You may kiss the bride.'

There's cheering from the congregation as I turn to Jake and he very tenderly lifts my veil and then brushes my lips with his.

Then he kisses me again, for a little longer. The kiss is beautiful, holding the promise of all the things we're going to do later on when we don't have to go full PG for the benefit of our audience, not least our wonderful eighteen-month-old daughter, Zara, who's on the front row being held by Jake's mother.

'I'm Mrs Jake,' I whisper to him.

'And I'm Mr Freya.' He grins at me and I beam back at him. I can't believe how lucky I am.

We've both learnt a lot more about ourselves over the past three years since the evening we agreed to officially date. Jake's learnt that he *does* have the right to be happy. And I have learnt that I really am good at loving people (Jake and Zara for a start) and that they love *me*.

We've also learnt that we both took a *very* surprise pregnancy in our stride. I did not adore pregnancy but I *love* motherhood, and Jake was wonderful while I vomited my way through not just my first trimester but also my second and most of my third, and is equally wonderful as a father.

'Looking forward to tonight when everyone's gone,' Jake murmurs into my ear.

'Shhh,' I admonish him. '*I'm* looking forward to having a fab day and evening with our family and friends.'

'Are you *not* looking forward to tonight?' He leans in and tells me some of the things that he's *particularly* looking forward to and laughs when I squeak out loud, because a couple of them are *naughty*.

'Maybe,' I say. 'But *first*, it's time to *party*.'

We've chosen to get married in the Devon village where Lizzie and I now have an alpaca farm business. We both still have our day jobs, so we have a farm manager, but we both visit as much as possible, and it's doing *very* well combining wool and milk production with alpaca experiences. We chose the village for the wedding partly because it's gorgeous and on the coast and we love it here, and partly because Sonja was threatening to gatecrash if we had it in London.

We've reached a truce with her. She's stopped trying to shit-stir (she was such a nightmare that we honestly both almost suspected her of somehow getting me surprise-pregnant so quickly just to test us) plus she finally gave me the autograph for Maud *and* agreed to meet her for lunch, which Maud adored, and in return we've agreed to go on her show every few months with a little update. Something that helped us a lot was that there was a huge public backlash against her nastiness to us and she had to fight to keep her job and promise to be a lot nicer from then on.

She and her producer did suggest that she attend our wedding and that they show footage of it on *Wake Up Britain*, to which Jake and I both had an immediate and massive reaction of *no way*. (I also refused point-blank to let her video me in labour. Obviously. And won't let her show photos of Zara. Obviously.)

Jake and I are in the middle of dancing in a group on the beach, me and Lizzie waltzing together, and Jake and Dan together (Lizzie and Dan are engaged and have three-month-old twins) when Max – whose debut thriller just came out to *huge* acclaim – wheels over to us. (The first time we spoke and he said he couldn't go places by himself because of his disability was a little lie to get me to visit him, a visit for which I never cease to be grateful.) He's in the wide-wheeled beach wheelchair that he treated himself to out of his advance, going at top speed (seriously impressive).

'That bloody woman's here,' he says.

'Not...' we all chorus.

'Yep. Sonja.'

'Fuck me,' Jake says.

'Later, sir,' I reply (okay, fine, I *have* had too much champagne, but in my defence it's *my wedding day*). 'And focusing on the essentials, I do *not* want cameras.'

And up pops Sonja in our faces with her phone camera held towards us.

I do my best smile while trying to put lots of other people between us and her, and then oh my goodness, the bliss, she's so intent on getting her photo that she doesn't notice a big wave coming behind her. It drenches her *and* washes her phone out of her hand.

'Wow.' I'm in awe. 'Karma in action.'

'I'm always grateful to Sonja and the programme, though,' Jake says as he begins to jog forward to haul her back onto her feet. 'For introducing us.'

'Me too,' agrees Dan.

'Yeah, fair enough,' Lizzie and I agree.

Fine.

Jake looks at me over Sonja's wet head and we nod at each other.

'We would love you to stay on condition that you take no photos,' Jake says as he and Sonja walk back towards us. He turns his own phone video on and says, 'I'm recording this. We request you not to take any photos of us and we *will* take legal action if you do.'

After Sonja has agreed – and has downed three glasses of champagne and is dancing with a delighted Maud on the beach – Jake says, 'The legal action thing. Easier said than done. We're in public and we're adults. She could *totally* get away with taking photos of us.'

'But she won't now,' I say happily.

Sonja is very good company once she's abandoned the idea of treating us like a story, and actually her presence is really no bad thing at all, because our story *did* begin with her.

In fact, after dinner (we hastily squish her onto a table of people around her age where she hits it off *very* well with my recently divorced Uncle Geoff), when we're doing our speeches (I do one too because I'm not going down the patri-archy route), Jake and I both reference her and thank her.

* * *

When the night draws to a close, a very tipsy Sonja, leading Uncle Geoff by the hand, comes over to us.

'I feel *so* fond of you both,' she coos, all rancour over the no-photo thing apparently forgotten. 'I feel like your fairy godmother. And now—' she leans in and does a stage whisper, which I'm sure can be heard by at least half of Devon '—I might be your new aunt.'

I sneak a sideways glance at Uncle Geoff, and, yes, he does look wide-eyed and jaw-dropped panic-stricken.

'Fingers crossed,' I say, crossing them for Uncle Geoff to make a safe getaway from Sonja rather than for her to join the family, as Jake laughs long and loud next to me.

'Thank you, Sonja,' he says. 'For the love challenge. I won, and found my amazing Freya and our happily-ever-after.'

'I might have lost the actual challenge but I won because I met you,' I tell Jake. It's totally fine to be super-sentimental on your wedding day. Obligatory, even.

He puts his arms round me from behind and I turn so that I'm facing him and wind my arms round his neck.

'I love you,' I tell him.

'Love you too.'

'You *both* won,' says Sonja fondly as Jake and I share a lovely long kiss.

* * *

MORE FROM JO LOVETT

Another book from Jo Lovett, is available to order now here:
    https://mybook.to/JoLovettBackAd

ACKNOWLEDGEMENTS

I've loved writing Freya and Jake's story – thank you so much for reading!

Huge thanks to my agent, Sarah Hornsley at PFD, for all her wonderful support and advice.

Thank you also to the fabulous team at Boldwood. Emily Yau is a fantastic editor and such a pleasure to work with. Thank you also to Helena Newton and Rachel Sargeant for their forensic copyedits and proofreads, and to Clare Stacey for designing the beautiful cover. And thank you to the wider team including Wendy Neale and Ana Carter!

Last but of course not least, thank you so much to my family and friends. Thank you to Liz Gale, Gilly Matthews and Fiona MacLennan, and enormous gratitude to my husband and children as always for putting up with my strange writing hours! Thank you – very much appreciated!

ABOUT THE AUTHOR

Jo Lovett is the bestselling author of contemporary rom-coms including *The House Swap*. Shortlisted for the Comedy Women in Print Award, she lives in London.

Download your exclusive bonus content from Jo Lovett here:

Follow Jo on social media:

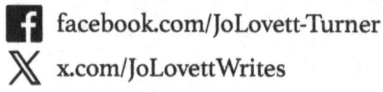 facebook.com/JoLovett-Turner
x.com/JoLovettWrites

ALSO BY JO LOVETT

Boldwood
EVER AFTER

x♡x♡

JOIN BOLDWOOD'S
ROMANCE COMMUNITY
FOR SWEET AND SPICY BOOK RECS WITH ALL YOUR FAVOURITE TROPES!

SIGN UP TO OUR
NEWSLETTER

HTTPS://BIT.LY/BOLDWOODEVERAFTER

Boldwood

Boldwood Books is an award-winning fiction publishing company seeking out the best stories from around the world.

Find out more at www.boldwoodbooks.com

Join our reader community for brilliant books, competitions and offers!

Follow us
@BoldwoodBooks
@TheBoldBookClub

Sign up to our weekly deals newsletter

https://bit.ly/BoldwoodBNewsletter